SKINS

SKINS

by Catherine O'Connell

DONALD I. FINE, INC.
NEW YORK

Dedicated with love
to my mother
Barbara King O'Connell

and

to the memory
of my belle-mere
Evelyn Venrick

PROLOGUE

From the distance, Jean McInerney could see the spotted coat of the lynx where it lay still in the snow. He pulled up alongside it and dismounted from his snowmobile, approaching the animal slowly, cautiously. Its left foot was held fast by steel bars, but years of trapping had taught him to be wary. He had been caught off guard by a live coyote once and lost a good part of his nose to it. Nostalgically, he put a gloved hand to the nub that remained. He must never forget that his prey could become quite vicious in its fight for freedom.

But in this instance his caution was unwarranted. The lynx was already dead. He was disappointed somewhat at having been cheated of the kill; to him it was an essential part of his work. He picked up the animal and examined it. A female and very thin. He hadn't been able to check this trap for over a week, perhaps she had starved to death. Fortunately, her coat was unmarked.

McInerney chucked the carcass onto the sled in back of his snowmobile and restarted the engine. He gave the lynx no more thought, his mind was occupied with far more pressing matters.

The outsiders were getting their way. They had forced through tough new laws to complicate the already harsh life of a trapper. These new laws dictated the type of trap he was permitted to use and how often those traps must be checked. Although the conibear traps were supposed to be more humane, they were difficult to set in freezing weather, and checking each trap within seventy-two hours was all but impossible along trap lines that could run as long as a hundred miles.

But even worse, the market itself was dying. The demand for

1

pelts had been falling steadily for years, and along with it the price. What would happen if the market were to disappear altogether? What would become of him and his people then? They couldn't make a living off of snow and ice.

They would have to move, but where? To the cities? They did not adjust well to change, his people. They were the hardy descendants of the French and English explorers who had passed through so many years ago. Many of them, like McInerney himself, also had Indian blood. The cities were no place for them.

The snowmobile was one of the few concessions they had made to modern times, and as McInerney urged his vehicle on through the shifting waves of white, his eyes watered into the wind as he searched for his next trap. He shuddered with involuntary anger as he thought once again of the outsiders, intruding upon an ancient way of life they could never understand, and he hated them for it.

I

MANHATTAN,
Monday, November 19, 1990

Evelyn Burhop did not like doing this. She was in no way a meddlesome type of person, and she feared she was violating the boundaries of neighborly concern. But it truly wasn't curiosity or any semblance of nosiness that was prompting her intrusion into Jennifer's apartment. Far from it, she was downright worried.

Her frail age-spotted right hand shook with apprehension and she had to steady it with her left as she held out the key to unlock 12 West. She inserted the key into the upper lock, the deadbolt, and turned it. It turned easily, too easily in fact. The lock had not been engaged.

"Jennifer," she called out once again loudly, and once again she knocked on the door. "Are you in there?" As before, there was no response. She tried the knob. It held fast. Still quivering, she used a second key in the knob lock this time and felt the tumblers disengage. She pushed the door open slowly.

From where she stood in the hall, the first thing to confront her was the unusual smell, something foul and unfamiliar, perhaps meat rotting in the disposal or an old carton of milk left in haste on the counter. Tentatively, she entered the marble foyer, the white polished stone cool and hard under her feet. She thought it odd that Chessie wasn't there immediately, rubbing against her ankles and begging for attention. The cat always came to the door.

Her gaze shifted to the living room. It too was calm, not a thing out of place, the yellow silk upholstered sofa plush and inviting, the weak afternoon sun filtering through the partially opened miniblinds. The only thing out of place was an open book that lay face down on the glass coffee table.

3

She stood there frozen. Her body trembled with fearful antici-pation as she tried to identify the smell, stronger now and even more acrid and unpleasant. She wanted to turn and run back out the open door and across the hall to the safety and security of her own home, but she had come this far and she was determined to finish what she had begun. She thought with disdain of the police and how uninterested they had been when she tried to report Jennifer missing. "Lady, this is New York," they told her. "People go away. Three days is nothing." But Jennifer seldom went away and never without telling her. Who would feed the cat? "Maybe she took the cat with her," was the policeman's cynical reply.

So the police didn't care, and that meant it was up to Evelyn to do something. She steeled herself to investigate further.

She moved forward into the spacious foyer, past the living room, taking tiny shuffling steps, at an excruciatingly slow pace, trying to forestall a discovery she dreaded. Evelyn looked to her right, to the Chinese console where she always left Jennifer's mail when she was out of town. There was a sheet of paper propped up on it. Maybe Jennifer had left a note after all.

Her eyes weren't as good as they used to be, and she had to pick up the sheet of paper and hold it at arm's length to make out its typed message. HOW MANY OF THESE WOULD IT TAKE TO MAKE A FUR COAT? it read.

Puzzled, she looked back to the console. There was something there she had overlooked before, something lying beside the note. With her blurry vision, it blended right into the deep, dark hue of the wood. It appeared to be a patch of fur, triangular in shape and covered with short, tightly curled hair, like the old Persian lamb coat she owned years ago. She picked it up and shrieked aloud when she saw the small pool of blood underneath it. HOW MANY OF THESE WOULD IT TAKE TO MAKE A FUR COAT? Sud-denly she knew for certain what that horrible odor was, recog-nized it without having ever smelled it in her life. It was the smell of death. The reality of what it was she was holding slowly dawned, and as it did, she screamed again. She dropped the vile piece of hair and turned on her arthritic heels, running from the apartment as quickly as her orthopedic shoes could carry her. Her hands shook more violently than ever as she tried to get her own key into her door. It seemed like an hour before she succeeded.

Inside she ran straight to the phone and called 911. They were far more attentive this time. It wasn't until she had finished talking with them, assured that they were sending someone out, that her stomach finally rebelled and she went into her bathroom to retch.

II

Karen Levinson did not look like the average criminal's idea of a police detective. Her poker-straight raven hair framed a narrow serious face distinguished by intense brown eyes and broad sensual lips. Right now she appeared to be gnawing on her long red fingernails, but in actuality they were far too precious to bite. She always unconsciously stuck them in her mouth whenever she was nervous or upset. Right now she found some kind of comfort in the clicking sound they made as she passed them back and forth against her teeth while she tried to ignore the wretched smell in Jennifer O'Grady's bedroom.

"Tougher than you thought it would be, Detective?"

The voice of her new partner, Tony Perrelli, was condescending, without a shred of sympathy and laced with the tones of his native Brooklyn. Yes, it was tougher than she had ever imagined, but she would never admit that to him.

Perrelli towered a full foot over her and his smooth olive skin and thick jet-black hair belied his forty years. He was the seasoned veteran, as he didn't hesitate to remind her as they stood together at the foot of Jennifer O'Grady's canopied bed looking at the grotesque spectacle that lay before them. Fighting back waves of nausea, she forced herself to study the barely recognizable remains of what had once been one of the most recognizable women in New York. The right side of her head had been bashed in and her luxuriant black hair was matted with blood. Karen forced her eyes to travel downward along the corpse. The upper body was still clad in a blood-soaked grey cashmere pullover, but the lower half was naked. Bile rose in Karen's stomach as she came to the spot between the legs where someone, not satisfied with killing her, had brutally mutilated her. She fought not to gag.

Even more macabre was what lay beneath the body. The killer had left her on top of a virtual funeral pyre of her own fur coats. One of the coats was of dark fur—mink, Karen thought—and did not show evidence of the violence that had occurred in the room, but the others, a silver fox, a coyote and a raccoon, were red with blood. They reminded Karen of road kill.

Gladly tearing her eyes from the corpse, Karen concentrated on studying the room around her. It was a warm and peaceful room, a feminine room with floral chintz draperies and bedclothes, an ironic contrast to what had taken place here. It was obvious that the owner had taken great care when decorating; nightstands at either side of the bed held delicate crystal lamps with pink silk shades. Karen noticed that on one of the nightstands a book of Emily Dickinson's poems lay open. Directly across from the bed was a large dressing table, skirted in the same chintz as the bed and windows, and an enormous array of expensive perfumes and cosmetics tidily arranged upon its beveled glass top. Along the same wall, a tall French armoire hid a television set.

There was only one aspect of the room that clashed with all this self-indulgent femininity: an entire wall of crowded bookshelves. There were more books stacked into dozens of neat piles on the floor.

Nathaniel Bradlee, the coroner, was there and he nodded to the two detectives as he methodically examined the body with gloved hands. "Do you know who she was?" asked Bradlee, not looking up as he worked the corpse's arm back and forth. It bent easily at the shoulder and elbow. He seemed unaffected by the rancid odor that filled the room.

"Yah," said Perrelli. "She was a model, the Swank Girl. You've seen her before, Nat, she's the one in all the fur coat ads. Guess she's had her last public exposure, there sure won't be an open casket on this one."

Karen blanched again, this time at the cold, impersonal attitude of her partner. Karen still couldn't separate herself from death entirely, and this murder of a woman so near her own age un-nerved her. In a strange way she was grateful for Tony's unflappable presence.

The coroner shook his head and continued his work silently, very professional and efficient. Tony tapped Karen's arm. He had seen enough for now.

"Where's the neighbor?" he asked one of the uniformed officers who had been first on the scene.

"The old lady? She's across the hall in her apartment. She's very upset. We told her that someone would be coming over to talk to her."

"What do you say, Levinson? Should we pay Mrs. Burhop a visit while the boys are finishing up here? Get a breath of fresh air perhaps?" He was teasing her, not bothering to hide his disdain for her. She knew she was probably as pale as a ghost, and she nodded readily, desperate for any change of scenery. She followed him eagerly as he led the way across the tiled hallway to 12 East. Their knock on the door was answered almost immediately by an elderly woman. She looked up at them from small intelligent grey eyes.

"Mrs. Burhop?" Tony inquired with uncharacteristic kindness. The older woman nodded.

"I'm Detective Perrelli and this is Detective Levinson," he said, moving aside to share a more equitable portion of the doorway with Karen. "We're from Homicide, and we need to ask you some questions."

It was obvious that the old woman was extremely upset, but she very graciously invited them inside. Karen's first thought as she entered the apartment was how different it was from the one across the hall. While the floor plan was a mirror image of the one they had just left, the decor was worlds away. The furnishings spoke of an entirely different time, an earlier era. The living room sofa and chairs were of good quality, but they were old and the heavy dark brocade was worn quite thin in some places. The walls were adorned with ancient still lifes, oil paintings of fruits in bowls and books lying in varying configurations. A polished cherry coffee table bore several leather-bound scrapbooks, and the matching end tables displayed numerous black and white photos in antique silver frames. An embroidery hoop lay abandoned in the middle of the sofa, giving the room the aura of a place that had been frozen in time many years ago.

From where she stood, Karen could see the East River, which shimmered in the quickly dwindling November light.

"Can I get you something to drink, some tea perhaps?" Mrs. Burhop offered. Evelyn's mother had raised her to always be scrupulously polite, regardless of the circumstances. Perrelli declined her offer, but Karen, altogether too aware of the bile her stomach was producing, said she would love some. This earned her a sharp glance from her partner. She still hadn't figured out his ways, but obviously he didn't subscribe to mixing too closely with witnesses. She decided to ignore his look, figuring he would much prefer to watch her drink a soothing cup of tea now than watch her vomit in the elevator later.

Mrs. Burhop emerged from the kitchen a moment later with a heavy silver tray that looked far too large for her to carry. She rested it lovingly upon the coffee table. It was laid out with a china teapot, cream, sugar, sliced lemon, a plate of small cookies and three cups. It was obvious that she had prepared for visitors. Her hands shook as she poured the tea, and Karen found herself wondering if the tremor was caused by age or fear. The old woman paused at the third cup and looked to Tony. He shook his head no, and then nodded impatiently at Karen.

Karen was taken aback. It seemed Tony wanted her to start asking the questions. It was the first time in the two weeks they had been paired together that he was permitting her to take any initiative at all. Then she looked back at the quivering old lady and she realized why. This was far too delicate a situation for Tony's brusque ways.

"Mrs. Burhop," she said gently, "can you tell us exactly what happened today and what you saw inside Ms. O'Grady's apartment?"

"Oh, yes, officer. Most definitely." She took a shaky sip from her teacup and began her story: how she had not seen or heard from Jennifer for three days and so took it upon herself to investigate.

"So you saw Ms. O'Grady fairly often?"

"Oh, yes. We have tea practically every day when she's at home. She's a model, you know, so she works irregularly. Sometimes she gets called out of town or is going to be late getting home, and then I feed Chessie for her."

"Chessie?" asked Perrelli.

"Her cat. I feed the cat for her whenever Jennifer is away. That is why I have a key."

"Did you see a cat in that apartment?" Perrelli asked his partner.

"No. Maybe in all the excitement it got out," Karen suggested.

"I don't think Chessie was there when I let myself in," Mrs. Burhop interrupted, "because usually she'll come running right for the door." She tried to take another sip of her tea, but this time her hands were shaking too fiercely and she spilled the contents of the cup all over the table, soaking the cover of one of the scrapbooks in the process. Karen swept the book up quickly and wiped the fragile leather cover with her napkin. She realized the woman's tremors were caused by more than age.

"Now look at what I've done," said Evelyn unhappily. She struggled to her feet. Suddenly the enormity of all that had happened came crashing down on her. She grew faint and fell back into her chair with a sob. Then she began to cry in earnest as Karen and Tony sat there awkwardly. After a while Karen could take it no more, and she went over and put one of her arms around the old woman's trembling shoulders.

"Poor dear Jennifer," cried Mrs. Burhop. "I know that she is dead in there, but did she suffer terribly?"

Karen thought of the mutilated body, the blood-soaked furs, the awful stench of death and decay. It was a good thing that Mrs. Burhop hadn't made it any further than the foyer. It would have been terrible if she had seen the rest. "No, I don't think she suffered," said Karen, not knowing whether she was lying or not.

The old woman seemed relieved to hear that, and she started to calm down. She dabbed a lace-edged hanky at her eyes, blew her nose into it loudly, and then folded it into ladylike squares, pressing it flat with the palm of her hand. "This would be so much easier if Mr. Burhop were still around," she said to Karen. "He was such a pillar of strength for me."

Karen nodded with understanding while Tony grimaced. She could tell he was eager to move on. His cold, callous style left little time for consoling bereaved neighbors.

When Mrs. Burhop finally regained her composure enough for them to continue, Karen began to extract what details she could from the old lady about Jennifer O'Grady. According to Evelyn, the model had no family to speak of and only dated infrequently in the years since she had moved in across the hall. She had very few visitors, and besides stopping in for tea with the old woman on a fairly regular basis, she didn't seem to have much of a social life. "But she didn't seem to care for it," Evelyn added.

"Did she have any visitors last Friday?" Karen asked.

"Not that I know of," she replied, "but I always watch my soap operas during the day and I have the set turned up quite loud. My hearing, like my vision I'm afraid, isn't what it used to be."

They had spent an hour with Mrs. Burhop when Tony, satisfied that they had learned as much as they could, signaled to Karen that it was time to leave. Before going Karen called the old woman's personal physician and got her a prescription for a sedative. She felt sorry for the elderly widow, alone in her home with her photos and her memories.

At the door it was Tony who spoke the last words. "Mrs. Burhop," he said in a stern tone usually reserved for impressing something important on a child, "it is imperative that you don't tell anyone, not anyone, what you saw in Miss O'Grady's apartment. I can't tell you how important it is." His voice held promise of the wrath of God were she to disobey.

She looked up meekly into his piercing brown eyes and nodded. "Yes, officer. I won't tell anyone," she said.

Nat Bradlee was just finishing up when they returned to Jennifer's apartment.

"What do we have here, Nat?" Perrelli asked.

Tony was almost as bigoted about blacks as he was about women, but Karen noted that he always addressed the coroner with the respect that came from working together for many years. As she listened to Nat Bradlee speak, she wondered how long it would be before she too had Perrelli's respect.

"It's pretty obvious that she died from the beating to the head. Although at this point we don't know what kind of weapon the killer used. Possibly a baseball bat. It appears that he used something sharp, probably a knife, to virtually skin the pubic area. From the lack of blood, we can assume that occurred after death. Since the rigor mortis has subsided entirely, I'd say she's been dead about three days. There doesn't seem to be any trauma to the vagina or anus, but I'll investigate it further at the lab. Do you want her for anything else?"

"Nah," said Perrelli. "We've seen enough."

The reference to "we" made Bradlee finally notice Karen, who was standing quietly at Perrelli's side, her intense brown eyes focused on him.

"New to homicide, young lady?" he asked.

"Karen Levinson," she said, extending her hand before remembering too late what type of examination he had just been conducting with his. Of course he had been wearing rubber gloves, but still the thought . . . She tried not to wince as he took her hand briefly. "Why any young lady would want to have anything to do with this sort of mess is way beyond me," he said.

"That's affirmative action for you, Nat," said Tony and he meant it.

Bradlee shook his head and followed the body bag containing Jennifer O'Grady as it was wheeled out of the door on a gurney, ready for transport down to a cold steel table at the city morgue.

Bob Falls, one of the industrious forensics men who had thoroughly explored every nook of the plush co-op in search for evidence, came up to Tony. "Doesn't seem to be much here I'm afraid," he said, disheartened. "There's no sign of forced entry. The deadbolt was left unlatched after the perpetrator left, and the lock in the knob locks automatically. Maybe she knew whoever it was and let him in. I picked up a few prints, but they're small. Look like women's. Probably belong to the corpse or the old lady."

"Thanks, Bob. You'll run them anyhow?"

"Of course."

"Where's the note?" Tony inquired.

The forensics man brought out a plastic bag and removed the single sheet of paper with a tweezer. HOW MANY OF THESE WOULD IT TAKE TO MAKE A FUR COAT? was neatly typed in the center of the page.

"It looks like a standard twenty-pound typing paper and probably a standard IBM typewriter. Only about ten million or so of them in Manhattan. I'll check it out though."

"Great," said Tony, handing back the note. "Oh, and listen, absolutely nothing, *nothing* about this note or the rug to the media, okay? Be sure to tell the rest of them. We'll be able to use this stuff when we nail the sicko. But if the press gets their hands on this, forget it. We don't want another Son of Sam circus and we don't want to set off any copycats."

"Right, Tony. I'll tell everyone. Anything else?"

"Yeah. Did you see a cat around here anyplace?"

"No, I didn't, although I noticed cat food in the kitchen and a litter box in one of the closets."

"Uh huh," said Perrelli. He pondered for a moment and then said, "Bob, I want you to take the litter box downtown and have somebody find out the last time the missing cat took a shit."

"I get all the good jobs," Falls said to Karen before heading off on his mission.

When it was just Karen and Tony left standing in Jennifer's bedroom, Karen walked over to the bed where the pile of fur coats remained. She looked under the bed, not knowing exactly what she was expecting to see. The cat perhaps? There was nothing.

She lifted one of the furs from the pile, the black mink that had lain directly under the body. The fur shone lustrous where it was not matted with blood.

"Wouldn't you rather be wearing one of those, playing the princess instead of the cop?" asked Tony. There was no humor in his voice. She was growing used to his slights and brushed it off. She lifted the raccoon coat from the pile. A piece of paper protruding from a side pocket caught her eye. She removed it and unfolded it.

"Hey, what's this?" she called to Perrelli. The top half of the flyer showed a picture of Jennifer O'Grady modeling a raccoon coat. Beneath was the photo of a scared raccoon caught in a leghold trap. IT LOOKED BETTER ON THE ANIMAL read the caption in large bold type.

III

Yolanda Prince loved her job best when she was out on the street in the middle of the action instead of inside the studio reading words off a teleprompter. In fact, it was her passion for reporting from the scene combined with her stubborn way of digging for all the facts on all sides of the issue that had gotten her where she was today: a feature reporter for Channel 8 News with her own "In Depth" specials featured regularly. Not too bad for a black, formerly fat girl from the Bronx. At twenty-eight, she had conquered numerous obstacles, and she had her sights set on much more.

Today she was standing in the raw November wind, fighting to keep a wool scarf wrapped around her neck and tucked into the collar of her camel's hair coat. She thought longingly of the warm new fox coat, in her closet, at home. Too bad her work required she wear something a little less controversial, she thought as she shivered against the biting wind.

Behind her the Christmas decorations of Fifth Avenue glittered in the premature dusk brought about by the dark, ominous clouds. In the early evening grey, the stores were bright and promising oases of gold and light and warmth.

It was the Monday before Thanksgiving, and the eager retailers were all geared up for the lucrative holiday season. However, the signs were none too promising this year; the economy was doing a backslide after the freewheeling eighties and war threatened to break out in the Gulf. If the country wasn't already in a recession, it seemed headed for one.

And among the retailers there was none with a more vested interest in this holiday season than Swank Furs, an ultra chic chain of furriers in front of whose flagship store Yolanda was now standing with her cameraman. Rumor had it that Swank was falling on hard times, and if true, it certainly wasn't being helped by the scruffy demonstrators picketing in front of the Fifth Avenue entrance.

With the concentration of a reporter, Yolanda watched intently as a middle-aged woman exited the store carrying a large black box embossed with the Swank logo, a white silhouette of a slim woman in a billowing fur coat. The woman had barely cleared the revolving doors when the demonstrators descended on her en masse. They began to encircle her, chanting "Shame." As they moved ever closer to her, she cowered before them. She looked helpless standing there in the wind, her salt-and-pepper hair blowing about uncontrollably, holding her box tightly at her left side, her right arm raised to protect her face.

"Don't you know 'Fur Is Dead,'" shrieked one of the protesters, a pock-faced young woman who carried a placard that voiced the same sentiment. The words were barely out of her mouth when she was pushed roughly aside by two Swank security guards who had noticed their customer's dilemma. A sizable white man and a lean muscular black woman dressed in impressive uniforms, they positioned themselves on either side of the frightened woman and steered her clear of the tumult. Undaunted, the demonstrators continued to call "Shame" to their backs and a few of the more motivated broke from the ranks and followed the woman and her two escorts, shouting all the way.

Yolanda's cameraman, Mark Slater, was recording it all. This should make tonight's news, Yolanda thought, if nothing more exciting came up in the next couple of hours. She smoothed a few unruly strands that had come loose from her French braid. Then she turned back toward the camera and pressed her lips together to even her lipstick, before gesturing to Mark that she was ready. She spoke directly at his camera.

"With the holiday season just starting, it seems most Fifth Avenue retailers are geared up for what is traditionally their most profitable season. With a recession looming before us, this Christmas season may well turn out to be a disappointment. Well, if this group of demonstrators has anything to do with it, there is one business that is going to be way off this year, and that is the fur business. We are in front of Swank Furs on Fifth Avenue where members of the animal rights group S.T.S. have gathered to protest what they call the inhumane act of purchasing and wearing fur."

Holding her microphone before her, Yolanda backed toward the picketers who, aware that they were being videotaped, became even more animated. They raised their voices and flailed their arms while maneuvering their slogan-bearing picket signs in front of the camera's eye. What a mixed bag, Yolanda thought, as she combed the picket line in search of a candidate for an interview. The marchers appeared to come from a variety of walks of life, although there was a marked predominance of women over men. There were quite a few aging hippies in faded jeans and army surplus; others looked like typical suburban housewives wearing corduroy slacks and neat little car coats. Yolanda noted one particularly odd character: an obese giant who stopped frequently to press literature on passersby who did their New York best to ignore him. Conspicuously absent was anyone dressed in business attire, but after all this was a Monday, and their sort were at work.

Yolanda's gaze met that of a rail-thin woman who had been

watching her intently and who immediately broke from the formation and approached her. Yolanda had Mark stop taping.

"You are . . . ?"

"Mary Ellen Fitzsimmons, president of S.T.S., Save Their Skins." The woman's words came out with a religious fervor, her narrow face gleaming with enthusiasm. She was red and raw with the cold and her long, mousey brown hair blew in a tangled mess of frizz about her. A red turtleneck peeked out from under a green nylon parka, and her faded jeans were frayed at the bottoms above her battered Nikes. She stood there blowing into synthetic knit gloves, trying to warm her fingers as her blue eyes watered above her clenched fist. Her face was makeup free. Creases around her eyes and mouth betrayed that she was in her early forties.

"Would you like to do an interview?" asked Yolanda.

"I would love to do an interview," replied Mary Ellen Fitzsimmons, stomping her feet impatiently against the cold.

Yolanda knew instinctively that she was dealing with a firecracker here, but that was part of the fun of the job. The unpredictability of people. It made doing face-to-face interviews such a challenge.

"Okay," said Yolanda. "Just be sure to look directly at the red light in the camera there. That means it's recording."

Mary Ellen was far from shy. "I know all about the little red light," she said. "I've done a few of these over the years."

Hoping she hadn't made a mistake, Yolanda nodded at her cameraman to roll.

"We're talking here with Mary Ellen Fitzsimmons, president of the animal rights organization called S.T.S., which stands for Save Their Skins. This group has been marching in front of Swank Furs since this morning. Mary Ellen, what do you expect to gain from this demonstration?"

Yolanda moved the mike over to Mary Ellen. Going from Yolanda's five feet eight inches to Mary Ellen's five-ten, the cameraman was easily able to keep them both in the camera's eye.

"Our goal," said Mary Ellen, straightening up as tall as she could and staring directly into the camera, "is to make the public aware that millions of animals are needlessly slaughtered in the name of vanity. We have chosen Swank Furs as our first target, because they are one of the biggest users of animal skins and therefore one of the worst offenders when it comes to violating animal rights."

Yolanda broke in. "I see. Now just moments ago we watched your people harass a customer leaving the Swank store. There have been numerous instances lately of people wearing fur being spit on or having paint thrown on them. Does your organization endorse such tactics?"

"We endorse any tactic that will stop cruelty to animals. If a person is insensitive enough to wear an animal's skin, then he or she had better be insensitive to some straight talking. If they can turn their backs on the pain of these animals, then they better be ready to hear about it. And while we don't condone destruction of someone's personal property, I can respect the bravery of those who throw paint on fur coats. Just like with the Vietnam War, just like with nuclear power, it takes the radical to draw attention to a terrible wrong. We have to make people think about what it is they are actually doing when they go out and buy a fur coat. I'm telling everyone out there, don't buy fur and if you already have fur, stop wearing it. Don't perpetuate the suffering of small, helpless creatures. Rise up against the greed-mongering fur industry and . . ."

Yolanda fought to regain control of the microphone, cutting Mary Ellen short. She had wanted an interview, she was not willing to provide the forum for a crusade.

"Thank you, Mary Ellen Fitzsimmons," she said curtly. "This is Yolanda Prince reporting for Channel 8 News in front of Swank Furs on Fifth Avenue."

The red light went out and Yolanda eased her grip on the microphone. She had lost control of the interview; her interviewee had taken over. Mary Ellen stood there before her looking very smug. "Is this going to make tonight's news?" she asked.

Yolanda shrugged. "Depends on what else is going on in the world today." She called over to her cameraman. "That's it, Mark." He began to put his equipment away.

"Well, let me at least give you one of these before you leave," said Mary Ellen. She reached into her jacket and pulled out a flyer which she handed over to Yolanda. Yolanda examined it. It was a picture of model Jennifer O'Grady wrapped in a raccoon coat positioned over the picture of a small raccoon with its foot caught in a trap. The raccoon's heartrending eyes, sad and frightened, seemed to plead for help. The caption read: IT LOOKED BET-

TER ON THE ANIMAL'S BACK. Yolanda folded it up and put it into her pocket.

"We have to get our message across," said Mary Ellen as she turned to rejoin the marchers. She took up her placard and fell back into the formation, which now was chanting "Real people don't wear fur." Yolanda watched and wondered what Mary Ellen would think of her new fox coat. Her thoughts were interrupted by the simultaneous arrival of four squad cars with their lights flashing and sirens blaring, as they came to a screeching halt in front of the Swank store. In the back seat of one, Yolanda could make out the greying head of the woman the demonstrators had tormented earlier.

Eight uniformed policemen carrying nightsticks emerged from the cars and approached the marchers. "Okay, let's move it out," one of them called.

"You can't do this," shouted Mary Ellen. "We have a right to be here."

"You don't have a right to harass innocent citizens," he responded as he tugged at the sleeve of one of the demonstrators.

"No!" screamed Mary Ellen as she threw herself at him. "That woman wasn't innocent. She was an accessory to murder." Mary Ellen began to claw and kick at the officer. The confrontation grew more heated and suddenly a melee broke and the police were shouting and wielding nightsticks and there were people screaming everywhere. Yolanda was yelling at Mark to set the camera up again, and to her relief he had everything rolling in minutes, just in time to get an especially good shot of a screaming and kicking Mary Ellen being loaded into the back seat of a squad car.

IV

The flickering red light of the answering machine on the counter shone like a beacon in the darkness of the kitchen, flashing on and off with the promise of rescue from the shipwreck of loneliness. Leslie Warning pushed the Play button before even bothering to turn on the overhead lights or take off her jacket. Her heart raced on as she stood there in the dark and heard a male voice; it dropped in disappointment as she realized it was only Larry.

"Give me a call, Sis," came the nasally whine. "I need for you to sign some things." There was a brief silence and then he added, "I see you guys are making it in the big time now . . . six o'clock news. Too bad Mary Ellen isn't a little more photogenic." He was taunting her in his typical way, attacking things and people who were important to her. The message ended and the machine clicked off. That was it—the one message only.

Tired and disappointed, Leslie began to peel off the heavy layers of clothing she had worn all day to protect her from the bitter November wind. She unwound a long scarf from her neck and removed her heavy outer jacket. Underneath she wore a thick woolen sweater and under that two cotton turtlenecks. She wriggled out of a pair of thick wool slacks and dropped them to the floor along with the rest of the clothing. As she stood there now, wearing only the tops and bottoms to her long underwear and a pair of thermal socks, the body that had appeared to to be stocky was actually revealed to be quite attractive. She was petite and soft and well proportioned to her diminutive height. She felt lighter already, having shed the clothes that had been weighing her down all day. She bent over and collected the discarded heap of outerwear and trundled across the room, passing through the swinging door of the kitchen to the back stairs.

The back stairs led up to a small suite of rooms once intended for the butler of the house. Leslie now used the rooms as her personal quarters. She felt more secure here, more sheltered, than anywhere else in the enormous old greystone mansion. She went into the bathroom and ran hot water into the tub. It would feel so good to soak her poor tired body. A grey-and-white cat came into the bathroom followed by an orange-and-white one, and the two of them rubbed against her legs, looking for attention. She patted their heads. "Hello Amanda, hello Edward," she cooed, stroking their silky coats.

The bath drained the last vestiges of cold from her, and after wrapping herself in a huge terrycloth robe, she went downstairs into the kitchen and prepared herself a bowl of soup, some hot bread, and a pot of tea that she carried back up to her small sitting room. She ate quietly and slowly in front of the television, talking occasionally to the cats and laughing halfheartedly at an old

"Andy Griffith Show" rerun. She remained there, unmoving, for most of the evening, sipping tea. From time to time she looked at the phone, willing it to ring, but it remained silent. As the late news was coming on, it rang. She pounced on it like a cat on a mouse. For the second time that evening her brother's voice dashed her hopes.

"Leslie, didn't you get my message?" he whined. "I've been waiting to hear from you for hours."

"I'm sorry, Larry. I was tired. I had a long day today."

"Oh, I thought maybe you were out with your new friend."

The reference to Neil stung, making Leslie painfully aware that it wasn't him on the telephone. "I haven't heard from him for a while," she said.

Her brother's response was too delayed, too calculated. "I'm surprised. Maybe he's got another heiress on the line somewhere."

"That's mean, Larry. Why don't you do me a favor and worry about your own love life and I'll worry about mine."

Larry backed off, although it was hard for him. He couldn't help it, his continual desire to aggravate her. Even though they were flesh and blood, having shared the same father, she bugged the hell out of him.

"I'm sorry, kid," he said with false sincerity. "I called because I want to talk to you about signing over that stock."

"Larry, I thought we were finished with this," said Leslie. She was irritated. "I don't want to let any more of the Warning stock go. I don't think that's what Papa would have wanted."

"But Leslie, it's at an all-time high . . ."

"I don't care." She tuned out her brother's pleading as the news came on. She hoped to see footage from the demonstration. The lead story caught her attention right away as the familiar face of a beautiful woman was flashed across the screen in a series of glamorous poses. In each she was wearing something fur: a fox cape, a mink hat, a lynx jacket. In a final shot, her sleek legs and smooth shoulders peeked out from a full length black sable coat. The clear message was that she was naked underneath.

"The body of fashion model Jennifer O'Grady was found today in her Manhattan apartment, apparently murdered, according to police. They would release no further details other than to say that she had probably been dead for a few days before a concerned neighbor alerted police. Miss O'Grady was a longtime spokesperson for the National Fur Council and was probably known best for her role as the Swank woman for the last twelve years, her face and figure automatically associated with the exclusive furrier. Police say they have no leads."

The newscaster continued with what he termed "a related story" as the footage cut to Fifth Avenue and the scene outside Swank Furs that afternoon where Yolanda Prince was interviewing Mary Ellen. Then it cut to a shot of the police breaking up the demonstration and piling Mary Ellen into a squad car.

"Leslie, are you listening to me?" came her brother's impatient voice.

"No, Larry, actually I wasn't. This is terrible. They just showed on the news that Jennifer O'Grady was murdered and then in the next scene they show the S.T.S. demonstration as if we had something to do with it."

"Jennifer O'Grady murdered?" said Larry, incredulous. "The Jennifer O'Grady. That beautiful creature. Wow. Maybe one of your nut cases did do it."

"Stop it, Larry, you're just being mean and I'm not in the mood for it right now. I'll talk to you tomorrow," she said, ending the conversation by hanging up the phone.

She loved her brother, but that didn't necessarily mean she liked him.

The phone didn't ring again, and after watching the rest of the news and a half-hour sitcom after that, Leslie got ready for bed. As she stood in front of the bathroom mirror brushing her hair, she frowned with dismay at the face that greeted her. It wasn't unpleasant, but even good clear skin and the soft, shiny brown curls that framed her face couldn't make up for its shortcomings. Everything in her small oval face seemed too close to the center, giving her a slight chipmunklike appearance, and it wasn't helped any by the way her tiny nose sloped downward on the end. Still, she had beautiful large eyes, brown bordering on hazel, that stared soulfully out from under thick brown lashes. Her father had often told her that her eyes let a person look into the soul of one of the loveliest human beings there ever was.

How she missed her father and the way they used to sit and talk. And her mother. She missed them both. A terrible melancholy passed over her, and she regretted having been so curt with her brother. In spite of his abrasiveness, she cared and worried about him. Neil said that she was always worrying about the whole world. As she pulled back the blankets and crawled into her bed, Amanda and Edward jumped up and settled in next to her, purring loudly. She turned out the light and lay back, and with only the cats to keep her company, she forgot about Larry and thought about how badly she wished Neil would call.

V

TUESDAY,
November 20

Michael Nilsson's mood was sour enough before Sarah, his secretary, announced that Yolanda Prince was waiting in his outer office. He realized he had made this appointment with her quite a few days ago, but how was he to know that between then and now his top model would be murdered. He told his secretary to have her wait, and he turned and looked out his window onto the traffic on Fifth Avenue as he tried to compose himself.

Jennifer . . . gone. It was still impossible to believe. When he received the call last night he had just sat down and cried. He had known her for twelve years, watched her go from insecure girl to mature woman, marveled as her beauty blossomed, shared in molding her into one of the most recognizable models in the city, perhaps the country. All because he had found her, had chosen her, had made her the Swank girl. The loss of Jennifer would be a hell of a loss for the business, that was for sure, but an even greater loss for himself.

He was interrupted from his pain by a knock on the door, and before he could respond it opened and his wife entered the room. She closed the door quietly behind her, and walked lightly, deferentially, over to him. At forty she was still a remarkable-looking woman, her frosted blonde hair piled full and high upon her head, her skin still smooth despite a few lines around her mysterious and challenging emerald eyes. She was dressed impeccably as always, wearing a beige silk suit that flattered the slimness of her figure, expertly concealing her bottom, which had only in recent years begun to broaden a bit. As always, he couldn't help but admire the way she carried herself, the way she was able to blend business and femininity with a panache few other women could carry off.

She bent down and touched his shoulders compassionately. After fifteen years together, she could read his moods. He appreciated that she was aware of his pain, although he was glad she didn't know the extent of it. And what about her? She must be in pain as well. After all, Jennifer had been her friend too.

"Are you all right, Michael?" she asked. The words came out with a soft Southern drawl. She had never lost her South Carolina inflection, nor the girlish nickname. Charlotte "Bunny" Walters Nilsson, former flight attendant, now vice-president of Swank Furs, Incorporated.

He nodded halfheartedly, and put one of his hands upon hers, patting it. "I just still can't believe it."

"I know, darling. It's too horrible." They sat there in silence, staring out the window. It was mid-morning and the pedestrian traffic on the sidewalk below was light. "At least those kooks aren't out there today. Do you think they are showing us some sympathy?"

"I don't know," he said flatly.

"Darling," she said. It came out dahlin'. "Yolanda Prince has been waiting out there with her cameraman for almost a half hour now. Don't you think you'd best talk to her?"

That was Bunny. She was all Southern soft, she was all Southern sweet, but when it really came down to it, she was also all business. That was the true reason she had torn herself away from monitoring the books and monthly sales figures. She always had the best interests of the business in mind. "I'll stay here with you if you think it will help."

"Just send her away," he said. "I can't talk about the business now. I can't go on camera the way I feel."

"Michael, we both loved Jennifer, we are both going to miss her. But it's so important that you do this interview with Miss Prince now. It's the holiday season, and sales are taking a beating.

You have to go on and give our side of the issue. You're the president of the National Fur Council, if you can't speak up for us, who can?"

He was tired and emotionally drained, but he knew she was right. It was something that had to be done.

"All right, send her in," he said.

Bunny picked up the phone and called the outer office. "Sarah, you can tell Miss Prince we are ready for her now."

Sarah placed the phone back on the receiver, relieved that she could finally tell the restless reporter that Mr. Nilsson would see her now. As it was, Sarah was embarrassed at having made Yolanda Prince wait as long as she had. She was famous, after all, there for all the world to see every night on the six o'clock news. "Mr. Nilsson can see you now," she said, jumping up to open the door for Yolanda and her cameraman. Yolanda stood up and straightened the jacket of her red suit, pulling it down around her hips, and then ran a hand briefly along the sides of her head, nervously patting her sleek French braid.

Michael Nilsson watched her enter his office. To him, she was the picture of cool confidence, or journalistic arrogance, as she approached his desk with her cameraman a few steps behind. Little could he know that he, the president of the largest chain of furriers in the country, a rich and powerful merchant with plenty of influence in New York's business, art and philanthropic circles, a man who in many ways epitomized New York, terrified Yolanda.

"Miss Prince," he said, coming out from behind his desk to greet her. "This is my wife, Bunny. We are awfully sorry to have kept you waiting, but as you know, Swank has suffered a personal tragedy, and frankly it has taken more out of us than we can say."

Yolanda sighed. "Jennifer O'Grady?"

Bunny spoke next. "Yes. As I'm sure you would assume, it was a terrible shock. Jennifer was like a daughter to us. She had been with us for twelve years."

"You mean with Swank?"

"Yes, of course, but with us too. My husband discovered Jennifer when she was seventeen and just out of high school. She had taken her first job as a secretary and came into this very store wanting to buy herself a fur coat. At that time most furs were beyond the reach of young working women. They had to be rich or movie stars to wear them. But when Michael saw Jennifer trying on coats, and he saw how stunning she looked in them, he had the idea that fur should be affordable for every woman. That's how we started marketing some less expensive furs, fun furs, and we also came up with an aggressive layaway plan. Business went through the roof.

"Jennifer was a perfect image for this new working woman we wanted to reach. She was so young and wholesome. We hired her then and there, and in fact she even lived with us for a while as we helped her get started. The rest is history," she said, and she choked slightly on her next words. "Until yesterday."

There was an awkward silence in Nilsson's office as Yolanda waited for the uncomfortable moment to pass. Bunny fought back a sob, and Mark, the cameraman, cleared his throat. Finally, Michael spoke. "But that's not what we are here to talk about today."

"No, of course," Yolanda almost whispered. She studied his face compassionately. He looked the worse for wear; his eyes were red and puffy and his face pale. Despite this, however, he was an extraordinarily handsome man with a Roman nose, a slightly cleft chin and a strong square face. He was pushing fifty, and his thick, wavy hair was turning grey. A pair of intense blue eyes, the type that never miss a trick, stared directly at her now, waiting for her to make the next move. It was, after all, her show.

"Uh, can we all sit somewhere, somewhere Mark can set the camera on us all?" she asked. Michael pointed to four leather chairs positioned around a coffee table, an area he liked to use for informal conferences.

"Perfect," said Yolanda. Michael waited until Yolanda and Bunny were seated before lowering his tall, muscular frame into the chair opposite Yolanda. "Now we are going to record everything we say here," she said, "but a great deal of it will be edited out. 'In Depth' is only a thirty-minute show, and there will be other people featured on it as well. But here's your chance to have your say." She smiled and nodded at Mark. The familiar red light came on.

"This is Yolanda Prince," she opened, "and I am here talking with Michael and Bunny Nilsson, the owners of Swank Furs. Mr. Nilsson, I believe that Swank is one of the oldest fur houses in New York."

"That is true. Swank was founded by my father, Lars, in the late thirties when he came here from Sweden," said Michael, speaking calmly and with authority. "He had been a trapper and later man-ufactured coats in Scandinavia, and he decided to set up his own business here in the United States. Swank is unusual among furri-ers in that we control all aspects of our coats. We have both a network of trappers in the Canadian northwest and our own ranches, and we produce all our own coats, jackets and fur acces-sories."

"It appears that the fur industry is under attack these days. There are many people today who take exception to the wearing of animal skins; they consider it cruel, inhumane. What do you have to say about that?"

"I have a lot to say," Michael Nilsson said. "I think that people need to be better informed. First let's start with the fur itself. Men and women have been wearing animal skins since the dawn of time . . ."

The interview lasted for over an hour and went very well, Michael thought. He had made many key points in defense of his sorely bashed industry, things he strongly felt the public had a right to know. He had spoken at length about the responsible nature of the fur industry and its place in America's history. He hoped it had a place in America's future.

Yolanda had been a fair and adept interviewer who kept the conversation moving smoothly. Only once did she try to lead him into some discussion of Jennifer O'Grady, but he cut her off im-mediately. Everything else had been perfect.

"When do you plan to air this show, Yolanda?" he asked as they waited for Mark to finish packing up his equipment.

"I'm shooting for the end of the week. What could be more appropriate than 'Fur Free Friday'?"

"Well, I just hope our side is heard over all those rabble-rous-ers," said Bunny firmly.

"Mrs. Nilsson, I always make a point of giving all sides equal time. I figure, let an informed public draw their own conclusions. I think we've got some really good tape here. You made a lot of valid points."

Bunny mulled this over and then asked, "Miss Prince, do you have a fur coat?"

Yolanda smiled and nodded her head. "As a matter of fact I just invested in a red fox this year."

"Red fox, what a delightful choice. That's a perfect coat for you, with your coloring. And a big fur like that looks so right on a tall woman like you." Bunny was relieved to know that the star of the show wore fur herself. That could only work in their best interest, she thought. She had an idea, and she made a mental note to herself to follow up on it.

After Yolanda and Mark had gone, Michael returned to his desk and swiveled his chair back around to the window view. What he saw displeased him greatly. They were out there again, like cockroaches, one story below him. There were fewer of them today, but they were there just the same, harassing any pedestrian in fur and discouraging potential customers from entering the store.

"Have they no compassion for human beings?" he said angrily, banging his fists on the windowpane. "They have no right to do this to us, today of all days. Don't they know what we're going through?"

"Can't we do anything about them?" Bunny asked dourly, looking out the window herself.

"This is America. They have their rights," said Michael. "It is we who have none. We have to sit by and watch them destroy our business."

It was not far from either of their minds that business had been down twenty percent last year and from what they were seeing so far this year, it wasn't going to improve any. Worse, a glut in pelts all over the world was depressing retail prices. He sighed into his hands and wondered how he was going to present all of this to his father. He shuddered to think about what Lars Nilsson's reaction would be when he learned that the Save Their Skins activists had singled Swank out as a target. And he also had to break the news to him about Jennifer.

His visit with his father this afternoon was going to be worse than usual and he dreaded it.

VI

Once outside on the street, Yolanda stopped to drink in deep refreshing breaths of the cold, wintry air. She took it in like a
woman suffocating, drawing a strange look from Mark, who stood
directly beside her.

"Sorry," said Yolanda. "I just got a sudden cramp in my foot.
Must be these new shoes. Give me a minute."

She stood there under his curious gaze, waiting for her head to
stop spinning, waiting for the tension to subside. Finally, away
from the confining walls of Michael Nilsson's office, she began to
feel the tight grasp of fingers loosen. The monster that had been
sitting on her chest, making her feel as though every breath was a
fight, was taking its leave.

She sighed. It was over, the attack had passed and she had
survived. But it left her drained and scared—it was so unpredict-
able. She wondered if Mark, standing patiently next to her, had
any idea of what she had been experiencing and if he would laugh
if he knew.

"Let's get going," she said with authority. They walked past the
small group of protesters and, as they did, Yolanda picked out
Mary Ellen Fitzsimmons, marching with as much vigor and enthusiasm as ever. A trip to the police station hadn't taken any of
the wind out of her sails.

"We will not give up," Mary Ellen shouted in Yolanda's direction, "until all living creatures are free!"

Oh Mary Ellen, thought Yolanda, you are one of the fanatics of
the world. It was getting harder for Yolanda to take these activists
seriously. She had met them all: Hare Krishna leaders who pon-
tificated about purity as they sent a force of brainwashed panhan-
dlers into the streets; gay liberationists paralyzing a hospital's
switchboard because it had fired a surgeon who had AIDS; rabble-
rousers in her old neighborhood who picketed for days in front of
a Korean grocery store because the owner had pushed out a shop-

lifter. The lunatic fringe, those eternally seeking the spotlight, they provided the news for Yolanda. They were her life's blood.

It was the way that Yolanda had always been able to conduct herself with them and get an interesting interview that brought the success she was just beginning to enjoy. They always loved to talk to her, dying for a few minutes in front of the camera. They respected her because, like them, she was the disadvantaged. With them, being black and a woman worked in her favor. They were so . . . easy.

The Michael Nilssons of the world were the other side of the coin for her. Just thinking of them struck terror into her heart. They were neither fanatical nor off-balance; they were the establishment. The white upper-class businessmen. They were the towers of steel who controlled the world, and in their presence Yolanda suffered uncontrollable anxiety.

Sure, things had changed in the past few decades. Black people had come a long way and women had surely made tremendous inroads, but Yolanda knew in her heart that for the most part it remained a white man's world. Successful as she was, she still found herself intimidated by the corporate soldiers of the world. They made her feel inadequate. Even at work, when she had to meet with a network executive, her legs would go to jelly and she once again became the young ghetto girl, uneducated, unsophisticated, poorly dressed. She felt she was nothing to these men.

It wasn't their power or their status or even their bank accounts that made them so different. It was the way they sailed through their lives. Commands fell easily from their lips, they shouldered responsibility naturally. Unlike celebrities, they were not dependent upon a fickle public. And everywhere they went, they commanded respect, moving in a cloud of self-importance that sprung from who knew where.

All that Yolanda knew was that they made her uneasy, made her feel small and unaccomplished and unimportant. How could this be possible when it was she who held the all-powerful microphone in her hand?

Feeling relieved that her anxiety had finally lifted, she mulled over the interview that had caused it. The hour with the Nilssons had gone fairly well; the material they had covered was strong enough to counter some of the animal rights claims as well as create some controversy. But Michael Nilsson had been so well prepared that he was able to control much of the interview. She had been irritated when he quickly cut off her questions about Jennifer O'Grady. Granted, the model's murder didn't have anything to do with the topic being covered on this week's "In Depth," but she was irked just the same that he had refused to talk about it.

Yolanda knew that one of the strengths of her "In Depth" specials was her ability to balance the program, to present equal arguments from two opposing forces. She didn't take sides. She didn't want to be Geraldo or Oprah or Phil, making their opinions known and their shows one-sided. Yolanda wanted her audience to make their own decisions.

But to make her show effective, Yolanda needed balance and counterbalance. She found herself thinking of the cool and self-assured personality of Michael Nilsson and she wondered who she could put up against him. Her original plan had been to interview Denise Segura of the Humane Society. Denise was a calm, rational person who could present a cogent view of the animal rights advocates. But the more Yolanda thought about Denise and her quiet inoffensive manner, the way her broad face was hidden behind thick glasses, the way she was constantly looking down shyly, the more she wondered if Denise was the right choice. How would a mild person like that stand up against the likes of a Michael Nilsson?

And then her thoughts flashed back to Mary Ellen Fitzsimmons marching just a few blocks away. Driven . . . uncompromising. She had shown her ability to do a strong interview yesterday. Mary Ellen could certainly hold her own against Michael Nilsson.

Yolanda stopped in her tracks so abruptly that Mark, loaded with equipment and following two steps behind, almost piled into her. "Mark, you go on to the van, I'll be right there," she said, starting back in the other direction. "I've just had an inspiration."

"Sure, Yolanda," he said. Eager to get out of the cold, he trotted on up the street, his long wool scarf flapping in the wind behind him, his shaggy brown hair blowing wherever it stuck out from under his cap.

"Mary Ellen!" Yolanda called out when she had reached the front of the Swank store. Mary Ellen, recognizing Yolanda, broke ranks with her fellow marchers and joined her. She was followed by another marcher, a skinny throwback to Haight Ashbury days who reminded Yolanda of a puppy the way he stayed at Mary Ellen's heels.

"Hi," said Mary Ellen. The hippie stood behind her, nodding impassively at Yolanda. Like Mary Ellen, he was tall and thin with ordinary features except for a thick beard that covered half of his face and ended midway down his chest. His soft brown eyes watered in his pale face, and his hair was straight and worn long, to his shoulders. He was dressed in blue jeans and a long green army coat. Mary Ellen wore the now familiar green nylon jacket and she stood there blowing into her gloves to warm her hands.

"A few less of you than yesterday," Yolanda commented.

"Yeah," Mary Ellen admitted. "We're saving bodies for the big push on Friday, Fur Free Friday. The day after Thanksgiving, busiest shopping day of the year. That's when we have our really big demonstration."

"We're just out here to maintain some presence today," said the bearded man in a surprisingly deep voice. "Keep everybody rattled." He extended a gloved hand to Yolanda. "Keith Geiger," he said. She took his hand and found herself meeting his eyes for what felt to be a moment too long. She saw something behind them, something cloaked and mysterious, and so unsettling that she quickly turned her attention back to Mary Ellen.

"I'm putting together an 'In Depth' on the fur controversy and I was wondering if you would be interested in doing a taping for it."

"Are you kidding? You bet I would," said Mary Ellen without hesitation. "Where and when?"

"I'd like to do it this afternoon if you're free. Do you have a headquarters?"

"We do now," she said. "In Soho. We've been blessed with a benefactor who's underwritten office space. You'll meet her when you come down." She gave Yolanda the address. "I can be there any time you want."

They agreed on two o'clock, and Yolanda hurried back down Fifth Avenue to where she knew she would find Mark waiting in the van. As she waited at a light, the face of Jennifer O'Grady stared up at her from the front page of the *Daily News*. MODEL FOUND MURDERED screamed the headline.

As she crossed with the light, she was already thinking about a possible topic for her next "In Depth." Jennifer O'Grady. Manhattan model murdered. Jennifer O'Grady wasn't the only model to have been a victim of violence lately. There was the model slashed by a jealous lover. And another who had been shot by an overzealous admirer who wanted to prevent anyone else from ever looking at her. Violence against beauty? It had possibilities.

The van's motor was running and inside it was blissfully warm. "Don't get too comfortable," Mark warned. "We just got a call. There's a fire in the east nineties and we're supposed to cover it."

"At least a fire is warm," Yolanda joked as she sat back. She rode the rest of the way in silence, mentally gearing up for her interview with Mary Ellen Fitzsimmons just a couple of hours away.

VII

Leslie looked up nervously at the two New York homicide cops looming over her desk. Neither was anything like she would have pictured a homicide cop to be. The man was very handsome in a dark, swarthy sort of way. The woman was about her own age with silky black hair, perfect makeup and long red fingernails. She looked back at the flyer they had just handed her. Of course she recognized it—it was one of theirs, the one Mary Ellen had designed. The picture of a beautiful Jennifer O'Grady wrapped in a lush raccoon coat was set over the picture of a frightened raccoon with its foot in a trap. IT LOOKED BETTER ON THE ANIMAL'S BACK.

"Yes, I've seen this," she answered. She craned her neck around, searching for something. The cluttered office was fairly large, and it held the standard office equipment: three wooden desks, a few extra plastic chairs, a typewriter, a computer and a photocopier. The atmosphere was one of gloom. Cheap veneer paneling made it darker than necessary, and morbidly graphic photos of animals in distress did little to lighten the mood. Leslie spotted what she was looking for—a stack of papers piled three deep and waist high, shrink-wrapped in cellophane.

"There," she said, pointing. "We printed twenty thousand."

Tony Perrelli rolled his eyes and smirked. "I don't suppose you could tell me how you distribute these?"

"We give them to volunteers who hand them out on street corners and at demonstrations," said Leslie sheepishly, hoping it wasn't illegal. Her soulful brown eyes were liquid as she looked timidly into Perrelli's hard ones. She shifted her focus to Karen, hoping another woman would be sympathetic. "We haven't done anything wrong, have we?"

"Do you know that this model was found murdered yesterday?" Perrelli asked.

"Yes," said Leslie, looking down to avoid his stare. "I saw it on the news last night. It's a terrible shame." She was uneasy in the presence of the police. She wished that Mary Ellen and Keith were there; she really didn't know how to handle this. But they were out demonstrating and she didn't expect them back in the office. She forced herself to look back at the detective. He started to ask her another question when to her relief there was the sound of loud voices outside in the hall.

"I love that idea," Leslie heard Keith saying as he opened the office door. "Maybe we could get Yolanda to let us give an award for the most inhumane person of the year. We could present it to Michael Nilsson, National Fur Council president."

"Hah! That one I'd like to present posthumously." Her hearty laughter faded when she saw the two serious-looking visitors standing before Leslie's desk. She looked at Leslie questioningly.

"Mary Ellen, this is Detective Perrelli and Detective Levinson from the police. They want to ask some questions."

Mary Ellen's expression hardened, her pupils narrowing to pinpricks. "If this is about the demonstration you can just talk to our lawyer. We know what our rights are."

"It's not about that, Miss Fitzsimmons," said Tony, straining to be civil. "We're from homicide. It's about the death of Jennifer O'Grady."

Mary Ellen's relief was obvious. She casually removed her coat and muffler and hung them on a rack near the door. "Oh that," she said, seemingly nonplussed. "A real shame. I suppose we'll have to change our flyers."

Keith shut the office door behind them, and he too took off his outerwear and hung it on the rack. He extended his hand to the officers. "Keith Geiger," he said.

"You are . . . ?" asked Tony.

"Vice-president of Save Their Skins. Mary Ellen is, of course, president."

Perrelli looked back at Mary Ellen. "Well, speaking of your flyers, one of them was found at the scene of Miss O'Grady's murder," he said, waving it in her direction.

Mary Ellen's face took on a more concerned look and she walked around to the back of the largest of the desks and sat down.

"Whew," said Keith as he dropped into one of the plastic chairs.

"This is terrible," said Mary Ellen. "We are basically a peaceful group. We do not condone violence."

Tony gave her a long, hard stare. "Well, that may be true, but I need to ask you some questions anyhow. First, how large is your organization?"

"A couple of thousand in the New York area. Wouldn't you say so, Leslie?" Mary Ellen suddenly looked disconnected, unsure of herself.

"Uh, yes, about two thousand locally."

"And how many of these people are actually active?" the cop asked.

"Oh, I don't know," she replied, shaking her head as if she were shaking off sleep. "A few dozen, I suppose. We keep a list of people we know we can count on for support."

"I'll need a copy of that list and a copy of your entire membership too. Does there happen to be anybody in your group who you might consider to be a little too overreactive, a little too gung ho?"

"You can't be too 'gung ho' when it comes to saving the animals," said Mary Ellen matter-of-factly. Her voice lacked its usual verve.

Keith picked up the reins. "There's no way anyone in our organization would commit murder if that's what you are hinting at. Our concern is for all living things."

"Uh-hmmm, no zealots then?" said Tony, looking more intently at his surroundings. To his left a large poster proclaimed, "Get a feel for fur, slam your fingers in a car door." Next to it was a picture of an animal's severed paw left in a trap. And next to that another poster screamed FUR KILLS in large blood-red letters. He meandered around, took in a few more unhappy scenes, and turned back to Mary Ellen. "If I could just get those lists from you, that's all we'll need for now."

"Leslie will get them for you," she said.

Leslie got up from her desk and went to one of the file cabinets. Tony looked carefully at her typewriter. IBM. One of millions in Manhattan.

Leslie fumbled around in the files and came up with a copy of the membership roster. She handed it to Tony along with a single sheet of paper that listed the most active S.T.S. volunteers in the New York area. She couldn't help but catch his eye as he took the papers from her, and she looked away timidly. She looked at the girl who was his partner. They looked good together, the two of them, both dark and intense. She wondered what it was like for a man and woman to work so closely in a dangerous profession. Just thinking about what they did, their proximity to death, made her skin crawl. Where emotions ran so high, did things develop between them? She noticed that neither of them wore a wedding ring.

Perrelli took out his wallet and flipped a few cards onto Leslie's desk. "My office number is on there and my beeper number. I want you to call if you think of anything that might help us." Leslie picked up the cards and took one for herself, handing the others to Mary Ellen and Keith.

Tony opened the door to leave, and then stopped as if he had suddenly remembered something. "Just for the record," he asked, "where were all of you last Friday?"

Mary Ellen huffed. "I was here all day working. So was Leslie."

Tony nodded his head. He really wasn't that interested in the women. He looked at Keith Geiger. "What about you?"

Keith's eyes darted about nervously for a moment before fixing themselves steadily on the detective's. "I was at home all day Friday. Alone."

"Hmmph," Tony grunted. Without another word he opened the door the rest of the way and stepped out. Karen, in his shadow, turned around and nodded good-bye apologetically before following him out.

"What a jerk!" said Mary Ellen after the two detectives were gone. Then her mood changed as she turned to Leslie and said excitedly, "Guess who's coming here to interview us this afternoon?"

VIII

Tony didn't say a word as they walked back to the car, a nondescript white Dodge parked in front of a fire hydrant. He hadn't said much to Karen all day, which was not unusual. His resentment was really beginning to grate on her. Like most other men on the job, he still couldn't accept the fact that women had a place in law enforcement. Stuck in a time warp, she thought. He was one of those who divided all women into two categories, wife or mistress, madonna or whore. And nowhere in this scenario did they have a place in the work force, and particularly not in a life-threatening occupation like police work.

Karen had a vague understanding of where he was coming from, and she knew she shouldn't care about his attitude. But she did, because she cared about her career. For most of her life she had wanted to be a cop, ever since she was a kid watching Peggy Lipton in "Mod Squad" and Angie Dickinson in "Policewoman." The strong independent women they portrayed appealed to her, and she set her sights on one day becoming a police officer. She studied criminology in college, and worked out constantly to get herself in the best physical shape, making her fine-boned frame surprisingly strong. She knew that women were becoming more and more an essential part of law enforcement, and she wanted to be in on it. Karen saw women as the true peace officers, often better able to defuse a volatile situation by using their heads instead of force.

But cops like Tony Perrelli were blind to this, doing everything in their power to make it rough on the women, to discourage them. How can you move ahead, thought Karen, when you have to constantly watch your behind?

Karen's promotion to homicide detective after only three years as a beat cop had come as a surprise to her, and at first she had been elated. Some of the wind went out of her sails shortly thereafter when she learned the real reason for her promotion. The mayor's office, under pressure from women's groups, had badgered the department to name more female detectives, and she just happened to be one of those who won the lottery. So it was luck and politics that had made her one of the very few women in homicide and certainly the youngest.

Fate had put her with Tony—his regular partner was out with hepatitis. She was immediately apprehensive about the assignment. He was reputed to be a fine cop, but his disdain for women on the force was legendary. Since their first day together, Karen had been miserable. He spoke to her seldom, took complete control of every call they made, and offered her little instruction. He never asked for her opinion. Yesterday at Evelyn Burhop's was the first time he had ever let her open her mouth, and she knew that was only because the old lady was so upset.

This wasn't how it was supposed to be. They were supposed to work as a team.

"So what did you think of them?" Karen inquired as they settled into the car, Tony at the wheel. "The S.T.S.ers."

"Weirdos."

"Do you think they killed the girl?"

Tony laughed aloud, a mean and hearty laugh directed at Karen. "This is our first call on this case, we haven't seen an autopsy report, and we know virtually nothing about the victim. I know you are new to homicide, but I would say it's a little premature to be leaping to conclusions. You've been watching too much TV." He threw the car into drive and pulled away from the curb.

"It doesn't work that way, you know," he continued. "Even if a guy's standing there with a smoking gun in his hand and a dead body at his feet with a hole in it and he looks up and says 'I did it' don't be so sure. As soon as you form an opinion you're closing your mind off to other possibilities.

"Like the guy with the smoking gun in his hand . . ." He turned and faced her, and although his tone was still tough, she had the feeling that he was going to share something important with her for once. "You know why I bring that up?" he asked.

She shook her head.

"Because it happened to me once, smoking gun and all. An older guy. Admitted he did it. He was convicted, and died in prison a few months later. Turned out he had terminal cancer and nothing to lose. The problem is that his son ended up killing a couple of other people, one of them a young mother, before we caught up with him. When he confessed to the murder his old man had gone to jail for, I was honestly sick. I realized then and there that it was my fault those other two people were dead. I was young and eager to get a conviction, and I didn't bother to look further than what was staring me in the face. Well, it turned around and bit me on the ass. If you think you're gonna stay in homicide, you'd do best to remember that. Don't go for the obvious."

His last words were icy, sort of a slap at the end of the lesson. His original persona had reemerged.

Karen had just about had it with his attitude. Sure, she was new to homicide and had lots to learn, but the way Tony was handling the whole thing wasn't fair. Even when he was teaching her, he was belittling her.

"You don't like me, do you, Perrelli?" she asked.

His eyes remained riveted to the street as he drove. "I can't say I don't like you, I'm sure you're a nice girl; I just don't like working with you. Unfortunately there's nothing I can do about it."

"Why don't you like working with me? Is it because I'm female?"

"That's part of it," he admitted, "And you're young, and you're practically a rookie, and you ask me a million stupid questions about things that your 'degree' didn't prepare you for. But mostly, yeah, it's because you're a woman."

"Well, if it's so tough why don't you put in for a different partner?"

"I already tried. I was shot down."

Karen was sullen. "Hey, I didn't give Concannon hepatitis."

"No, and I didn't ask to have a spoiled little princess for a partner."

The words stung. Until now, she hadn't realized how deeply he resented her. Unfortunately for him, however, he didn't have the first inkling of her tenacity. She had defied her family to become a cop and stuck out her first three years on a street beat. As far as she was concerned, Perrelli had just challenged her. She was prepared to lock horns and fight. Not just yet, but when the time was right. Oh yes, Detective Perrelli, to hell with you. Someday you're going to get back what you dish out.

Tony was weaving his way through the heavy traffic as they headed toward midtown and their next stop, Swank Furs. A stony silence prevailed until they reached the store. They parked in the delivery ramp.

"Okay. We're going to talk to the Nilssons now," he said, "but I don't want you to say anything. I just want you to be like a fly on the wall. Sit there and listen. Got it?"

"I got it," she said, trying unsuccessfully to stifle the edge in her voice. He looked at her for a long second before getting out of the car. Was it him, or did she suddenly seem the slightest bit sarcastic?

They were ushered into Michael Nilsson's second floor office overlooking Fifth Avenue. His wife was there with him, and she guided them over to the conference area where the Nilssons had sat with Yolanda Prince a couple of hours earlier. Tony settled his long frame casually into the soft leather chair, sitting back as though he were in someone's living room waiting for a cocktail. Karen sat forward on her chair, her back straight, her attitude alert and attentive as she took in the fine furnishings around her.

"Thank you for seeing us," said Tony after introductions had been made and the Nilssons were seated. "We need to ask you some things about Jennifer O'Grady." He waited a polite moment to defer to the grief he sensed in the room. "To the best of our knowledge, there is no family?"

"That is correct," said Michael dourly. "Both of her parents are dead, and she had no brothers or sisters. As far as aunts or uncles, she never mentioned any."

"I understand that she worked for you for quite some time. Did you know her well?"

It was Bunny who broke in now, interrupting her husband. Her voice was wistful and melancholy, the Southern drawl twinged with sadness. "We knew her more than well. We were her family. She spent the holidays with us, dined with us regularly, counted on us to help with her finances. Michael was practically a father to her, the father she never really had, guiding her along from when she first came to us."

"And that was when?"

"Twelve years ago." Her eyes darted to her husband's, and he nodded his head in quiet approval. "I hope this can stay in this room, because it is contrary to popular knowledge, but Jennifer

O'Grady was little more than a street urchin when we met her. We were coming out of a Saturday matinee of *A Chorus Line* and in a hurry to get out of the area, it's grown so seedy as you know, I'm sure, when this girl, this street person, came up to us asking for spare change. She looked so hungry, she was so thin, and she was dressed in rags. She was filthy and unkempt, but even then, it was obvious that she was very beautiful. There was something about her that Michael and I saw immediately, a combination of beauty and vulnerability, of wholesomeness and sensuality.

"We bought her lunch and learned that she had very little recollection of her father, and she had been living hand-to-mouth since her mother's death a year earlier. She was a baby, yet she was old beyond her seventeen years.

"At the time we were looking for a model to represent Swank exclusively. Once again, Michael and I were thinking along the same lines. Could this girl possibly be the one?

"We took her in and polished her up, a Pygmalion sort of thing. We changed her name, she was Sophie Tochowitz at the time, and taught her how to carry herself, and the Swank girl was born. We invented the story about her being a secretary, we wanted to market a wholesome image, and she was an immediate success. Before long, she was famous."

Bunny dropped her eyes, a slight pooling of tears evident in them. "She went from so little to so much . . ."

"What about friends, boyfriends?" Tony queried. "Did she have many?"

Michael spoke next. "I guess you could say we were her best friends. She dated infrequently, and seemed to have few friends. For the most part Jennifer was a very private person. She spent most of her free time reading."

So we noticed, mused Karen, thinking back to the stacks of books that lined the wall of Jennifer's bedroom.

"Did Jennifer ever mention threats of any kind?"

"No, nothing," replied Michael, but his wife stopped him short.

"There was something," she said as if just recalling it. "Jennifer mentioned to me recently that one of those animal kooks had harassed her a few times when she was on her way home. He said some nasty things like she should be skinned herself, or something like that. She didn't seem concerned about it. She just mentioned it to me in passing."

Tony was interested. "Did she tell you anything more about him? What he looked like?"

"No."

"And she never reported it to the police?"

"No, I don't think so. She was irritated, but that's all. I don't think she felt she was in any danger."

"When was the last time you saw Miss O'Grady?"

"When she was here last Thursday."

"But neither of you saw her at all on Friday?"

"No," said Bunny. Tony looked to Michael Nilsson. He shook his head.

"Hmmmph," said Tony to no one in particular. He stood up abruptly, signaling that the interview was finished. Once again, before leaving, he pulled out his wallet to leave his card. But instead of throwing a few down on the table as he had at the S.T.S. headquarters, he handed them directly to Michael Nilsson. "Please call me if you can think of anything at all that may be of importance."

Michael Nilsson was holding the heavy oak door open for them, and as Karen passed him on her way out, she could read the unhappiness in his face. Something compelled her to stop, and she looked first to Michael and then to his wife. "I'm very sorry about your loss," she said.

When they were alone in the office, Michael turned to Bunny and asked coldly, "Why didn't you tell me that someone was following Jennifer?"

"I'm sorry, honey. It just didn't seem all that important, and certainly not worth worrying you about."

Michael looked out the window and onto Fifth Avenue and the pedestrian traffic below. Thankfully the marchers were gone for now, but like the pesky insects they were, he knew they would return.

"Do you think one of them killed her?" he asked.

Bunny looked at him blankly and shrugged.

IX

The S.T.S. headquarters, in which she now sat, was certainly a far cry from the luxurious offices of Swank Furs. Yolanda looked around the good-sized room with its cheap furniture and gruesome posters, and shivered. She turned her head away from the poster of a trapped fox, it's glassy eyes staring helplessly into hers. She wondered if it was he who was hanging in her closet at home.

She waited as Mark set up the equipment, a captive audience to Mary Ellen's incessant chatter.

"I'm just an activist at heart, that's all. When I see something wrong, I have to do something about it. Vietnam, nuclear power plants, women's oppression, I've demonstrated against all of them. And I've gone to jail more than a few times for my beliefs too. Used to drive my parents crazy. They live in upstate New York, that's where I'm from. But I guess with ten kids they couldn't let little Mary Ellen's trips to the slammer be that devastating." She laughed aloud. "My poor parents, it's a miracle they survived us. But they are wonderful people. They encouraged all of us to be individuals, and that's what they got. Ten individuals. I'm not even speaking with five of those individuals at present. Political differences."

"All ready," Mark called out, much to Yolanda's relief. She had heard enough of Mary Ellen's personal history. She was beginning to have doubts about featuring her in this special.

"Now remember, Mary Ellen," she instructed. "Please stick to the issue. This will be edited anyhow, but the more you stick to the subject of the fur industry, the more likely that you'll see it on TV. Okay?"

"I guess that means you don't want me to go into the Draize test and how many innocent rabbits have been blinded so that women can wear mascara?"

"Exactly," said Yolanda. "Maybe we'll do the laboratory issue some other day."

"Don't you see, they're all the same issue," said Mary Ellen, but upon seeing Yolanda's exasperated look she backed down. "Okay," she said, feigning surrender.

Yolanda was exhausted when they finished up the interview an hour later. Mary Ellen could certainly be a draining subject, her dedication to her cause was unwavering. She had been surprisingly good about staying on the subject, probably because she wanted to get as much air time as she could, but she did manage to compare the death of six million Jews in World War II concentration camps to the slaughter of billions of broiler chickens. Even Yolanda's cameraman, the usually unflappable Mark, seemed stunned by that one.

Keith Geiger, who had sat quietly by during the interview, asked Yolanda when the program would air.

"Friday," she answered. "I thought it would be appropriate to show it on Fur Free Friday."

"That's great," said Mary Ellen, as she watched Yolanda and Mark gather up their equipment. "Say, what do you think about the murder of the Swank girl?"

"I think it's a tragedy," said Yolanda, her mind fluttering once again back to the subject of Jennifer O'Grady. For some reason, she was becoming obsessed with it. She wished she knew more about the murder—the police had released few details. Found dead in her co-op, blow to the head. No robbery, no suspects. Violence, violence against models. She would start that story after she finished with this one.

"Well, it's too bad she died, but maybe it will discourage some people from buying fur," said Mary Ellen.

Yolanda looked at her with true amazement. This girl is a nut, she thought.

"Did you know they found some of our literature in her apartment?" Mary Ellen asked.

"No, I hadn't heard that," replied Yolanda, suddenly interested, sniffing some hard news.

"Yeah, I'm sure they think one of us did it," she cackled, and then she said no more.

Once outside, Yolanda started to think more seriously about what Mary Ellen had said. Was it possible that some deranged animal rights protester had murdered Jennifer O'Grady? Why hadn't the police mentioned finding S.T.S. literature in her apartment? What else were they hiding?

She made a mental note to talk to whomever was on the story when she got back to the studio.

The phones had been unduly quiet during the interview, and when the one on Leslie's desk jangled noisily, she jumped in her seat.

"Good afternoon, S.T.S.," she answered.

"Hello, stranger."

Her heart sank in her stomach before rebounding into her throat and then slowly settling back where it belonged. It was Neil. There was a God. Her prayers had been answered.

"Hi," she said shyly, and then, surprised by her own boldness, she asked, "Where have you been?"

"Oh, around. I've been exceptionally busy trying to drum up some business. You know how that goes, or then again, maybe you don't. Anyhow, if you're still talking to me and you're free tonight, I'd like to buy you some dinner."

She had no plans, but she wondered if she should tell him otherwise. It had been so long since he called, she feared he'd lost interest. She knew it wasn't smart to be too available, but she hated playing games, so she said, "I'm free."

"Good. I'll pick you up after work. How does Eye-talian sound?"

"It sounds wonderful." He could have fed her dirt for all she cared as long as she was with him. She hung up and her whole being was aglow. She noticed that Keith and Mary Ellen were both looking at her.

"Was that the Yuppie creep?" asked Mary Ellen.

"I know you don't like him."

"I don't like gold diggers, and that's what he looks like to me. Just after your money, Leslie, so he can get himself a nice BMW with a cellular phone. Watch out for him, that's all I'm saying."

"Thanks, Mom," she said, "but he didn't even know I had money when he met me." And then to herself she thought, *Aren't you after my money too, Mary Ellen?* Sometimes it seemed that everybody was after her for something.

X

Michael noticed that traffic was lighter than usual as he passed easily through the Lincoln Tunnel and moved along at a good pace on the Jersey Turnpike. A lot of people must have already left town for the holiday, he thought. Just his luck that today of all days it would be a breeze getting to his father's house in Upper Montclair.

His regular Tuesday visit with his father was the thing he most dreaded in life. For a few hours he would have to sit and listen to Lars Nilsson tell him how he should be doing things and exactly what it was that he was doing wrong. A series of strokes should have taken some of the wind out of his sails, but the physical disabilities only served to make his mind more focused on what he wanted, and his demands on Michael had become more stringent than ever.

While his mother was alive, at least it had been tolerable. Her gentle presence could defuse his father's tirades. Sometimes she would even interrupt him, and come to her son's defense, just as she had ever since he was a little boy. She was the only one who could ever break through Lars's cold exterior. Michael could picture her reprimanding him on Michael's behalf and Lars turning his partially paralyzed face toward her in anger at first, and then softening at the sight of her. Michael sorely missed having her as his ally.

She had been dead three years now, drifting off in her sleep one night, leaving life as quietly as she had lived it. And leaving Michael alone to deal with his father.

Years of therapy had taught him that his father was simply a selfish, demanding, mean-spirited person. He thought of how incensed Lars would be if he ever discovered how much money Michael had spent on psychiatrists to come to that conclusion. Lars would have been happy to tell him so for free. But even knowing that the problem lay with his father and not with himself, it still took Michael days to recover from one of his visits with him. One hour with Lars Nilsson could erase weeks of therapy and seriously erode Michael's self-confidence.

It had been that way his whole life. No matter what, Michael could never do enough, and most of what he did wasn't right. When he was growing up his grades hadn't been good enough and his athletic performance wasn't aggressive enough, and now the way he handled business certainly wasn't successful enough.

Inside Michael still lived that little boy who wanted so hard to please his father, to win his love. With a still vivid twinge of pain, he thought about the year he had built his father a replica of a Viking ship for his birthday. He had worked so hard on the little balsa ship, and had been so eager to give it to him. Beaming with pride, he had gone into his father's office in the big house and presented him with his masterpiece. His father took one look at the gift and laughed.

"Now what on earth would I do with something as useless as this?" he thundered. "I hope you didn't waste a lot of time on it." And then, without bothering to thank or dismiss his son, he had returned to the everpresent pile of paperwork on his big, polished desk.

When he snuck back into his father's office that evening he was devastated to find his precious boat in the wastepaper basket. His little boy's heart broke and he cried as he picked the crumpled pieces out of the trash. He realized then that he was not crying over the boat, nor over his father's coldness, but because he truly believed he could not do anything right.

Michael knew of only two things he had done in his life that his father approved of. The first was marrying Bunny; Lars was very fond of her. The second was discovering Jennifer for the Swank girl. Otherwise his father considered him a dismal failure.

As he turned off the turnpike, he was a tormented soul, wondering how he was going to break the news about Jennifer to his father.

Michael swung his Jaguar into the circular driveway and pulled directly in front of the great Tudor mansion. It looked cold and foreboding in the winter dusk. The trees around it were stripped bare, and even its coat of ivy had been reduced to a patchwork of twigs. The house loomed black and dark. All that was missing, thought Michael, was a bolt of lightning behind it to illuminate it.

He rang the bell as he always did despite the fact that he had a key. Within a minute his ring was answered by Maria, the Filipino housekeeper who had been with them for years. She was a saint as far as Michael was concerned, weathering his father's outbursts and abuse with a chaste smile. Michael wondered if it had gotten any better for Maria since his father had been in the wheelchair, no longer able to follow behind her making a point again and again.

"Your father is in his den," she said agreeably, her English pleasantly singsong. Michael walked down the hall to the dark oak-paneled room where he had once dug his Viking ship out of the trash. A fire blazed in the fireplace and his father was seated in a massive leather chair set before it. Beside him, in a straight back chair, sat his father's plump, grey-haired nurse, Maureen. She was reading to him from a leather-bound copy of *Gulliver's Travels,* the sound of her soft lilting Irish brogue bringing a warmth to the room no fire ever could. She stopped abruptly as Michael entered the room, her broad Celtic face looking up at him. His father turned his head as best he could, his body crumpled and awkward as he twisted it in the chair.

"Continue, Maureen," he said after setting eyes on his son. "Finish the chapter, Michael can wait." Without otherwise acknowledging his son, he turned back around to listen, his body falling helplessly back into its original position, slumped against one side of the chair.

Michael felt his cheeks burn red as the rage he always had to keep in check burned at his vital organs. Maureen looked at him apologetically and turned her attention back to the book. She resumed reading aloud. When she had finished the chapter she closed the book. "Is there anything else, sir?"

"That's fine, Maureen. You may leave us now," he said, waving her off with his right hand.

Michael walked over to his father and self-consciously took the chair that Maureen had just vacated, bracing himself to announce Jennifer's death. He knew Lars would not have heard of it, he refused to read the newspapers anymore with the exception of the financial sections that he had Maureen Donovan read to him. He never watched broadcast news; he considered television a medium worthy only of peasants.

"How are you, Father?" Michael asked in his most pleasing voice. He looked into the narrow, pinched face, so unlike his own. The vertical, craggy lines of his father's face met in a grimace. He still had a full head of hair, but its youthful blondness had faded to steel grey. One might be fooled for a moment, thinking there was some humor in the twinkling blue eyes under the two thick grey eyebrows, but one would be mistaken.

"How do you think I feel?" the old voice said sourly. "Fine, for a man who can't read because he sees double of everything, and has to have his ass wiped by a fat Irish nanny because he'll fall off the goddamn toilet if he tries to do it himself."

The air was chilly despite the roaring fire before them, and as it crackled and spit, throwing an occasional ember against the black mesh screen that enclosed it, Michael stared into its depths and summoned the courage for what he had to say.

"Father, I'm afraid I have some rather unpleasant news, bad news, to report to you."

The old man, his senses as sharp as ever, stiffened in his chair. Using all of his energy, he turned his body as directly toward his son as his semi-paralyzed left side would permit. "What is it?" he demanded.

"Two things," Michael began cautiously.

"The Save Their Skins people picketed the Fifth Avenue store all day yesterday and were there again this morning. They are harassing our customers on the street. For some reason we are their main target. I don't know what to do about it; the police can't help, they say these people are within their rights. God only knows what Fur Free Friday will bring." Michael waited for some response from his father. There was none. "Business is off twenty percent," he added.

He could see Lars grimace, a barely visible gesture in the cold, lined face.

"What's the other news?" he asked.

Michael swallowed hard. "It's about Jennifer, Dad," he said, his voice quavering. "She's dead."

If this information shocked the old man, the intense blue eyes registered nothing more than a flicker. They seemed to go into themselves for a moment and then they reemerged, full and strong, intent on Michael as ever.

"Tell me everything about this."

"She was found yesterday in her co-op by a neighbor who hadn't seen her in days, and let herself in to check on her. She was murdered, Dad. Bludgeoned to death."

"Do the police know who is responsible?"

"Not yet."

Lars eased himself up with his right arm, his useless left side following along. He clucked to himself, a gesture Michael knew signified deep thought. "You know who's responsible for this, don't you?" he asked finally.

Michael shook his head.

"Them, you imbecile. Those idiots picketing in front of our store. It has to be them." He railed on. "They're the only ones crazy enough to do such a thing. All they care about is their precious animals, they don't give a hoot about human life. Look at what they did to the Inuit eskimos up in Canada, forcing most of them to turn to drugs and alcohol and suicide after their livelihood of seal hunting was taken away from them. Ruined the entire seal market, these Bambi lovers. What will they ruin next?"

Michael sat frozen, not daring to stoke his father's ire. Maybe he had overestimated his father's lucidity. What did all this ranting about eskimos have to do with Jennifer's death? Perhaps the strokes were finally affecting his mind.

"You know these people are dangerous," Lars continued. "You should have known from last year that it would only get worse. We must find some way to discredit them. We must find something that will expose them as the fools they are."

He clucked to himself again as Michael sat in stunned silence. It was as if the issue of Jennifer hadn't mattered for anything.

"I know what we are going to do," said the old man after a few minutes of thinking. "I've got it." The withered old body shook with excited anticipation as he continued on, the challenge of the problem before him bringing him to life. "We are going to start a program for the hungry."

He leaned his craggy face as far forward as he could into his son's startled one. "Yes, a program for the hungry. That should get to all those bleeding hearts. But it must be right away, we have to get the publicity for the Christmas season.

"We will announce that fifty percent of the profit we make on the sale of every fur this holiday season will go to feed the hungry. Find a good organization, one of the shelters or some distribution program, and do it in conjunction with them. Have Bunny handle it—she knows the charities. We will show the world that Swank cares about human beings; we are humanitarians. Show them that we don't share the misplaced priorities of these animal fanatics. I'll bet you we can even get the city in on it and we'll look like goddamn saints. Every time one of these morons tries to prevent the sale of a fur coat, they will be taking the food from the mouth of a human being. How do you like that?" The old man was trembling with excitement, very pleased with himself.

Now Michael was convinced his father was slipping. "But Father, fifty percent? Can we afford it?"

"You fool," his father exploded. "We can't afford not to. Besides I said fifty percent of the *profit* on a fur coat, you know how those figures can be worked over. No, we must launch this program, and we must announce it right away. We can't afford to let business slip another twenty percent."

Michael was feeling the usual impotence his father invoked in him. "Yes, but part of that was because last winter was a warm one, and . . ."

"Warm, my ass," his father howled. "It's because of them, all because of them. Look what they've done in Europe. They've destroyed the market. We have got to go after them! Fight fire with fire." Sure that the issue had been resolved, he quieted down and returned to the subject of Jennifer.

"What about the funeral? We're taking care of it, aren't we?"

"Yes," said Michael, nodding.

"Let me know the arrangements. I want to be there."

Michael was surprised. His father rarely left the house these days. He was content to sit before his fire and run his empire through his son. Was he actually showing some emotion? Maybe. After all, he had been there when Jennifer O'Grady was created. And he had shared in the visibility and profits she brought to the Swank chain.

"They are doing an autopsy, of course," said Michael. "And then there's Thanksgiving, so the service will probably be Friday."

Suddenly the old man looked tired. He had obviously expended more energy than he was used to. He lowered his head, closing himself off, making it clear that he was finished with his son. "Send in Maureen," he said impersonally.

He looked as though he were falling asleep as Michael got up to leave. But just as he reached the door, his father's voice called out clear and strong, "Get Bunny going on this hunger thing right away. She knows everybody on every goddamn committee in New York. Right away. There's not a moment to lose."

After Michael had gone, Lars sat staring intently into the fire for the two minutes it took for Maureen to reappear. "Bring me my telephone," he said gruffly, "and then leave me alone."

XI

Yolanda, with her cameraman in tow, spent the remainder of the afternoon doing "man on the street" interviews, approaching pedestrians at random for their opinions on the fur issue. She was surprised at the high percentage of people willing to respond to her questions—evidently she had chosen a hot issue. She never received half as much cooperation when she was dealing with anything political.

By the time Yolanda decided she had gathered enough "color" for her purposes, it was dark. They headed back to the studio, where Yolanda got herself a steaming mug of coffee, and settled down in front of a monitor to watch all the footage they had taped today. She was eager to see what she had.

The first person to come on the screen was a tall, well-dressed woman who stood before the camera wearing a voluminous coyote coat. The woman identified herself as a banker. "What do I think when people say they don't like my wearing fur? I don't say anything. I'm not about to argue over it. If they don't like it, then too bad. I'm warm and they're not."

The next subject was another woman, well-dressed, petite, and wearing a full-length cloth coat. The collar was turned up against the cold, and she held it closed tightly about her neck as she spoke into the mike. "I think the wearing of fur is shameful," she said unequivocally. "It's a travesty that animals must suffer to provide luxury for a few. You would think mankind had advanced past that.

A middle-aged man in a suit: "Haven't given it much thought, actually. My wife likes fur though."

Young male in blue jeans and leather jacket: "It's the rich pigs who are into money and status who will wear animal skins." When it is pointed out to him that his jacket is made from an animal hide, he mumbles something about that being different, and he takes off down the street.

Yolanda took an hour to watch the remaining footage of the street interviews. Next, she watched the tapes from her interview with Michael Nilsson at Swank and Mary Ellen Fitzsimmons at S.T.S. Working from two separate machines, she watched them both through fully and then played them back, one against the other. The interviews came off so differently from each other. Michael Nilsson appeared to be self-confident and assured, level and rational. Mary Ellen was, well, Mary Ellen, radical, aggressive and quirky.

Michael Nilsson spoke with authority on behalf of an industry and a long-established family business. This country was explored and settled by trappers, he explained, men who traded in animal skins. It was they who opened the frontiers. Wearing fur for warmth was a long-standing tradition, he continued. A fur coat was not only glamorous; it provided excellent protection from the cold. It could last for decades. Environmentally safe, and biodegradable. Every woman should have a fur coat, and every man too for that matter.

Mary Ellen didn't mince words. She called fur coats advertisements for cruelty, prizes won as a result of the suffering of defenseless animals. She emphasized that trapped animals died painfully, often prisoners in the steel-jaw leghold traps for days before meeting their demise at the hands of the trapper. And so-called improvements like mink ranches were no better. The animals were raised in deplorable conditions, she said, destined to spend their entire lives in overcrowded pens, sometimes cannibalizing each other for food. And the "humane" manner in which they died? Electric prods shoved up their rectums, which could take up to two minutes to kill. Or excruciatingly painful suffocation by unfiltered automobile exhaust. "Do you find this more humane?" she asked.

Back to the Nilsson interview: "The animal rights activists will talk about the inhumanity of traps, but the truth is we are constantly working on better regulation and monitoring of trapping. With the type of leghold traps used now, the animal only feels a slight pinch to its leg. Often trapped animals are found sleeping next to the traps. A newer trap, called the conibear, which kills instantly, is being used widely now. And legislation has just been passed in this country and in Canada to insure that the trap lines are checked frequently."

Mary Ellen: "An estimated thirty million animals are trapped in the United States alone every year. And believe me, they feel pain. Not only that, many of them freeze or starve to death while trapped. A very high percentage of them will actually chew off a paw to escape. The trappers even have a word for it. 'Wring off' it's called."

Michael Nilsson: "People don't realize that nature itself is not kind. Wild animals seldom die of old age. They succumb to other predators, or the weather, or starvation. Wild animals will kill other animals. Mink, for example, are known to go into killing frenzies, wiping out entire dens of muskrats. This is how it is in nature."

Mary Ellen: "By buying one mink coat, you are responsible for the murder of between thirty-five and forty-five animals."

Yolanda liked it. It was working, the play-off of one side versus the other. The dialogues dovetailed perfectly, and with the occasional "street interview" slipped in, it was going to make a very interesting segment for her "In Depth" show.

She played the Michael Nilsson tape again, and listened to Michael speak about the firm his father founded. He talked about how they had always stressed quality and how he had dreamed of bringing the luxury and practicality of fur to the average working woman. Well, that part would have to go, thought Yolanda. She wasn't providing any free commercials here. Then she watched, with interest, his reaction when she brought up Jennifer O'Grady's murder. He deftly changed the subject, saying it was a tragedy indeed and that he didn't care to discuss it. Despite his cool demeanor, Yolanda could read pain in his face. Deep pain. She played the tape back again, watching his face more intently this time. The name of Jennifer O'Grady definitely struck a chord. Then again, why shouldn't it. Admittedly they were close.

But the pain she saw in his face looked like more than the loss of a treasured employee or beloved daughter figure. It appeared to go deeper than that.

Yolanda was intrigued. Maybe there was something more to his relationship with Jennifer O'Grady than anyone knew.

She called down to the news desk. "Who's covering the Jennifer O'Grady murder?" she asked the spry little editor-on-duty, John Walsh.

"Suzy Harking. She's here if you want to talk to her," he said.

"Yeah, put her on," said Yolanda excitedly.

Whenever she heard Suzy's thick Brooklyn accent, Yolanda had to wonder how she ever got into broadcasting. But Suzy was known for her persistence, some people might call it pushiness, and it was that trait that got her to the meat of many a story and made up for her shortcomings in diction.

"The O'Grady murder? I can't tell you squat about it. The cops have clammed up, which tells you there's something they're not letting out. But I can't find out what it is. All they're saying is what you've seen on the news, found beaten to death in her apartment."

And I think I might know what it is they are not letting out, thought Yolanda, tapping her teeth with a pencil, the eraser bouncing off the flawless enamel. Thinking, thinking. The S.T.S. flyer in the apartment. She didn't want to give this one to Suzy. She wanted it for herself.

"Wasn't she found by a neighbor?"

"Yep. Little old lady who lives across the hall. Hadn't seen her in a few days and got worried. According to the police, she let herself in. Her name is Evelyn Burhop, but forget trying to see her. The police put the fear of God into her, and she isn't speaking to any reporters."

Reporters maybe not, but someone doing a special interest story on Jennifer? Perhaps. "Do you happen to have her number?" Yolanda asked.

Fifteen minutes later, Yolanda hung up the phone and hummed contentedly to herself. She opened her appointment book and turned to the next day, Wednesday, November 21. In it she wrote, "Tea, Evelyn Burhop, 4:00."

XII

His drive back into the city did not go as quickly as the drive out to Upper Montclair had. There was never any predicting what New York traffic would be. It operated on a mind of its own, free of any sense of rhyme or reason. But one thing was for sure, the grey clouds that had been hanging overhead had finally turned into snow, which would only serve to further foul things up.

As Michael sat motionless in his Jaguar, he took small consolation from the fact that things had gone far better with his father than he had expected. His biggest fear had been that his father would fly totally off the handle, but the old man had taken both pieces of news far better than Michael had expected. He had even thought he detected some actual pain in his father's face upon learning of Jennifer's death. Maybe the old man did have feelings.

An accident on the turnpike mucked up the inbound traffic even further, and as Michael inched along at a snail's pace, he realized it would be at least another hour before he got home. Dutifully, he picked up the car phone and called Bunny. Her light and charming voice offered an aural oasis in his world of aggravation and disappointments. It was always pleasant and welcoming, promising a warm and stable refuge. He told her that he was running late, and she assured him that dinner would keep. She asked about his father. He would tell her over dinner, he replied.

Having checked in with Bunny, he had fulfilled all of his duties and obligations. It had been a day packed too full of them. The interview with Yolanda Prince this morning, the police, breaking the news to his father. Tomorrow there were funeral arrangements for Jennifer to be made. But for now, in the ever thickening snow along the Jersey Turnpike, he finally had a few minutes of his own. Propping his head up with one arm against the window, his eyes began to fill with tears. A solitary drop slid down his cheek at first, but just feeling it fed his grief and he indulged himself with a sob. One tear turned to two, a choked sob turned into a muffled cry, and soon he was weeping in earnest. Oh, Jennifer, my pretty young Jennifer, what did they do to you?

Against his will, his thoughts fluttered back to her, to Jennifer, the Jennifer he had known so many years ago. She had been so beautiful, so needful, so trusting when he and Bunny discovered her. But there had been another side to her too, one that only he knew, a side that showed her to be wise and cagey beyond her years. She was, after all, a wild animal who would do anything to survive.

She must have feared that they might reject her—send her back to the streets. It was she who had come to him. In his mind he could still smell the fragrance of her, the clean shampoo scent of her long, thick hair. He could feel the silky weight of it against his face. Only in his imagination could he once again enjoy the sensation of her long, slender arms and legs as she wrapped them around him and brought him to her, a wicked and wonderful little girl. Up until the day she approached him those many years ago, he had thought of her only as his ward. Afterward, he would never look upon her in a fatherly way again. On that day, some twelve years ago, a seventeen-year-old girl had taken him, some twenty years her senior, and made him feel for the first time that he knew something of the ways of love.

Bunny had been out at one of her brunches that Sunday afternoon. Jennifer was living with them at the time, and Bunny had been working closely with her for weeks, preparing her, grooming her, teaching her the tricks of modeling. So it did not seem odd to Michael when Jennifer appeared in the doorway of his study and asked if he would mind watching her demonstrate a few poses. She was wearing a white terrycloth robe, and her hair was still damp from her shower. She smiled broadly, girlishly, when he told her to go ahead. Pretending her robe was a fur coat, she proceeded to model for him. As he watched her move, he began to comprehend how truly marvelous she was. She had the endearing and playful qualities of a kitten, but the mature size and grace of a cat. It was impossible for her to make an awkward move.

He applauded her as she finished, and she clapped her hands together, jumping up and down in childish delight at his approval. And then she changed, her expression becoming serious as she looked him straight in the eyes. "I want to thank you for saving me," she said. Without another word, she walked towards him and the terrycloth robe fell open. He found himself looking at her long, lean body with its narrow sloping waist and lengths of smooth, shaped thigh. She wore simple cotton underthings, and they looked absurdly innocent on so fine a body. At first he thought it might be an accident that her robe had fallen open, and he averted his eyes. But when he looked into her face he could not mistake her intentions, and he found himself suddenly both excited and terrified. She reached his chair and took his newspaper away, parting her legs over his and lowering herself onto his lap. He could have stopped it there, he knew, pushed her away and reprimanded her. But the thought of having this child who was so willing, so open to him, consumed him and he put his hand out to rub her fine breasts through the simple white bra. Gently, he pulled it aside to look at the rosebud nipples that had grown firm and pointed under his touch. He placed a hand behind her neck and drew her face slowly toward his until he tasted her lips, so smooth and damp and cool. The taste of youth. He stood up with her then and urgently lowered her to the floor, pulling the cotton panties away. He lowered his pants and entered her. She wrapped herself around him, long young arms and legs, and surrendered herself to him.

When it was over, he felt more alive than he had ever dreamed. He was a king, a conqueror. For despite all his good looks and sharp business dress, his basic insecurities extended to sex, and this was the first time in his life that he felt in charge. It was so different from sex with Bunny, who was always calling out instructions when they made love, making him feel inadequate. Jennifer made him feel virile and godlike.

They were to make love time and time again. Whenever they were together, he was relieved momentarily of his insecurities. She always let him take the lead and she placed no demands upon him either verbally or with the motions of her body. She was a magnificent work of living art for his use, and she always gave herself unselfishly to him.

For years Michael enjoyed what he considered the best of both worlds. He had a wife who was a perfect partner, brilliant and loyal. In fact, truthfully, she had a better head for business than he had. And then he had his two or three times a week of absolute heaven, sneaking off to see Jennifer, who by now was living in her own place, a smart little uptown apartment that Bunny had found for her. It was a good run for Michael, securely happy with his beautiful wife, exceedingly pleased by his young, wildly sexy mistress.

For six years it went on like this. Jennifer made him feel whole, filled the empty spaces inside him. She never asked anything of him, never pushed him in any way, and seemed perfectly content to leave things the way they were. His life was in perfect balance as far as he was concerned, his afternoons occasionally enhanced by a foray with Jennifer in a dressing room at Swank, his evenings spent with his elegant wife.

He should have known it couldn't go on forever. He had been stupid to think that he could hold onto an eager young woman on such empty terms. As Jennifer's success grew and she became more firmly established in the fashion world, she became more secure in herself. She started reading voraciously, and was not such a lost little girl anymore. And then she began to deny him that to which he had become so accustomed.

At first, their trysts were only less frequent, Jennifer making excuses why she couldn't meet him. But finally the day came when she cut him off altogether. She just said it was time to end it. Michael had been tormented for the six years since.

He had carried the hope that he could be with her again, could savor the sweetness of her touch, the unequaled sensation of her yielding to him. He longed for her twenty-nine-year-old body as dearly as he had her seventeen-year-old one. As long as she had been alive, it was possible that they could come together again. Now even that slim hope had been wiped out and replaced by an emptiness that made his heart ache.

He forced himself to stop crying, and turned the rearview mirror to get a good look at his face. How ridiculous he looked, his distinguished features bloated and red, puffy like an hysterical woman's. How would it appear to anyone who deigned to look in the window of his forty-thousand-dollar car to see a grown man crying like a baby. Crying like a little boy. One who couldn't do anything right. He was glad it was dark and snowing and he hoped that if he stopped crying now his face would clear up by the time he got home so that Bunny wouldn't notice.

XIII

Karen was exhausted. It had been a long day. Tony had dragged her from one end of Manhattan to the other. They had interviewed every model and photographer who had ever worked with Jennifer O'Grady, and they had come up with basically the same responses. Nice, friendly, hard-working, kept to herself. It didn't appear that Jennifer had any close friends in the world besides the Nilssons and Mrs. Burhop. She confided in no one, if she had anything, indeed, to confide. Everyone they talked to mentioned that Jennifer loved to read. She was always lugging a book along to her various shoots, and whenever there was a down minute she could be seen burying her nose in it.

It was confirmed that she had no living relatives, and that she had been born Sophie Tochowitz and changed her name at the behest of the Nilssons during her "remake." Karen had laughed to learn the beautiful Irish lass was actually Jewish.

Tony and Karen visited Mrs. Burhop once again, and she was able to give them little more. Jennifer had never mentioned friends or enemies. Most of Jennifer's visits, it seemed, were spent listening to Evelyn reminisce about the good old days when she and her husband Henry would go ice skating at Rockefeller Center or dancing at the Biltmore.

"Did she ever mention anyone harassing her, Mrs. Burhop?" Tony had asked.

"No," she replied, and then she stopped. "Wait . . . she did mention once that some man had followed her, said nasty things to her. But she didn't seem to be terribly disturbed by it, just perturbed. This was maybe a couple of weeks ago."

Tony was interested. "Did she say what he looked like?"

"I'm afraid not," the old woman replied, sorry she couldn't be more helpful.

Before they left, Tony had made it a point to remind her not to say anything to anyone about what she had seen in Jennifer's apartment. "It would make our job very difficult, and then we might never find the murderer," he said. "And you don't want that to happen, do you?"

"Oh, no," replied Evelyn, shaking her head in fierce agreement. "The reporters have been ringing my phone off the hook, but I've refused to talk with them, just as you instructed me."

"Good girl," said Tony, patting her on the arm. She was surprised at his gesture, and drew away ever so slightly.

Karen, embarrassed by Tony's condescension, took Mrs. Burhop's hand in hers. "Thank you once again for your help," she said. "Are you okay here?"

"I'm fine," she replied. "It's just that I'm going to miss Jennifer and Chessie so very much. Please stop and have tea with me some time."

"I'll try," said Karen.

Next on their agenda was the Humane Society, where they spoke with Denise Segura, her broad face open and nodding, anxious to be of help. No, she wasn't aware of any fanatics in their ranks. She turned over a membership roster to them gladly.

The people at the Animal Rights Mobilization, the Animal Liberation Front, and People for the Ethical Treatment of Animals (PETA) were quirkier and not nearly as friendly as Denise Segura, but they grudgingly came up with their membership lists nonetheless. Karen had never realized that so many organizations existed solely to promote animal rights. She marveled at their dedication, and wondered what might happen if they were to ever throw some of that enthusiasm toward their fellow man.

She and Tony arrived back at the office weighted down with the membership lists and scads of literature the various organizations had foisted upon them.

"What a day!" cried Karen. She was drained, both physically and mentally, as much from dealing with her partner's disdain as from the investigation.

"It ain't even begun, babe," Tony said cockily, dropping another stack of papers onto the pile on her desk. More membership lists. "We start right here on the computer and we go all the way down the list, looking for anyone with prior arrests or anyone with a history of mental problems."

She looked at the mound of paper in front of her, and glared back at him. "And what are you going to do?"

He quickly reclaimed half the papers. Backing away in mock

fear, he said, "I guess I'm going to do some of these too." He smiled at her, a big, cheesy smile that showcased his perfect teeth, lined up like rows of white kernels on a corncob. "Don't worry," he added. "I wasn't going to leave all the paperwork for you."

Karen looked down, embarrassed. She knew if she hadn't opened her mouth he undoubtedly would have stuck her with all the paperwork. But instead now it was she who ended up feeling small about the whole thing. She stoically choked back her aggravation, and picked up the roster from the Humane Society. That was as good a place to start as any.

Hours later she had come up with nothing. Her stomach was growling, her back ached, and she was tired and wanted to go home. Tony was on one of his frequent trips to the men's room when Bob Falls, the forensics man who had been at the O'Grady residence the day before, approached her desk.

"I believe somebody here wanted some information about a cat box," he said, holding a report out to Karen. It was snatched from his outstretched hand by an eager Tony, who had reemerged with remarkable timing.

"Thanks, Bob," he said, quickly perusing the single page.

"By the way," Falls volunteered, "I checked out the type used for the note. IBM Wheelwriter 4, 5, or 6. Virtually indistinguishable. Like I said, one of millions."

"Figures," said Tony, his eyes still glued to the report. "Uh-huh!" he intoned upon finishing it.

"What?" Karen demanded intrigued. "What does it say?"

He looked at her like she was a pesky fly on the wall. "It says the cat eats Nine-Lives's Gourmet Dinner." Karen did not look amused. "All right," he surrendered, "it says what I already figured was true. The last time that cat used its litterbox was Friday, which means that the murderer must have taken the cat when he left."

"So what do you suppose that means?" asked Karen, mystified.

"It means that whoever beat Jennifer O'Grady to death was too sensitive to leave a poor defenseless creature alone to fend for itself until Jennifer's body was discovered. A true animal lover." He picked up the stack of names that sat before him on his desk. "That's what makes me think we just might find our killer in this mess."

*   *   *

An hour later, Karen's stomach was really rumbling, but at this point even Tony was diligently working away, tapping name after name into the computer, and she didn't want to be the one to suggest they take a break. Thus far the only thing of interest that had surfaced among any of the animal rights advocates was a case of shoplifting. All in all, the Humane Society was a pretty peaceable group. Trying to ignore her hunger, she finished up with the last of its members, and was about to start working on the next group when two loud, gruff male voices burst onto the scene. Karen recognized them as belonging to Bruce Bobovich and Charley Haines, two veterans of homicide.

"Hey, Tony," called Bobovich, "We're going down to Italian Gardens to grab a sausage sandwich. Want to come with?"

"Yeah, I could eat," replied Tony, glancing at his watch and pushing his chair back from the desk. Karen's groaning stomach heaved a sigh of relief, and she straightened in her chair. She could already smell the Italian sausage. Her mouth watered in anticipation.

It was all for naught. "Levinson," her partner clucked in her direction, "I'll be back in about an hour. Take a break if you need one." He pulled on his jacket, and the three men left the room, talking and joking noisily among themselves.

Karen fought back tears of rage. She pretended to be intently interested in the papers that lay before her, afraid to look up lest anyone in the half deserted room notice that she was upset. That would be exactly what they would expect from a woman, she thought, and she wouldn't give any of them the satisfaction.

That son of a bitch, she thought. Maybe she wasn't one of the guys, but he could at the very least extend the courtesy of treating her as a fellow human being. He could have asked her if she wanted to join them; after all, she was his partner. Oh, he made her angry, so very angry. She hated him.

After the red flush of anger and humiliation had finally subsided, she let out a long sigh and sat back in her chair. She opened a drawer and took out her leather bag, fishing around for a few dollars. Reluctantly, she went down the hall to the vending machines where she bought herself a microwave hamburger and a bag of Cheetos, which she ate solemnly at her desk. She washed them down with foul stationhouse coffee, then went back to work with a vengeance, checking name after name until late into the night.

XIV

Leslie fumbled nervously at her plate of angel-hair pasta and wished she had worn more makeup. She was painfully aware of being plain as she looked around the busy restaurant and observed the handsome couples gathered over the red-and-white table-cloths. Everyone looked so attractive in the glow of the flattering candlelight. She found herself praying fervently that the lighting had the same effect on her.

"How's your food?" Neil asked casually as he stuffed a large forkful of chicken cacciatore into his mouth and chewed with pleasure. He washed it down with a long swig of Chianti. She could see his tongue move along under his lips as he checked his teeth for food before giving her a broad grin. She loved his grin, the slight gap between his front teeth making him even more endearing. She couldn't help but smile back despite her nervous-ness.

"Mine's very good," she said, struggling to spin the lengths of frail pasta around her fork. Her best efforts still left long strings dangling free. Afraid of looking ridiculous, she aborted the effort and tried again. Neil laughed, took her fork from her, and helped himself to the tablespoon beside her plate.

"You do it like this," he said, centering the unmanageable glob in the spoon. Deftly, he wrapped it around and around until it was a tidy ball, then offered it to her.

"Thank you," she said sheepishly. "I guess we never ate much Italian food when I was growing up."

"Neither did we, that's why I can't get enough of it," said Neil. "My mother was the Irish cook personified. Lots of stew. Every-thing tasted the same. I guess when there are eight kids stew's about the easiest thing to make."

"Eight kids, wow," said Leslie, gleaming at him over the table as she chewed her pasta. He was so very handsome, she was thinking. She loved his classic features, the thick crown of auburn hair and the square freckled face. He had a slightly sloped, perfectly proportioned nose and small neat ears. But it was his eyes that mesmerized her; they were blue with a permanent teasing look about them as if he harbored some hilarious secret.

He was still wearing his business suit, one of obviously good quality that hugged his broad shoulders and tapered along his narrow torso. His starched white shirt had a spread collar and on one of his cuffs the embroidered initials N.P.H. peeked out. Neil Patrick Harrigan. His yellow silk tie was a print that Leslie was vaguely familiar with—she associated it with one of the many trips she had taken to Paris with her parents.

Leslie found herself regretting her own wardrobe. She was wearing simple black wool slacks and a black turtleneck sweater. How her lack of interest in clothes used to drive the saleswoman at Bergdorf Goodman crazy when her mother sent her to be outfitted twice a year! With Neil sitting across from her, clothes took on a new significance, and she made a vow to herself to go back to Bergdorf's soon. The woman would probably faint when she saw her. She had probably assumed that Leslie died along with her parents, it was so long since she had been in.

Neil was still eating with relish, and he looked up from his plate to catch Leslie staring at him. She looked away quickly, staring off into the recesses of the restaurant, back towards the kitchen where the waiters moved in and out with self-importance. She pretended to be absorbed in watching them flit about, not wanting to meet Neil's eyes again. He reached a sure hand across the table and turned her chin toward him.

"What is it?" he asked.

Unable to contain herself anymore, the shy mouse spoke. "Neil, where were you? I mean, after we met, we saw each other practically every day for a week, and then I don't hear anything from you for two weeks. I was afraid you wouldn't ever call again."

Neil looked moved. He spoke to her tenderly, seriously, but still as one might speak to a child.

"Leslie, I really enjoyed the time we spent together too, but you have to understand I have a lot of things going in my life. My work is important to me, and it's not easy making any money in commercial real estate these days. It's like trying to get tickets to *The Phantom of the Opera* on a Saturday night," he joked.

She smiled slightly too.

"And," he added, "I have to be honest with you. I do have other friends. I do see other . . . people."

"Oh," she said, feeling the inevitable disappointment. Her eyes darted back to the kitchen doors where she could pretend the waiters' show interested her more than what was transpiring at their table. She thought about where she was and the man who was sitting across from her. What did she really know about him, and furthermore, what did she really expect from him? He was the result of a chance encounter in Central Park that had led to some museum visits and a boat ride around Manhattan and some other touristy things neither one of them had ever taken the time to do before. She had no right to place demands upon him.

"I'm sorry," she said honestly. "I just want to be your friend."

"And I want to be yours," he said with finality, flashing that infectious smile of his, tearing at her whole body and soul with his beauty. He chucked her cheek affectionately and resumed eating his chicken cacciatore.

"This is so good," he said, cutting a piece and extending it toward her. "Would you like to try it?"

She shook her head no. He withdrew the fork.

"You vegetarians," he teased. "You don't know what you're missing." He chomped away. "How are things in the animal saving business these days anyway?"

"It's crazy," said Leslie, relieved to be on another subject. "Mary Ellen is going to drive me insane. She's getting worse as we get nearer to Fur Free Friday. She's a real energetic and dedicated person, but she's also one of the most disorganized people I've ever met. She makes appointments and forgets them, doesn't pay the bills on time, and goes around getting herself arrested. I get to do a lot of her clean-up. She's going to be on 'In Depth' by the way."

"Is she now?" said Neil. "I like Yolanda Prince. She's not one of your usual media scumbuckets."

"She seemed pretty nice."

Neil speared another piece of chicken. "Do you think poorly of me for being a flesh eater?"

"No, I think everyone is entitled to his own opinion."

"I bet Mary Ellen wouldn't like it."

"Mary Ellen thinks poorly of anyone who wears leather shoes. She's religious about only eating plant material, and she refuses to buy any product that was tested on animals—including medicine."

"That's fanatic. You're not fanatic like that, are you?"

"No. I just can't eat meat. It started when I was a child." Leslie's eyes drifted back to another point in time, and a soft smile touched her lips. "My parents had a ranch in upstate New York, and we used to spend summers up there. I grew so fond of the animals, I couldn't imagine eating them."

Then the softness faded and a harsh, stony look came into her face. "And then there was my brother. He could be so terribly mean. I'll never forget some of the things he and his friends did to little animals, and sometimes they would make me watch. One time they got hold of a baby squirrel and . . ." She stopped short, realizing he was still eating. "Well, I'm not going to tell you, but let me just say it wasn't very pleasant. The memory of watching that little squirrel suffer has stayed with me for most of my life." She paused in sad reflection.

"So that's when you stopped eating meat?"

"Well, not exactly. I was only seven and my parents wouldn't stand for it. I used to hide it in my napkin and flush it down the toilet when I excused myself from the table. They were so worried I wasn't eating right. I think that was the only thing we ever fought about. Finally, I agreed to eat fish, and they stopped trying to force me to eat meat."

"And your brother Larry? Did he ever outgrow torturing animals?"

"He's my half-brother, actually, from Papa's first marriage, and I think he's just moved on to torturing humans. He really resents me, because our father left control of his estate to me. My father knew Larry and his weaknesses, and I guess he figured if he left his money where Larry could get his hands on it, he would blow it on women or horses or some stupid business deal."

Leslie ordered dessert, and Neil finished the wine, following it up with a Sambuca. Leslie noticed that he had taken on a slightly inebriated glow that made him appear more impish than ever. She found herself trying not to stare at him, but her eyes kept wandering back.

"What are you doing for Thanksgiving?" he asked out of the blue.

She sighed. "I'm supposed to go out with my brother and his mother," she said dourly. It was at the holidays that she missed her parents most.

"You don't seem too excited about it."

"I'm not," she replied. She thought of the year before. Larry had drunk too much wine, and Sheila had barely bothered to disguise her contempt for her.

"How about joining my family for dinner? It's crazy and crowded, but I can guarantee you won't be bored. Of course, we are Neanderthal enough to serve turkey, but there are plenty of vegetables. You won't go hungry."

Leslie was so excited she could barely speak. "I'd love to join you," she said breathlessly, getting the words out quickly, before he could take back his invitation.

Leslie's heart was fluttering as she cut through the kitchen, past the flashing light of the answering machine, and floated up the back stairs. As she crawled into her bed, the cats jumped in beside her, fighting each other for the best space along her outstretched body. She could feel their purring as they nuzzled alongside her, and it matched her own contentment. She felt the happiest she had ever been as she recalled the soft warmth of Neil's lips on her own when he had kissed her good night. She was floating above the stars. And then a funny notion ticked into her mind, breaking into her euphoric state. She didn't know why she was thinking of it now, but suddenly she wondered how Neil had known her brother's name. Certainly she must have mentioned it at one time or another, she thought. Yes, that must be it. Eager to return to her blissful state, she buried any unpleasant notion she might have had, and fell into a deep trouble-free sleep.

XV

Bunny greeted Michael at the door with a chilled martini in a stemmed glass, the lemon twist a bright splash of yellow in the pool of icy gin. He took it from her thankfully and drank a good-sized slug before putting it down and removing his coat. Bunny took the coat from him and hung it neatly in the oversized entry closet before putting her arms about his neck and kissing him on the lips. He pulled away.

"Michael, honey, are you okay?" she asked with concern, her deep Southern drawl always an aural caress.

"I'm sorry," he replied. "You know how spending time with my father always depresses me."

"I know, poor child." She took his hand in hers and held it up against her cheek, turning it and kissing the palm. Then in a brighter voice she said, "Well, I'm making paella for you, and I've banished Emily to her quarters for the evening so we can talk freely. I'm sure you've got a lot on your chest. Now go and enjoy your martini while I set the table, and I'll come for you when it's ready. Then you can tell me all about it."

He watched as his wife walked from the entryway and as she went he couldn't help but appreciate her. She had so many good qualities: beautiful, smart, a shrewd businesswoman, and an understanding partner. He picked up his drink and walked down the hall to his favorite room, his study. This was the room in which he had first had Jennifer. That was the first thought that came to his mind as he entered. A fire crackling in the fireplace distracted him and he noticed a newspaper neatly folded on his favorite chair. Bunny never overlooked anything, he thought gratefully. He lowered himself into the chair with a fatigue more mental than physical, and opened his paper, attempting to concentrate on it. But his mind drifted continually back to Jennifer, her spirit was there with him in the room. The calming influence of the gin was beginning to take hold, and he changed his focus to the fire where he watched the yellow and orange of the flames as they lapped at the logs, at times diminishing and then coming back stronger alto-gether. He was mesmerized, watching the fire in a way he proba-bly hadn't since he was a little boy, when he was suddenly aware of Bunny's presence in the room. He looked up abruptly.

"Dinner's ready, love," she said.

He followed her into the dining room where a low lit chandelier hovered over a large table dressed in white linens. Two places were set, one at the head, the other to its right. Two candles glowed in heavy silver holders.

He took his seat and Bunny poured him a glass of wine, a Spanish Rioja to go with the paella. She was an excellent cook and preferred to do her own cooking whenever time permitted. Emily, their longtime British housekeeper, tended to prepare food on the bland side. But with their hectic schedules and frequent evenings out, Bunny seldom cooked more than twice a week. Whenever she did, though, it was a culinary event.

The paella was excellent, loaded with tasty lobster and shrimp, tender pieces of chicken and spicy chorizo sausage, set on a golden bed of saffron rice. Michael appreciated good food and wine. Even when he was feeling his worst, he was always able to eat, and he ate the paella with gusto, washing it down with fre-quent sips from his wine glass.

Bunny's pace was slower, more demure, as she sat quietly to his side. In the flickering glow of the candlelight, Michael noticed how attractive she looked this evening. Her frosted hair was piled atop her head, but little wisps of it had escaped and they fell in soft spirals about her face. Her green eyes were luminous and reflected the emerald color of her cashmere sweater, its buttery-soft material folded in a flattering shawl collar.

The subtle changes of middle age befit her, he thought. Though she was still a far cry from stately, she was no longer young, and the fine lines that had formed about her eyes and mouth added depth and character to her lovely face. He was glad that she wore her age gracefully instead of fighting it like so many of her peers. He had a great distaste for those desperate women who flocked to plastic surgeons, seeking face lifts and tummy tucks to ward off the inevitable ravages of time.

Her gaze upon him was loving and reassuring, and the two of them ate at first in companionable silence. After a while, Bunny put her fork down gently on her plate, and leaned against the high back of her chair. She picked up her wine glass by the stem and swirled the wine around inside it.

"So, Michael," she said, sipping lightly from her wine. "Are you ready to tell me how it went with your father?"

Michael sighed. It was a light sigh, however, not nearly as deep as it would have been an hour ago. The anesthetic properties of the martini had combined with those of the heavy red wine to numb his pain a bit. *Forget about Jennifer for now. Let's talk about Father.*

"Oh, Father," he said with exasperation. "He was his usual self, letting me stand there for minutes before deigning to acknowledge my presence. But once that was out of the way, he behaved better than I expected, so I guess I shouldn't complain."

"How did he react to the news about Jennifer?" she asked.

"He surprised me," Michael replied, as he toyed with his glass. "For a minute there, he looked sorry. It was the most emotion I've seen from him since Mother died." He stopped talking and took another sip of his wine. "He even wants to attend the services."

"See," said Bunny. "I told you that underneath it all he has a heart."

"You say that because he likes you. He certainly does a good job of hiding it from me."

Bunny waited for Michael to offer more, but when he didn't she pressed on. "And what did he say when you told him about the demonstrators and business being off so badly?"

"That he did not take so well as Jennifer's death, although it served to give him an inspiration, and that made him happy. In fact, I am supposed to pass this inspiration on to you, and you are to do something about it."

"I'm afraid to ask what it is," she said dourly.

"Dad seems to think that we can beat this animal rights thing by having Swank Furs do something humanitarian. He wants us to donate fifty percent of all the profit we realize on the sale of each fur coat to one of the local charities that feeds the hungry."

"Fifty percent!" she cried. "Has he had another stroke?"

"A stroke of genius if you ask him. He says we can't afford not to do it, and we have to do it in a big way. We have to discredit these people, he says, and what better way than by saying they are taking food out of the mouths of the hungry each time they discourage the sale of a Swank Fur."

Bunny made a temple out of her fingers and thought. Slowly a smile lit her face. "Your father . . . what a mind. He's right, when you think of it. Not only will it make us look good, but it should help to pick up things during this flat holiday season. We might even pick up the borderline customers who weren't really sure where they stood on the issue. Now they'll be able to do something for the good of humanity by buying the fur coat they really wanted in the first place. And Swank will be the furrier they come to. Think of the publicity! Old Lars, I really have to hand it to him."

Michael chewed on a piece of lobster and watched Bunny as she withdrew into thought for a moment.

Bunny's mind raced as she thought about how she was going to handle this. The hungry. This was a whole different ball game. Most of the charities and philanthropic activities she was involved in, like the board of the Metropolitan Museum or the American Cancer Society, were chosen because they were prestigious. Everyone approved of them. She had even helped raise funds for a home for abused children. Children's charities were always in vogue. Well, the times were "a changin'" she realized. One saw more and more on television regarding the indigent and the homeless.

The hungry. Now who did she know who was involved with the hungry? Suzanne Ricing was on the board of something for the hungry, but that was national. Bunny wanted something local to be sure to draw lots of local press. She searched her brain, she knew there was something . . . and then it came to her. Of course, the Hunger Exchange. She had attended a dismal fundraiser for it a few years ago as a favor to Amanda Warning who was the chairperson. Amanda was dead now, killed in that terrible car crash, but Bunny was willing to bet that her dreary little daughter was still involved. Now what was her name? Leslie, that was it. Poor little mouse of a thing to come from such well-known and influential parents.

"I've got it, Michael. I know exactly what I am going to do. I'll call Leslie Warning. I'm pretty sure that she is active with the Hunger Exchange; they feed New York's homeless and poor and provide hot meals at home for the elderly. I'm sure she can help me get on the right track.

"And as soon as I get that set up, I'll get the press onto this. Maybe give Yolanda Prince a call. She'd like this one, I'm sure."

Michael was feeling drunk now, and as he regarded his energetic wife, he felt the same amazement she always inspired. Wherever did she get it from? He wished he were able to harness some of her energy for himself. No wonder his father thought so highly of her, she was in so many ways everything Lars had always wanted Michael to be, smart, energetic, quick to act.

"Do you know where to reach this Warning woman?" he asked.

"She must be in my directory, or her mother's number at least. The last I heard she was still living all alone in their huge greystone over on Sutton Place. I'll bet she's still there. I'll call her tomorrow; no, I'll call her tonight and set up a lunch meeting for tomorrow. We have to move on this quickly if we want to make it effective for the holiday season. There's not a moment to waste. Too bad we couldn't have gotten this in place for Thanksgiving."

Bunny got up and went to make her call, and as Michael watched her go he was once again grateful she was his wife. She would take care of everything. She was back in a few minutes.

"Did you reach her?" he asked.

Bunny shook her head. "No, she was out, but I left a message on her answering machine to call me as soon as possible."

Michael leaned back in his chair and poured out the last few drops of wine into his empty glass. He was feeling much better now. He wanted more wine.

"Bunny, open another bottle." It was a command, not a request. She started to object, but it was so unusual for him to make any demands that she decided not to deny him this one. It was obvious that he was feeling worse than he would admit, and she knew why. So she got up and went into their wine storage and brought out another bottle of Rioja which Michael proceeded to finish off there at the table without any help from her.

XVI

Early Wednesday morning found Karen back at her desk feeling as though she had never left it. Tony wasn't in yet, and she was glad. She wanted to be waiting for him when he came in, to see his smug face when she told him what she had uncovered late last night while he was off stuffing his face with Italian sausage or stuffing his Italian sausage into someone's face.

She had finished up her half of the background checks around two A.M., her eyes so droopy that she kept nodding off, her entire body a giant yawn. She was going to call it a night, disappointed that she had come up with nothing more from the ranks of the "Bambi lovers," as she was starting to call them, than a few shoplifters. She was exhausted and she could hear her bed calling to her. But before leaving she happened to glance at Tony's desk, and she noticed the S.T.S. file sitting on top. It must have been the next one he was going to work on. She was amazed he hadn't started working on it immediately, considering the radical nature of the group.

Digging deep inside herself for a second wind, she took the file from his desk and started with the first name on the list.

Fitzsimmons, Mary Ellen, she typed into her computer. There was definitely some action here. A rap sheet a mile long came up. Karen read through it with a great deal of interest. Most of the citations were for civil disobedience, and dated back to the middle sixties. Disorderly conduct, resisting arrest, illegal assembly. Mary Ellen's legacy of rebellion was right there before her in glowing green letters. Karen read on for further details of Mary Ellen's counter-culture years. Arrested for refusing to move from the path of a train on its way to a nuclear facility. Arrested for defacing public property by spray-painting "Animals here are being held against their wills!" on the walls of the Bronx Zoo. She was arrested in connection with a breaking and entering at the medical research facility at New York University where hundreds of laboratory animals had been set free, effectively flushing untold dollars and years of research down the toilet. No charges had been filed due to lack of evidence. The list went on and on.

Most recently there was a harassment charge filed by one of her neighbors. It seemed the poor woman had the misfortune to own a raccoon coat and live in the same building as Mary Ellen. She had already suffered untold verbal abuse from Mary Ellen when gruesome photos of dead animals began turning up on her front door. The judge had issued an order barring Mary Ellen from going near the apartment when a second neighbor witnessed her tacking the picture of a skinned sable on the victim's door.

The latest charges: interfering with the police. That was her arrest on Monday in front of Swank. Well, this girl certainly had no fear of jail.

Now wide awake, Karen went on to the next S.T.S. member.

Keith Geiger, the consummate hippie. The only thing missing from him was the flower in his hair. Karen reflected on his vaguely unsettling looks. He was a cross between a young Moses and Charles Manson. His eyes were at once piercingly sincere and disturbingly shielded.

Keith's record sort of paralleled Mary Ellen's. There were numerous arrests for minor civil infractions. But as she went back to the seventies she saw something that nearly pulled her out of her chair. Keith Geiger had done time in prison . . . a military prison. He had been court-martialed in 1970. What for? she wondered. She made some notes.

She moved on through the S.T.S. membership. This was a more exciting crowd than the other organizations, she discovered. By the time she had finished going through their roster it was four A.M. and she had uncovered three more persons of questionable background. People they would have to talk to. There was John Abbott, convicted of breaking and entering, sentence suspended. And Christian Petersen, who had a long record of priors ranging from resisting arrest to corruption of a minor to selling pornographic material. And the last was Sylvester K. Wolfe. He had served time for assault with a deadly weapon, exposing himself and pandering. He also had been written up for numerous violations of the city's animal code.

An unusual collection, Karen thought to herself, before shutting down her terminal and heading home for a few brief hours of sleep.

*   *   *

Tony finally rolled in around nine o'clock looking frazzled around the edges. He made no apologies to Karen for not returning the previous night. She decided against even trying to elicit one. She was too excited that they finally had some hot leads.

She walked over to Tony's desk and slapped the file down in front of him. "I hope you don't mind," she said, "but in your absence I took the liberty of checking into these names. I think you'll find some of them interesting."

He looked back at her slowly, his response as measured as her approach. His pupils were mere pinpricks of black in his coffee-colored eyes, and the eyes showed no signs of contrition, regret or appreciation. Instead they appeared to be rather amused. Without a word he took the file from her, opened it and read quickly. A sinister smile spread across his face, revealing those tight fine white teeth.

"Good job, Levinson," he said. "Now all we have to do is finish up the rest of these names, and we can hit the street." He tapped the remaining pile in front of him.

Karen was incensed. Not only had she already done her half, but part of his, and now she was going to have to spend the rest of the morning plugging in more names. Slowly it dawned on her that this had been his scheme all along. Getting her to do most of the grunt work.

"Do you know I was here until four o'clock working? If you had been here to share the work we would have been finished by now. Where the hell were you anyway?"

"Sorry, I got waylaid," he said, indifferent to her anger. He got up and went to get himself a cup of coffee.

Furious, she took a pile of the lists and went to fume in front of her computer. She thought of her partner out in some bar last night with his fellow cops, not her fellow cops, and her anger roiled. Waylaid! I'll just bet. Leave out the "way" and that would probably be more like it.

She looked at the sheet of paper in front of her. The Society Toward Animal Rights Today. START. Painstakingly, she typed the first name into the terminal. Altman, Susan.

XVII

Leslie pulled on her usual uniform of baggy, comfortable slacks and a sloppy, shapeless sweater and looked at her image in the mirror. She shook her head angrily. She had never been vain, so it was hard for her to put more effort into her appearance. But the memory of how dull she had felt among the glamorous people in the restaurant last night still lingered, and she pointed an accusing finger at her reflection.

"You wished you had taken the time to dress up yesterday, and here you are again looking like a slob. It's time you made a change here, Leslie," she berated herself. She thought of her mother and how hard she had tried to get her to care about clothes. Leslie had never been interested, just as she had never been interested in other things her mother cared about, like cotillions and coming out parties, and knowing the right people in New York society. Leslie had always found those people shallow and boring, and she had shunned them. But now that she knew Neil, she understood why a woman would want to look her best. It was because there was someone for whom she wanted to look beautiful.

The servants' quarters, in which Leslie had taken up her residence, had a single exit that opened into a narrow hallway at the top of the back stairs. Leslie walked out into the hallway, but instead of heading down the stairs, as she usually would, she turned to her left and padded down the hall, following it around to where it opened up into the main hallway of the house's second floor. Everything seemed alien to her as she walked along the Oriental carpets that ran the length of the hall. To her left was a series of closed doors. To her right the hallway was open to overlook the huge black-and-white marble entry below. She could see up to the ceiling at the third floor where the grey daylight came in through a huge beveled glass skylight.

She stopped before the fourth door, and hesitated before turning the knob. She almost felt like an intruder, it had been so long since she had ventured out of her warm safe cocoon in the servants' quarters and into the main terrain of the house; the memories of her parents were just too painful. Yet she couldn't bring herself to sell the house either.

Her old room was a shrine to her past. It was still decorated as it had been when she was in college, yards and yards of white dotted swiss on the windows and bed. In a corner her collection of dolls was stacked in cribs and on satin pillows. The oldest of them were delicate and cracked porcelain, dolls her grandmother had once played with. Her mother's dolls were there too, pretty babies with golden locks and blue velvet dresses with starched collars. One of them even wore a mink coat, something she guiltily permitted because after all, it had been Mama's.

She opened the huge walk-in closet and scanned the orderly clothes that hung inside. She browsed through the racks. Nothing had been updated for three years, but the classic styling of most of the clothes she and her mother had selected was such that they could withstand the test of time. Like her dolls.

She took off her dowdy clothes and changed into a cream-colored silk blouse and a pair of winter white gabardine slacks. She was tired of black. She tied a multicolored scarf around her neck and moved to her dressing table and put on some makeup. Then she looked at the results in the full-length mirror. Oh well, it was some improvement anyway.

Down in the kitchen, she prepared her morning coffee and fed the cats who wound themselves around her ankles crying. She noticed the answering machine blinking. She didn't really care that she hadn't checked it last night, the only person whose call she could have cared about had been with her. Now in the cold morning light with her head out of the clouds, she played back its messages.

The first one turned out to be from her brother Larry. Call me immediately, it's urgent, he said. It was over money, she was sure. Let it wait.

The second call was a surprise. "Leslie dear, this is Bunny Nilsson. I don't know if you remember, but we met at the fundraiser for the Hunger Exchange that your mother . . . that your dear mother chaired quite a few years ago. I need to get in touch with you very soon. Could you please call me." The soft Southern voice left a number.

A third call was her brother again. "I don't know where you are . . . are you out with Mr. Wonderful? Call me, please."

The machine clicked off. Her spirits were far too good to have them ruined by her brother, but she was intrigued that Bunny Nilsson wanted to talk to her, and she returned the call. She immediately recognized Bunny's drawl.

"Mrs. Nilsson?"

"This is she."

"This is Leslie Warning."

"Oh, Leslie dear," the voice effused over the line. It was like honey, thick and sweet, dripping with good intentions. It was a voice that could catch flies. "I'm so glad to hear from you. I have some very exciting news to tell you about the Hunger Exchange. You *are* still involved with them, aren't you?"

"Well, yes," said Leslie.

"Wonderful. I can hardly wait to tell you all about it. Are you free for lunch today?"

Leslie didn't know what to say. She was supposed to work in the S.T.S. offices in the morning and then join the picket line in front of Swank in the afternoon. She wondered what Bunny Nilsson would say if she knew about that! She really didn't want to have lunch with her, but since it involved the Hunger Exchange she felt she had to.

"I'm free."

"Marvelous," spewed Bunny as if they were old friends. "How about the Russian Tea Room at noon? I haven't been there in ages. Is that all right with you?"

"That would be fine," Leslie replied.

After hanging up Leslie wondered if she had made the right decision. But if Bunny Nilsson was offering something to the Hunger Exchange it had to be something big. Bunny Nilsson was one of the most powerful fundraisers in New York, and the Hunger Exchange had always held a special place in Leslie's heart. It had been her mother's pet charity. Since her mother's death she had drifted away from the group. Oh, she still sent them a generous annual contribution in her parents' names, but she was turned off by all the infighting among the socially ambitious fundraisers.

In fact, it was after leaving her last meeting as a board member on the Hunger Exchange that Leslie had met Mary Ellen. It was a sunny afternoon, and she had been wandering through Central Park, when she saw this mesmerizing woman standing on a make-shift stage, brandishing animal traps and shouting at the top of her lungs. Intrigued, Leslie stopped to watch and was totally taken in by the vocal, energetic figure on the stage. Her slight frame belied the strong voice that carried over the crowd without aid of a microphone. The woman was demonstrating the use of a trap, a mean-looking contraption of steel jaws lined with jagged teeth. She opened it until it yawned to a size nearly half her body. It looked horribly painful.

"You tell me," she was shouting, "that getting your leg stuck in this would feel the same as slamming your fingers in a car door. Well, that's what the fur industry, what the trappers are trying to sell us. They are trying to tell us that an animal feels no pain from these traps." She looked around the gathered audience. "Sir," she called out to a man in a suit. "Yes, you. Would you like to volunteer to come up here and put your arm in this trap?" He shook his head fiercely with a "no-way" gesture and hurried on.

"Do you see? Do you see what I mean? Do I have any volunteers who are willing to put one of their limbs into these ruthless steel jaws?" When no one was forthcoming, she went on. "This year in the United States alone seventy million animals will be murdered for their skins, and twenty-five percent of them will have been caught in traps such as these," she shouted, waving the open trap with a vengeance. "Now I ask you, should any living creature suffer something like this, something that tears at the flesh, rips the ligaments, crushes the bone . . ."

Leslie was moved, and when the rally was over she went up to the speaker and shyly introduced herself. She had spare time she wanted to give, she told Mary Ellen. Mary Ellen hadn't been overly receptive at first, until she learned who Leslie was. Mary Ellen warmed considerably when she discovered Leslie was an heiress, and put her arm around her in a motherly fashion. "Leslie," she said, "we've been looking for someone like you."

It wasn't until weeks later, after Leslie's money had helped them secure their first office space, that Leslie saw the horrible traps again. Mary Ellen had returned from a demonstration and brought them into the office, dropping them to the floor with a clang. Leslie mentioned the gruesome nature of the traps, how the sight of them had moved her to join S.T.S. in the first place.

"Especially that large one with the jagged teeth," she had said, shuddering at the thought of it.

"Oh, that one," said Mary Ellen nonchalantly. "It's a terror, isn't it? It's an old bear trap. Luckily they've been outlawed for some time now."

"They have?"

"Yeah, but I still use this one for my speeches because it's so mean looking, and it always draws a response from the crowd. I don't get nearly the same effect from this," she said, holding up an innocuous looking pair of padded steel bars set on steel jaws. "It's just not as fierce looking, but the result's the same: paws chewed off, animals starving, etcetera, etcetera. I go for the effect," she said, rattling the old bear trap.

Leslie wasn't sure how she felt about that. She had to wonder about the scruples of deceiving people that way.

But after working with Mary Ellen for a while, Leslie came to appreciate her eccentricities. She knew that she was simply, totally, dedicated to her cause, and that to serve that cause she would let nothing get in the way.

Looking at the clock, Leslie started. It was getting late. She finished her coffee quickly and gave the cats a loving pat good-bye. But before leaving, she ran into the first floor powder room and took another look at herself. She was thinking of Neil and feeling very special. She wanted to look that way.

And then she was out the door and on her way to the S.T.S. office, oblivious to the cold and grey of yet another dreary November day.

XVIII

Larry Warning barged into the office, his arrival creating a burst of wind that sent papers scattering about the small room. Startled, Leslie looked up from her desk, and her expression turned to fear and displeasure as she saw her brother hovering over her desk.

"Jesus, Leslie," he said coldly, his voice filled with barely controlled anger. "Where in the hell have you been? Don't you return phone calls anymore?"

"I'm sorry, Larry," she responded meekly. He frightened her when he was angry like this. She hated confrontation more than anything else, and especially with her brother. "I forgot to check my machine until this morning, and then I was running late. I was going to call you in a little while."

Her soulful brown eyes looked into his, and his hostile demeanor began to soften. The red in his round face faded, and his color returned to normal. Wordlessly, he found a metal folding chair and pulled it up in front of her desk. His soft wide face took on an appealing glow and she felt the old urge to pinch his cheek like a baby's.

He was thirty-two, five years her senior, but he looked much younger. His immature features were framed by a head of loose black curls cropped short in a round halo about his face. A pair of blue eyes, clear and deep as a cloudless sky, were his best feature. His worst was his mouth, a fleshy pair of lips so purple that he always looked cold, and small white teeth that were pearls far too tiny for his broad face.

He was her older brother and her only living relative. Half of the blood that flowed through her was the same as his. Despite his shortcomings, she couldn't help but love him.

"So how are you, little sister?" he asked finally.

"I'm fine. How are you?"

He studied her for a moment. She looked different. Makeup, that was it. And she was actually wearing decent clothes. He was perplexed, and almost lost sight of his mission.

"I'm fine too," he said nicely, and then coming back to his senses, he added, "Except that I am extremely frustrated. Leslie, I am a grown man who's supposed to be worth millions, and I can't get my hands on a dime because my little sister controls the purse strings."

"Larry, that's not fair. You have to stop blaming me for what Father did. He wrote his will, I didn't. I'm able to live quite well on my trust fund. I don't see why you can't."

"The trust fund just covers my living expenses. It doesn't allow for anything else, don't you see, Les? I need to have more money, money for investments, money that I control."

"How about getting a job?" she asked.

He looked startled for a second. She was normally so timid. Was it possible there was a tiger under that mousey facade? Where did this new spunk come from?

He stared at her pleadingly, aware that he was in no situation to bully her, and that perhaps he would do better by appealing to her sympathetic nature.

"Leslie . . . I want to be free to live my own life, make my own decisions. I have a right to that. We've been offered an unreal amount of money for our company stock. Please consent to sell it."

"No," said Leslie firmly. She stood up behind her desk. "Warning Mills was Papa's company and his father's company before him. Even though you and I aren't active in it, it's still a part of us. I don't intend to let it go. Not now anyway."

"Or ever," countered Larry. "C'mon, Leslie, when are you going to let go? They're dead. Your mother is dead. Our father is dead. Holding on to the company isn't going to bring them back. I want to see my half of the money and move on. You should do the same."

"I don't need the money," she said obstinately, "and I don't want to sell."

"Jesus," said Larry, his anger rising. Leslie wished there was someone else in the office. He held his hands together tensely as if fighting the urge to wrap them around her neck. As he clenched them together in his lap, he spoke in a mean, tight voice. "Why I have to be tied to you I'll never know. You drive me crazy with your weird dolls, your cats, your moronic job."

He leaned forward now and his hands clutched the sides of the desk, clinging to it with magnetic force. "If one of your stupid little charities asked you to sign your life away you'd do it on the spot. But you won't help your own flesh and blood, your only brother. You're selfish, Leslie, thinking only of what makes you feel good."

His arms released the sides of the desk now and flailed about in frustration. "You already give most of your trust fund money to this dump . . . if you sell the stock you'll have more to give to them. That should make you happy. You could do it in your parents' honor or rename S.T.S. the Warning Foundation for Abused Animals." His voice was verging on hysteria now, and in his tantrum he swept his arm across her desk, sending most of its contents flying.

She got up slowly, watching him deliberately, and began to pick up the pens and papers he had scattered on the floor. She wasn't angry with him; she couldn't be when he was like this. She felt sorry for him. She remembered so clearly how he used to do this when he was a child. Always doing something to draw attention to himself. She knew he had resented her existence from the start, and in a way she didn't blame him. His mother, who was never able to get over the divorce, had turned him into a very sad and embittered little boy. She was sure that when they were children, he had hated her. It was she who got to live with two parents who loved each other while he shuttled back and forth between two people who were barely civil toward one another. Larry's mother had done everything in her power to turn Larry against his father and his baby sister.

Leslie thought sadly of how she had tried to win her brother's love. She had always saved things for him and shared with him. She had badgered her father constantly to include him on any special outings. But to her frustration, Larry had always thrown her kindnesses back in her face, batting away the love she so willingly offered him. During their adolescent years, Larry's obvious dislike had yielded to a grudging tolerance. Leslie had been encouraged by this, because she knew that eventually she could get through to her brother's heart.

But since the day of the accident, Larry had reverted to his old attitude. It was as if he blamed her because their father had left everything, with the exception of their trusts funds, and the house —which went to Leslie—to the two of them jointly, including the huge block of stock that was still the controlling interest in the company.

She knew why he had done it. Had he left them each half of the stock, Larry would have sold his and diluted the Warning control of the company, making it vulnerable to a take-over. There was too much sweat, blood and history in the company to let it go to strangers.

Larry sat quietly as Leslie straightened things up. He neither offered to help nor did he make any further disturbances. When she had replaced everything on her desk, she said quietly but with finality, "Larry, I'm not selling, and that's it."

His white face flushed red once again, and then returned to its normal pallor. He stood up and sighed in defeat. "I don't know why you want to hurt me so, Les," he said. His shoulders sagged inside his large soft frame, and he looked so vulnerable for a moment that Leslie ached for him.

"What about tomorrow?" he asked, changing the subject so quickly that it took her by surprise. "Are you joining us?"

Leslie thought of how miserable the holidays were when she spent them with Larry and his resentful mother.

"Oh, Larry, I forgot to tell you. I've been invited to a friend's home for Thanksgiving."

He seemed genuinely surprised that she had other plans. "Who? Mary Ellen? What are you having? Bean curd with alfalfa stuffing?" he teased. "Well, Mother and I will think of you as we dine on roast turkey and trimmings at the club."

"You know I don't eat that anyway," she said.

"Oh, Leslie, you are a pip. What a waste . . . It's such a shame that you don't have a clue how to enjoy life." With that he turned and walked out the door without even saying good-bye.

When he was gone the office returned to its former state of silence and Leslie felt an overwhelming sense of loneliness come over her. She couldn't sell the stock, she simply couldn't, even if it meant further alienating her brother. And in a way, she pondered, the stock was keeping them together. If she ever did agree to sell it, she wondered if she would ever see him again.

XIX

"This was just delivered for you."

It was Elliot from the receiving room who was interrupting Yolanda at her work. A simple man of indeterminate middle age, he had worked for the station longer than anyone else she knew of. It was believed that he was the feebleminded cousin of an executive long since purged during a ratings war. Elliot remained as his legacy.

Yolanda took the large round box wrapped in brown paper from Elliot's eager hands and gave him a smiling thank-you. He nodded excitedly in return, and retreated happily, his mission fulfilled. Yolanda watched him as he went, his clumsy walk light with self-importance. Too late, she thought to ask him about who had brought it. Newscasters could get nervous about that sort of thing.

Her uneasiness was dispelled as soon as she removed the brown paper wrapping. The signature glossy black-and-white packaging of Swank Furs reflected the overhead fluorescent light. Gingerly, she pulled the top off the box and a low "oooh" escaped her lips. Inside was a red fox hat, its fur rich and gleaming. She removed the hat from the box; it was as soft and delicate to the touch as silk. She pulled it on, the wide brim of fur encircling her head like a halo. Without looking, she knew she looked terrific . . . she could just feel it.

A few of the girls in the newsroom came over to comment.

"Oh, Yolanda, is that ever beautiful."

"It looks terrific on you. Where did you get it?"

Yolanda glanced back into the box that was still sitting on her lap. There was a card inside and it bore the same logo as the hat box: the slim silhouette of a woman wrapped in a large billowing fur coat. And it was engraved with Bunny Nilsson's name. Beneath it was a handwritten note: "I thought this might go nicely with your coat. I know the color will be fabulous for you." It was signed simply "Bunny."

"Boy, this lady doesn't miss a trick," said Yolanda. "I wonder if I should keep it?"

"Why not?" asked one of the girls. "I'd never turn away any gift that was fur," she added wistfully.

"Well, I think it's disgusting," came a third voice. It was Pam Young, one of the associate producers of the local news. "You might just as well put a crown of thorns around your head for the suffering that little piece of vanity represents." She gave the handful of papers that she was holding a smart little shake at Yolanda's head and sighed with disgust before continuing on her way.

Yolanda took the hat off her head and held it at arm's length, examining it. "It sho' is mighty fine, tho," she said, slipping intentionally into a street accent. She replaced the hat in the box, and slid it under her desk. She would decide what to do about it later.

It was generous of Bunny Nilsson, she thought, but then again every gift had its price. Did she think Yolanda would give Swank more favorable treatment in her "In Depth" if she accepted it?

It wasn't as if Yolanda couldn't afford to buy her own fox hat. She was finally reaching a point in her life where she could afford luxuries—things that she once could only dream about—things she had thought only rich, white, Connecticut housewives could afford. Now many of those things were within her reach, and it was because of one of those housewives—and Ellie—that it was so.

Sadly, Yolanda reflected on the first time she had met Mrs. Hutchinson. It was an oppressively hot day in June, and Ellie, her grandmother's sister, had stopped in her Bronx apartment only to find Yolanda left alone in the stifling heat. Ellie carried her along to work that day, taking Yolanda for her first train ride, her five-year-old eyes widening at the wonders she saw as they moved farther and farther away from the city. Yolanda remembered being awed by the trees, so green and lush, so dense and healthy. In the housing projects trees were rare, and those that did exist were scraggly and blighted, stunted by city air and concrete.

When they disembarked from the train in Westport, Yolanda marveled at how different the air was; cool and breezy under the broad shade of huge trees and rich with oxygen instead of smog. Mrs. Hutchinson was there to meet them, and Ellie was quick to apologize for bringing Yolanda along. But Mrs. Hutchinson had been kind from the beginning, fussing over her, saying that she would be no problem. When they arrived at the huge white clapboard house, Mrs. Hutchinson insisted that Ellie go on with her chores, and she took Yolanda out onto a cool shaded porch overlooking a lush, wide ravine where she fed her milk and cookies. Yolanda was enamored with the friendly white lady who smelled like talcum powder and dressed in such pretty clothes.

But it was what happened next that would have the biggest impact on Yolanda's life. Mrs. Hutchinson disappeared momentarily, and when she returned she was carrying a stack of books, children's books left over from her own children who had grown up and gone away leaving their mother to putter around her large house by herself all day. What a world those books opened up to Yolanda! They were nonsensical, many of them, with stories of talking fish and animals who drove cars, and they tapped right into the fertile imagination of a little girl. She listened, entranced, as Mrs. Hutchinson read to her. Up until that point in her life, no one had ever read a word to her. Mesmerized, she begged the white lady to read the books to her over and over again.

A door had opened for Yolanda. Once a week, she would ride the train to Connecticut with Ellie, and while her great-aunt did the housework, Yolanda would read with Mrs. Hutchinson. When she started school in the fall, she was way ahead of her peers, and it was largely because of Mrs. Hutchinson's help that she was able to make sense out of what she was being taught in the woefully inadequate inner city schools.

For years she would look forward to school holidays and summer break so that she could once again go up to Connecticut with Ellie. Through Mrs. Hutchinson's sad, lonely eyes she was introduced to a world of literature and beauty and fine things. She learned table manners and proper pronunciation, things for which she was chided by some of her classmates who called her white and uppity. But Ellie saw what was happening and was glad—she wanted more for Yolanda than cleaning houses.

The saddest moment of Yolanda's young life occurred on a beautiful summer day when she was thirteen.

She and Mrs. Hutchinson had been sitting on the porch reading aloud from Shakespeare's *Sonnets* when out walked a tall white man with serious black spectacles and a serious grey suit to match. Mrs. Hutchinson looked surprised to see him, and Yolanda sensed fear rising in her. She recognized Mr. Hutchinson from photos she had seen around the house. His wife rarely spoke of him. With a single withering glance, he pulled Mrs. Hutchinson from Yolanda's side and drew her into the house. The sound of sharp words from inside followed, sounds Yolanda could not decipher except for the occasional word "girl" and "help." When Mrs. Hutchinson reappeared on the porch she looked shaken. She closed the book of sonnets with its well-worn leather cover, and handed it over to Yolanda.

"I'm afraid you won't be able to come out with Ellie anymore, Yolanda," she said timidly, her mild grey eyes looking pained and lonely. Yolanda wanted to cry—she knew what she was losing. But then, with a wisdom she had never known she possessed, she realized it was Mrs. Hutchinson who was losing more. From that moment, Yolanda hated Mr. Hutchinson. She longed to go inside and corner him, to demand an explanation. But she didn't, and when he passed through the room later as she and Ellie were getting ready to leave, his presence so huge and self-important, she knew that he could never care about anything she had to say to him. That bothered her more than anything. To him, she simply didn't exist.

Two years later Mrs. Hutchinson died of cancer. Ellie told her about it, and Yolanda read the obituaries to find out where the funeral was being held. She took the train to Westport and walked five miles to the church. There she sat anonymously in the back, watching the polite tears of the grey, impeccably dressed offspring of her mentor as they stood tall and erect beside their father. A few people turned to study Yolanda, and once Mr. Hutchinson looked her way, but his glance was fleeting and Yolanda knew that he had no idea who she was. At that moment her hatred for him burned deeper than ever. She would show him, she thought. Him and everyone like him. She would become not only someone he recognized, but someone he had to respect. That was the only way she could win.

Her mind came back to the present, and she thought about Bunny Nilsson's gift, the fur hat. Things sure had changed; now she had white people sending her presents. She had come a long way, and it hadn't been easy, but she still had a long way to go.

XX

Karen and Tony pulled up in front of the old frame house and in a rare display of camaraderie, they looked at each other quizzically. The ramshackle bungalow stood out among the other tidy houses on the well-kept Brooklyn block. It looked barely habitable. Broken glass and crushed cans littered the weeds of what had once been the front lawn, and all but one of the windows were boarded up, further adding to its general appearance of abandonment.

"Does somebody actually live here?" Karen asked.

It was their third stop since leaving headquarters. They had already checked out the two other S.T.S. members Karen had turned up on her computer search. The first, John Abbott, the second-story man, was working in construction and had been on a job all day Friday. Christian Petersen, the pedophile pornography enthusiast, was confined to a hospital bed, close to death from AIDS. That left Sylvester K. Wolfe, in front of whose residence they now sat. Wolfe had once been charged with pistol-whipping a neighbor who had complained about his animals. The neighbor hadn't shown up in court, so the case had been dropped, according to the arresting officer whom Karen had contacted. "But I'd be careful around this guy," he had warned. "He's a real piece of work." His words echoed in her ears as she got out of the car and hesitated before the crumbled walk. Tony came up behind her and waved his arm, pointing graciously toward the house. "Ladies first," he said.

"Thanks for nothing."

As they walked along the badly cracked pavement, a terrible apprehensive feeling seized hold of Karen. Once again, she was grateful for Tony's strong presence, and when she turned to look back at him, she noticed he had opened his jacket and taken the safety off his revolver. She did the same.

Once they were standing on the sagging front porch, their noses were assaulted by a horrible stench. It was the pungent smell of animals, musty and heavy, a head-turning smell. Karen grimaced at Tony before knocking on the rotting wooden door. The sound set off a round of baying and loud barking from the dogs inside. Karen found herself secretly hoping that no one was at home.

But it was not to be. A hoarse male voice could be heard inside chastising the dogs. Their barking ceased abruptly, then the voice addressed them through the still-closed door.

"What do you want?"

"Is this Sylvester K. Wolfe?" Karen asked with all the authority she could muster.

"Who wants to know?"

Karen glanced at Tony, who proffered his hand as if to say "it's all yours." Thanks again, Tony, she thought. Trying to overcome her nervousness, she said shakily, "I'm Detective Levinson from the New York Police Department, Mr. Wolfe. Detective Perrelli and I would like to ask you a few questions."

"What department are you with?" the voice rasped out.

"Homicide."

There was a moment of silence and then the sound of several locks being unbolted. The door opened a crack and a bloodshot grey eye peeped out at them from behind the false security of a chain.

"Identification?"

Karen and Tony complied, holding up their N.Y.P.D. badges and identification cards. Wolfe eyed them briefly and then closed the door again. When he reopened it, he had removed the chain.

"As long as you aren't from animal control," he said, gesturing for them to enter. "Come in quickly now, before anyone gets out." Four dogs of assorted size and breed struggled against his legs, eager to get at the interlopers. Karen hesitated.

"Go on," urged Tony behind her. She remained semi-frozen and turned to him tensely. "I'm afraid of dogs," she whispered.

"Well, you'd better get over it," he snapped, forcing himself past her and into the house. Unsteadily, she followed.

The stench outside had been nothing compared to the odor inside the house. The strong stink of animal feces and cat urine lingered in the air. The dogs, instinctively sensing Karen's fear, nosed at her crotch and growled at her in low tones. Fighting the impulse to turn and run, Karen stood pat and quickly surveyed her surroundings.

They were in a small front room containing a few pieces of shabby furniture. Along one wall was a battered old sofa over which an old green bedspread had been thrown. On it lounged at least a dozen cats in various states of repose. A few of them looked up to take in the visitors, eyeing them lazily before returning to their previous positions. Next to the sofa was a La-Z-Boy recliner, its imitation leather cracked and open in gaping holes from which peeked its yellow synthetic stuffing. A portable TV set was on a folding table. Sylvester Wolfe had been watching "The Honey-mooners." The only light, other than that cast by the television screen, came through the yellowed shade that was drawn over the only unboarded window.

Karen turned her attention for the first time to their host. Although his voice had sounded like an old man's, she saw readily that he was much younger, somewhere in his late thirties. And huge. He was about six-three and at least three hundred pounds. His dark, messy hair was streaked with premature grey as was the stubble on his pasty pouchy face. More than ever, Karen felt ill-at-ease.

She was glad when Tony took over right away. It was obvious that he too was none too comfortable standing in the stink of Wolfe's house, with Wolfe's dogs sniffing curiously at his feet and groin.

"Mr. Wolfe, we are investigating a murder and we need to ask you some questions."

"Me? I can't imagine why. I don't know anything about no murder."

"I hope not," said Tony with an unconvincing smile. "But it's my job, so I just have to ask. You happen to be on the mailing list of an animal rights group that, for reasons I can't say, might be connected, so we are checking everyone out. No need to be alarmed."

Sylvester did not look relieved. Karen watched as his eyes darted about the dimly lit room until they came to rest atop the TV set. From where she stood, she could barely make out what was on top, but finally she recognized what it was. It was a small stack of the same S.T.S. pamphlet that they had found in the pocket of Jennifer O'Grady's coat. She saw that Tony had noticed this too, and at once all three of them averted their eyes as if they had seen nothing.

"Mr. Wolfe," asked Tony, "did you know Jennifer O'Grady?"

"Jennifer O'Grady, Jennifer O'Grady," he said, repeating the name over and over again like a parrot. Finally, as if arriving at an answer he had been seeking for some time, he said, "The model."

"The model," concurred Tony. "Did you know her?"

Sylvester walked over to the television stand and picked up one of the flyers. "From this," he said, waving it at them.

"Have you ever met her?"

He rolled his big eyes back in his head. "Met her?" he asked innocently, and then firmly he said, "No."

"You've never seen her on the street or spoken to her?"

Sylvester once again appeared to be thinking and then repeated his answer, "No."

"Where were you last Friday, Mr. Wolfe?"

Refusing to be rushed, the big man paused for another interminable wait before responding. "Home. I was home all day last Friday." His voice had taken on a hostile tone and upon hearing the change, the dogs began to growl, low threatening sounds emanating from deep within their narrow throats. Karen's heart clutched as one dog, a mix with a high percentage of Doberman in him, bared his teeth at Tony.

"Can anyone confirm that?" asked Tony.

Sylvester looked about the room at his gathered menagerie. "They all know I was here."

Karen, still cowering from the snarling dogs, was surprised when Tony totally changed his line of questioning.

"Mr. Wolfe, you seem to be quite the animal lover."

"Oh, yes," he effused, his tone turning warm and friendly. The dogs eased back from their hostile posture and lay down on their haunches. The Doberman mix relaxed his curled lips so that his teeth were no longer exposed. He lay his head down upon his front paws and watched.

"Tell me," continued Tony, "don't you hate people who harm animals?"

"Of course. Anyone who could hurt a defenseless creature is, well, they're . . . despicable," he said, finally settling on the right word. "Yes, despicable. That's where I've gotten most of my pets, from people who didn't take care of them. People who didn't love them. They didn't deserve them."

"What do you think of people who wear fur coats, Mr. Wolfe?"

A hateful, sour look came across the pasty face and the dogs began a low level of growling again. "Someone should pound their heads in," he snarled.

Karen breathed deeply of the fresh Brooklyn air, gladly taking deep gasps of the sweet fumes of pollution and exhaust. Anything was preferable to that stench inside Sylvester Wolfe's home. Her legs were still a little shaky from being around the dogs, so she was happier still when she was securely seated in the car, even if she had to be in the company of her ever hostile partner. Bad as he was, she would take him over the dogs any day.

"Pound their heads in?" she said, repeating Sylvester's words.

Tony looked at her like she was an imbecile. "I noticed, thank you." He drove silently, obviously in deep thought, before finally saying, "I think we should go back over to Jennifer O'Grady's apartment and see if we can't find a picture of that missing cat of hers. Who knows, we might just find that little critter wandering around inside Mr. Wolfe's house."

Karen thought of the wretched house, of the stinking menagerie inside. "Aren't there laws against having that many animals in one place?"

"Yeah. Maybe when this is over we'll give animal control a call, but for now I want to leave everything just the way it is, until we can find out if old Chessie is in there."

Sylvester watched the two detectives walk down his damaged sidewalk and get into their car. He saw how they looked at his house with disdain before they pulled away. So maybe he did need to fix it up, make it more the way it was when his mother was alive. He had promised her, before she died, that he would take good care of it.

Mama had been so wonderful. She had loved him so much, loved him when the others didn't, made him fudge brownies when he came home from school crying because the kids had teased him. She had even arranged it so that he would be financially secure for the rest of his life. He had been her baby, and she had looked after him.

Now he had his babies to take care of. He picked up a large tabby that rubbed against his ankles and stroked its neck fondly. "Don't worry, children," he called out to the rest of the animals in the room. "I will always take care of you. No one will ever take you away from me."

XXI

Leslie was just getting ready to leave for her luncheon date with Bunny Nilsson when the phone rang. She rushed to pick it up before the answering machine came on. It was Mary Ellen calling from a Fifth Avenue pay phone. Leslie could barely hear her over the din of traffic.

"Leslie," she shouted into the phone. "Could you do me a favor and see if I left my engagement calendar there. I think I might have made an appointment for today."

Leslie put down the phone and went over to Mary Ellen's desk. The top drawer was a disorganized mess, a plethora of hastily scribbled notes, office supplies and candy wrappers. Laying atop the piles of junk was a tattered book marked "Engagements," its cover barely held on by strands of fiber, the inside pages falling out in entire months. It's a good thing it's almost the end of the year, thought Leslie. She opened the appointment book. There was something marked for Wednesday in Mary Ellen's illegible scrawl.

"It looks like you have something here at eleven-thirty," said Leslie, squinting to make out the name.

"Damn," said Mary Ellen. "I can't believe I forgot about it. The woman called last week and said she wanted to share something with me that would make S.T.S. very happy. I think she wants to give money."

"Well, no one has shown and it's eleven-thirty now."

"Leslie, will you hang around until she gets there and make some excuse for me? Don't tell her I spaced on it. Get all the info from her and whatever?"

"Mary Ellen, I have a lunch date . . ."

"Oh, c'mon, make him wait. It's good for them to have to wait once in a while."

Leslie didn't feel like telling Mary Ellen who she was lunching with or why, so she acquiesced. "I'll wait for a little while."

"Thanks, Leslie, you're a trooper," Mary Ellen screamed. Then the noise and traffic of Fifth Avenue was gone and the line was silent in Leslie's hand.

She waited until noon, and the woman still hadn't shown up. Deciding she had already waited longer than she should have, she taped a hastily scrawled note to the door, set the answering machine and abandoned the office. She struggled in vain to flag down a cab in the midday Soho traffic, until she drew the attention of a battered taxi that barely appeared roadworthy. However, its rooftop light was lit, meaning it was available, and that made it a precious commodity regardless of its condition. She scrambled gratefully into the back seat and fell into the indentation that thousands of customers over the years had worn into its uphol- stery.

She had plenty of time to wonder what it was Bunny Nilsson had to offer the Hunger Exchange as they puttered along, the old cab stuck in traffic as she watched the light at the intersection turn red for the third time. It was taking them forever to just cross Houston Street, and she was becoming anxious. Her mother had always considered tardiness to be the ultimate in rudeness.

She watched the light turn to green for the fourth time, and this time they were able to negotiate their way through the busy inter- section, through the heavy stream of pedestrians, and head up- town. It was twelve-thirty when the cab finally came to a halt in front of the 57th Street restaurant, and Leslie paid quickly and rushed inside.

Bunny was on her second glass of wine, and none too happy, when she looked up to see the maître d' escorting a flustered looking Leslie across the crowded room to her corner table. Nor- mally Bunny would have insisted on being seated more centrally, in the stream of action, nearer the ebb and flow of the movers and shakers. But she had remembered Leslie as being shy and re- served, and had opted for a quieter table. Over to the side no one would disturb them or eavesdrop on their conversation.

Bunny tried to mask her irritation at being kept waiting, and she waved with polite eagerness in Leslie's direction. Bunny hadn't seen her in years, not since the last time the girl had ac- companied her mother to a luncheon fundraiser, and sadly her looks hadn't improved. She still carried herself with utter lack of confidence and dressed dreadfully.

In a wave of uncharacteristic charity, Bunny found herself pity- ing Leslie. It couldn't have been easy on her, losing her parents so suddenly like that. Maybe Bunny should take her under her wing. Go shopping with her and update her less than stylish wardrobe. Get her to invest in a new hairstyle and some makeup. The girl did have beautiful skin and gorgeous huge brown eyes. With a little jazzing up she could be transformed from the ugly duckling into a beautiful swan. Well, maybe not quite a swan, but certainly im- proved.

The girl's mother had failed her, thought Bunny. Then again, Amanda Warning had been a little strange herself. She and her husband had practically shunned New York society, preferring to keep to themselves, leading a rather insular life. Amanda was always turning down offers to sit on the most visible and prestigious of boards, like the Met or American Ballet Theatre, opting instead to work for obscure causes like the Hunger Exchange. Downers, as Bunny referred to them. Causes Bunny normally shied away from. Wasn't it ironic now that at the behest of her father-in-law, she found herself about to aid one of those very causes.

Bunny rose and hugged Leslie with a familiarity that made Leslie uncomfortable. She pulled back shyly. Bunny pretended not to notice the slight rebuff.

"Please sit down," she said, and once they were both seated she placed a manicured hand warmly on top of Leslie's. "How are you, dear?" she asked, looking directly into her eyes, telegraphing to Leslie that they were both thinking of the same thing, Leslie's deceased parents.

"I'm fine," said Leslie, choking up. Her eyes welled momentarily as they always did when someone expressed sympathy about her parents. She never failed to be amazed that it still drew such a strong reaction from her. She hated it, hated that they knew about it, and hated that they were probably conjuring the same gruesome mental picture she lived with every day of her life.

"They were wonderful people, your parents," said Bunny with her cozy Southern sincerity. "They are sorely missed."

"Thank you," said Leslie, further embarrassed by Bunny's attention. She pulled her hand back and placed it in her lap under the table. Happily, the waiter chose that moment to break the awkwardness by making his appearance.

"Something to drink, ladies?" he asked hurriedly in a clipped Middle Eastern accent.

Leslie ordered a mineral water, and Bunny had yet another glass of wine. The waiter retreated quickly, and Leslie made her apologies for being late.

"I'm sorry to have kept you waiting, Mrs. Nilsson . . ."

"It's Bunny, please."

"Bunny. Anyhow, something came up at work, and I was detained. An appointment that never showed up."

"Don't we all know about that," laughed Bunny, her weak smile fading quickly. "I wasn't aware that you had a job."

Uncomfortably, Leslie said, "Yes, I do," and eager to change the subject, she asked, "So what was it you wanted to discuss with me about the Hunger Exchange?"

"Something I think you will find fabulous. But first, let's look at the menu so that we can order. I'm starved. Then we'll talk about the Hunger Exchange."

The waiter returned with their drinks, and they both ordered luncheon salads with goat cheese. Then Bunny got down to business.

"I want to help the Hunger Exchange. That is, the Nilsson family and Swank Furs want to."

Leslie sat mute as Bunny explained. "We, my husband, my father-in-law and I, were thinking, 'What can we do for mankind this holiday season? Something important, something that gives back a little of that which we are so lucky to have.' And then my wonderful husband Michael came up with a marvelous idea. Swank Furs is going to give away fifty percent of the profits we make on the sale of every fur coat we sell this holiday season. And we want to give it to a needy cause. Well, what better cause is there than the Hunger Exchange? So, remembering how involved your mother was with the Hunger Exchange, I naturally thought to call you right away. I assumed you would be carrying on her tradition." Bunny was gleaming, triumphant at what she had to offer. Proud of her grand generosity. She waited for Leslie's response.

Leslie's mind was racing, digesting what she had just heard, wondering what she could possibly do. What a dilemma. The promise of a large cash infusion for the Hunger Exchange required condoning the ongoing slaughter of helpless animals. What should she do? She looked into Bunny's face, the perfect eager smile poised for praise and thanks. Leslie knew she had to be honest.

"Uh, Bunny, there's something I don't think you are aware of," said Leslie. The words came out with difficulty and she held her breath before moving on, speaking quietly and with a silent strength she had summoned up from deep within her. "I must be honest with you. Most of my time these days is spent working for S.T.S. I don't know if . . ."

Bunny cut her short. The blood had drained from her face, even the white of her lips shone through the waxy layers of her expensive lipstick. She stiffened, sitting up very straight in her chair, and said, "Are you referring to Save Their Skins, the animal rights fanatics? The misdirected and misinformed terrorists who have turned my life into a living hell? You work for them? Is that what you are telling me?"

Leslie's cheeks burned in confused shame. The last thing she wanted to do was upset Bunny Nilsson. She nodded her head in embarrassed confirmation.

"My dear," said Bunny in a voice she was barely able to control. "We are talking about people who are starving. Are you placing animals above them? Do you know that since the beginning of time man has relied on animals to survive? They have supplied his food, skins to keep him warm . . . Do you think we would be here now if mankind hadn't made use of that which God provided for him?"

Leslie just stared back at her meekly. Disgusted, Bunny took her napkin from her lap and laid it on the table before her, her rage evident despite her outward civility. Fighting to maintain her dignity, and resisting the urge to pick up her wine glass and dash the liquid into the girl's face, she stood slowly. "Well, I guess we have nothing further to discuss here. You will excuse me, but I have just developed a terrible headache. Please enjoy your lunch, I did invite you. I will take care of the check on my way out." And with that she departed, shaking with anger.

Leslie felt as though she might cry. She should have known that such a scene would be the result of meeting Bunny Nilsson for lunch. But worst of all, she had come on behalf of the Hunger Exchange only to take the very bread from its mouth. Certainly Bunny would find another organization to support now.

She pushed her chair back from the table and stood sheepishly. She avoided eye contact with the curious waiter as she passed him on the way out. Once safely ensconced in a cab, she gave her home address. There was no way she would be marching in front of Swank today, not now. No, she was heading home, to her house, to the safe cocoon she inhabited with Amanda and Edward, to her shelter from the outside world, to her room.

XXII

There were only about twenty of them marching today, but Mary Ellen wasn't concerned. Twenty people were fine; their very presence was having a crippling effect on Swank's business. She was glad that creepy fat guy wasn't marching with them today; she hadn't seen him since Monday when the police broke up the demonstration. Perhaps that had scared him off.

She didn't know why he bothered her the way he did; she was usually very tolerant of misfits and eccentrics. She remembered the day he first wandered into the S.T.S. office looking for flyers to distribute, and she had given him a handful. He had surprised her by saying he wanted to give a donation and handing her one hundred dollars, and Mary Ellen, ever eager for the green, had put him on the mailing list. Sylvester K. Wolfe was his name, she remembered, and she hadn't seen him again until last Monday when he joined them in the march, if you could call what he did marching. He just kind of waddled along, stopping often to rest on the sidelines. She wondered if he would be there on Friday. She hoped not. He really made her skin crawl, and a person had to be pretty bad to get that kind of response from her.

Friday! It was almost here, her day, Fur Free Friday. It was the biggest shopping day of the year, and this year they were expecting a larger turnout than ever, a show of unity that would awaken the whole world to the righteousness of their cause. It was through their hard work and sacrifice that people would be educated to see the senseless cruelty that was being inflicted upon the small helpless creatures of the world. Marching in the cold was a small sacrifice for a freedom fighter like Mary Ellen.

It was lunch hour, and the passersby on Fifth Avenue gawked at them. Mary Ellen shifted her placard from one shoulder to the other as she batted her free hand against her leg in an effort to warm it. Keith was marching right in front of her, his thin body swimming in his huge army coat. She knew he must be cold too, his frame was so skeletal, and as she walked in his steps she felt a small pang in her heart. He was so dedicated to their cause, she mused. He worked so hard for it. She admired him, both for his strength and his sensitivity. She knew things about him that no one else knew, and she grieved for the pain he lived with.

She fell into rhythm with his peppy step. She continued on this way for a while, in his shadow. She forgot her surroundings, and was just another human being on a long march to destiny. Maybe she was a prehistoric woman, climbing over formidable mountains and crossing arid plains, carrying her burden without complaint. Her feet were leathery tough and the muscles of her body thick and developed from days of long work in fields and . . .

"Shame!"

Her fantasy life disappeared abruptly, and she snapped her head to attention. Keith and the others had broken ranks, and were bearing down on a woman who had actually had the audacity to purchase something at Swank. She was exiting the store, proudly carrying a garment bag bearing the Swank logo. She was on the young end of middle age, and she bowed her blonde head into the wind as she rushed to get past the demonstrators, ignoring their taunts and jeers. But when she was a safe distance from them, she did a most unusual thing. She turned around and stuck her tongue out at them, before hurrying on her way.

Mary Ellen saw a strange look come over Keith's face as though he had just received a titillating invitation. He glanced at her for a moment and then, like a flash, he was running down Fifth Avenue, chasing after the woman. Mary Ellen watched as he caught up to her and walked along with her until they disappeared from sight.

The demonstrators resumed their march, Mary Ellen jumping right back in, wondering all along what the hell Keith was doing. It was fifteen minutes before he returned, his cheeks flushed and his face glowing with excitement. "Well, I tried," he said. "I was hoping I could talk her into seeing things our way, and returning that symbol of death she had just purchased."

"And were you successful?" asked Mary Ellen, caught up in his excitement.

"No," he laughed, "but it was fun just the same." He shouldered his FUR IS DEAD sign, and took up the march again, Mary Ellen marching alongside him this time. She was trying not to think about how cold she was, when a taxi pulled up directly in front of the store and a woman wearing a voluminous Finnish raccoon coat and matching hat stepped out. She stood defiantly at the curb. It was Bunny Nilsson.

A chant went up among the marchers. "Murderer!" they cried. Bunny took them in with a broad glance, and then sashayed past them, her eyes forward, her pace deliberate and measured, amid the torrent of accusations being hurled at her back. When she reached the store's revolving door she stopped abruptly, her face turning an angry red. A security guard materialized and tried to guide her into the store, but she broke his grasp and turned to face her accusers. She leveled her eyes at them, and in a clear, loud voice she shouted, "FUCK YOU. FUCK ALL OF YOU." Then she turned and went into the store.

A cheer went up among the marchers and Mary Ellen turned triumphantly to Keith. "I think we're getting to her," she said.

Keith face was still flushed and excited. "We are getting somewhere, aren't we?" Their eyes met and locked for a long second, before Keith looked down at his cheap wristwatch. "Wow," he said, "I didn't realize what time it is. I've got to run."

Mary Ellen looked at him curiously, hoping he would offer some explanation, but none was forthcoming. "See you Friday morning?" she asked.

"You bet." Then, in a gesture very uncharacteristic of him, he grabbed Mary Ellen by the shoulders and gave her a quick hug. "Have a happy Thanksgiving," he said, staring at her a moment longer than necessary. Mary Ellen watched him head down Fifth Avenue once again, his body erect and unbending against the knifing wind, his hands stuffed deep into the pockets of his flapping army coat, and once again she couldn't help but feel that small pang.

XXIII

Bunny sat in the window of her husband's office and waited for him to come back from lunch. She gazed down at the straggly group of marchers below and only half-regretted her outburst.

She knew she should have maintained control—her action had only put her on their level—but she could not contain herself any longer. What was it with these people anyhow? Did they never give up?

She was more disturbed, however, by the words she had screamed at the animal people. Her whole life she had tried to distance herself from that kind of language and the class of people who employed it. It was the kind of language her mother used when she was angry. And when she wasn't. Her poor mother! She was such an ignorant hick, never making anything out of herself and her beautiful face and body, wasting her life on a truck-driver husband who loved her dearly enough to only slap her around when he was drunk. Bunny had never even known her real father.

The house she grew up in had been filled with shouting and swearing, and she had longed for a more peaceful existence. The noise often forced her to take refuge in her cubbyhole of a bedroom, and it was there she would pore over fashion and travel magazines and picture a better way of life.

When she reached eighteen, she went in search of that life. She packed her bags, said good-bye to her mother, ignored her stepfather, and headed to Atlanta, that mecca to which thousands of country girls flocked in hopes of finding that perfect job or man, preferably the man. Bunny got work as a cocktail waitress in a popular hotel. There, for the first time, she met men like the ones in her magazines, men who wore something besides T-shirts and celebrated with more than beer from long-necked bottles. She made up her mind that she was going to get herself just such a man, one who wore immaculate suits and starched shirts and silk ties. She had seen enough of life at the bottom—she was heading for the top.

It so happened that the hotel where she worked was one that was used by the airlines to put up their flight crews during layovers. Bunny was impressed by the stewardesses, or flight attendants as they preferred to be called. They seemed so sophisticated, so worldly, and they also commanded a lot more respect from men than a cocktail waitress did. Bunny heard stories of girls who had gone from rags-to-riches after meeting wealthy men on their flights. Bunny decided that working for the airlines was the next step toward accomplishing her goal.

She had no trouble getting a job as a flight attendant. She was attractive, she was tall, and most of all, she was smart. She flew for years, biding her time and waiting for the right man to come along. One day he did, in the person of Michael Nilsson. She took one look at the handsome well-dressed man sitting in first class, wearing no wedding band, and her sights were set. She flirted with him lightly, learned his name, and used that information to find out when his return flight to New York was scheduled. She called in a few favors, juggled her schedule, and two days later she was a passenger herself, and in the seat beside him. There she discovered the key to snaring Michael Nilsson. She had been so taken with his good looks and wealth that it came as a surprise to discover that he was basically insecure. But sitting next to him on the plane, she picked up on it right away and used it to her advantage. She began a crusade to build up his self-esteem. He was charmed by the soft-spoken Southern woman who in a short time was able to point out to him a number of his strong and positive qualities. She was so compassionate and understanding, quite different from the demanding, hard-boiled women he knew in New York. He took Bunny to dinner that night, and that was it; she won him over totally. But when she won over his old man as well, she cleared the way to becoming Mrs. Michael Nilsson, and that had given her the social position and financial comfort she had always longed for.

There was only one flaw in their relationship: Michael was a terrible lover. Still, she was more than content. Sex was, after all, necessary to solidify a good marriage. Beyond that it held no great appeal to her. Years of listening to her mother's panting and screaming at the hands of her imbecilic husband had convinced Bunny that she could live without the amorous side of life. Michael's fumblings were fine with her.

There was something far more important to their relationship. They had a great partnership, one that worked well for both of them. Bunny managed their social life and the household, but she had also made herself indispensable to the business. Her vision had helped them to push Swank to record profits in the eighties, and brought Michael the only thing he really wanted, the begrudging respect of his father.

Michael, in turn, had introduced her to the world of her dreams. In many ways she was just like Jennifer, Bunny thought.

A survivor. And she still had to remember sometimes not to let her true roots show as they just had in front of the Swank store.

She watched the crowd below, looking for any signs of Leslie Warning. That little bitch certainly couldn't have the nerve to show up outside there now, could she? Bunny clenched her fist at the very thought of it. Who would have thought that mousey little creature would become another thorn in her side?

The door to the office opened and Michael stepped in. He looked tired, even more so than he had yesterday. Bunny knew the endless stress was taking its toll. Jennifer's murder, the never ending torment of the demonstrators, the dramatic decline in business. They were all eating away at him and she regretted that she had to give him more bad news.

"It's a no-go with the Hunger Exchange," she said curtly.

His look of fatigue turned to one of irritation. "What? How could they turn down an offer like that? What went wrong?"

"Leslie Warning is what went wrong. It seems her charitable interests extend beyond the human realm."

"Bunny, you are talking in puzzles. What is it you're trying to say?"

"Amanda Warning's little girl works for S.T.S. She wasn't interested in our money."

Instead of becoming more upset, Michael seemed to be amused. "Wouldn't that just figure?" he said, shaking his head.

"Michael!" Bunny cried. "I can't believe you're taking this so calmly. I was fit to be tied when she told me. Someone with her background caught up with a group of fanatics like that. Talk about misplaced priorities . . . to refuse aid to the hungry because of some wacky allegiance to animals. I don't understand it —I just can't understand it!" Bunny banged her small fist repeatedly against the windowsill, the dull thuds echoing lifelessly in the room.

"Whatever will we tell your father?" she asked. She too feared the old man's wrath.

Michael remained amazingly calm. "Call the P.R. firm. They should be able to come up with something."

"I suppose so," Bunny sighed. "But the Hunger Exchange would have been so perfect. It's so clear what they do. We could have made the announcement on Friday. It would have completely overshadowed their Fur Free Friday."

Michael didn't seem to hear; he wasn't paying attention to her anymore. He flopped into a chair and gazed out the window, his eyes focused somewhere off in the distance. He didn't want to think about marches or fur sales, all he could think about lately was Jennifer. He pictured her as she was years ago, the street urchin with the unmistakable promise of beauty. All gone now, her head bashed in, her perfect face gone forever. He choked at the thought of it.

"Michael, are you okay?" Bunny went to him and rubbed her hands through his hair.

"You know," he said sadly, "right now I couldn't give a rat's ass about all this. I just can't stop thinking about Jennifer."

"You really loved her, didn't you?" asked his wife.

Michael looked up, astonished by her knowing tone. She continued to speak. "I know all about it—I knew then. Do you think a wife can't tell about these things? But it's been over for years, hasn't it?"

He nodded feebly, still looking into her eyes, afraid to break away.

"I know you love me, Michael, and I knew that someday your infatuation would pass. To have made an issue of it then would have forced you to make a decision. I never wanted to risk losing you, you are the most important thing in the world to me. So I closed my eyes to it, and I'm glad I did.

"Don't feel guilty about it now, it's too late for that. Before, yes, now, no. It was over."

Michael felt like a fool. All those years he thought his affair was a secret, and she had known all along. She was too smart for him.

He bowed his head and searched his soul, wondering if he should tell his wife the whole truth. Honesty won over and he went for the clear conscience.

"Bunny, there's something I have to tell you. It's true the affair had been over for years, but Jennifer called me Thursday night and told me she had to see me the next day. At her place. She said it was important. I felt compelled to go.

"When I got there about four o'clock I rang her buzzer, and there was no answer. I thought she had changed her mind about . . . whatever . . . and was ignoring me. I left. Now I know she was already dead."

He was ashamed to confess how quickly he had responded to

Jennifer's request. As he looked back into Bunny's eyes he expected to see pain and hurt, but was surprised to see something else lingering behind the clear, cool green. It was a look of puzzlement, as if she didn't quite understand what he was saying, and then it turned to a look of fear.

"Michael, no one saw you there, did they?" she asked. He knew she was thinking about the police, a thought that had already crossed his mind more than once since Monday.

"No, I don't think so," he said, sounding as though he was trying to convince himself. "There was this one kook on the street, but he was just that, a kook . . ."

"Oh, Michael, of all times for you to have slipped. What if the police find out that you had an affair with Jennifer, and that you were seen in her neighborhood Friday afternoon? It wouldn't look good."

"I know," he admitted. "And to be frank, I'm scared. I didn't say anything about it before because of you; now I can't tell them because it would look like I was hiding something."

Bunny's face took on a look he had seen often during important business negotiations. She became the mother lion protecting her cub.

"Oh well," she said finally with a lightness that belied what they had just spoken of. "I guess if anyone had seen you, you would have heard by now." And then her tone grew sterner. "But you and I, that's a different story. We have a lot to discuss tonight, Michael."

She walked to the door and stopped, her hand upon the brass handle. "I've got a lot of work to do," she said. "I'll see you at dinner."

Her tone made Michael suddenly shiver. It reminded him of his father.

XXIV

Yolanda dialed Evelyn Burhop's code and waited for her to answer. It took eight rings.

"Oh, yes, Miss Prince, I remembered. I was just getting tea ready. I'll buzz you in now. It's 12 East, dear."

Yolanda grabbed at the door while the electronic sound of the security system echoed through the small marble-tiled lobby. The building was on the older side, built prior to World War II and not so fine and ostentatious as many built since, but it had a certain charm to it.

Yolanda waited for the ornate brass door of the elevator to open and she stepped into the small carpeted box. It carried her up at a snail's pace, stopping at twelve with a jerk. The doors opened and she stepped into a small carpeted hallway. There were only two apartments, 12 East was Mrs. Burhop's, 12 West had been Jennifer O'Grady's. It was still draped with bright yellow tape proclaiming it a crime site.

Yolanda hesitated between the two doors. No sign of forced entry at the 12 West apartment, the police had said. Did that mean Jennifer O'Grady had known her assailant? Then again, the building's security system was hardly foolproof. Ring enough buzzers and eventually someone was going to let you in. Or wait and grab a door behind someone leaving. Those were the easy ways; a creative thief knew of at least a dozen others.

She knocked tentatively on Mrs. Burhop's door, and she heard footsteps. Knowing she was probably being viewed through the peephole, she waved and called out. She heard a series of locks being unbolted and a chain sliding off the door.

A distinguished-looking old lady opened the door, her face a combination of welcome and apprehension. "Please do come in," she said graciously. "I do hope I've done the right thing by letting you come here."

"I promise you, you have, Mrs. Burhop," said Yolanda, twisting her head as she looked around the apartment. The place was a virtual museum, the only concession to modern times the huge television in the living room.

"Please sit down," said Mrs. Burhop, indicating a well-worn sofa that despite its age still showed signs of great quality. Yolanda sank down into the dark green brocade while her hostess excused herself. Mrs. Burhop soon reappeared carrying a silver tray that contained a tea service.

"This was something I often shared with Jennifer," Mrs. Burhop said wistfully. "She was such a fine young woman, a good listener. It seems that most of the young people today are so involved in themselves. They don't have time for anyone else.

"Jennifer would come over and sit with me for hours. She loved to hear my stories of how fine New York used to be, how my late husband and I would dine and dance and walk on the streets at late hours. Oh, the way Broadway used to be, and how everyone danced in the streets the day the war ended. Life was so much grander then. There was elegance—things you don't find much of anymore."

Yolanda took a cup of tea that was offered to her in a china cup. And my people, she thought. Were the times better for them back then too? Did my grandmother clean your apartment? How many black women dined at the *21* in the grand old days?

"Mrs. Burhop, as you know, I want to do a special on Jennifer O'Grady," Yolanda said.

"Well, of course, that's why you're here, isn't it? You know, the police have been adamant that I not talk with anyone about what happened here, so I can't say anything about that. But I want to say good things about Jennifer. The poor thing left no survivors. I do so want people to remember her fondly."

"I'll be sure that people do."

"You know, I can't understand why someone would do that to her. She didn't have an enemy in the world. Then again she didn't have many friends either. Just her cat. She loved her cat. And poor Chessie has disappeared."

"I know what it's like to love a pet, I had Mr. B. for years." The silver-haired woman picked up a framed photo of a miniature poodle, its face raised towards the camera like a true ham. She looked at it lovingly. "Mr. B. was a great comfort to me in the years after Mr. Burhop died. But when he went I couldn't bear to replace him; I thought it would be unfair to his memory."

It didn't seem Mrs. Burhop replaced anybody, be it dog or man, thought Yolanda, but she sure didn't let go of their memories. For the next hour Yolanda sat patiently, obliged to listen to Mrs. Burhop's stories, gems out of her past that she reveled in taking out and polishing for anyone who would listen. Yolanda's tea grew cold and her eyelids grew heavy. She felt sorry for this proper old lady who probably had enough money squirreled away to take care of her practical needs but no people to take care of her emotional ones. Yolanda's mind drifted, and she was no longer paying any attention to what Mrs. Burhop was saying when she heard the word "Jennifer" and it pulled her back to attentiveness.

"She was such a kind girl. To die so horribly," said Mrs. Burhop.

"Was it so horrible?" asked Yolanda.

"It was terrible," Mrs. Burhop continued. Her hand shook as she replaced her cup and saucer on the table. She leaned forward to Yolanda, her face red with embarrassment. "You mustn't tell that I told you, but it was hair that I found. The private kind. I knew it the minute I touched it. And there was a note too. I can't remember exactly what it said, I was so shocked, but it was something about making fur coats out of that hair."

The aged grey eyes with their fine yellow film of cataract looked deep into Yolanda's brown ones, searching for her reaction to this horrifying revelation. Yolanda felt her blood pressure rising as she grasped what Evelyn Burhop was saying. What a story she had here! Pubic hair skinned from the victim, a note about fur coats. Yolanda thought about her special due to air Friday. A segment about this could send her ratings through the ceiling.

Suddenly Yolanda was standing and thanking Mrs. Burhop for the tea and the conversation. She had to rush off, she said, tomorrow being Thanksgiving and all. She left the old lady standing in the doorway a little confused and wondering if she had made a mistake.

Yolanda willed the elevator to move faster, urging it onward in its snail-like descent. She was excited beyond belief. She had in her hands a hot potato that nobody, nobody, could imagine. Her reporter's blood told her this was truly, truly hot. A reporter's dream.

Once outside the building, she rushed to hail a cab. As she sat back to enjoy the ride to the studio, a disturbing notion crept into her head. Had she promised Mrs. Burhop that this revelation would be in confidence? She couldn't remember.

Her blood was pumping and her stomach had an excited thrill to it, and she had to tell herself to calm down. Chill out, Yolanda, she kept thinking. What would a responsible reporter do here?

She knew the answer before she had even finished asking herself the question. She had to be responsible first and foremost. That meant checking out the facts. She couldn't go on the air with a shocker like this and then later discover that the old lady was senile.

Damn, she thought. That meant she would have to talk to the police. She would find out from Suzy Harking who the detectives on the case were. Before she did anything else, she had to talk to them.

XXV

Evelyn Burhop was surprised to hear her buzzer ring for the second time that day. Guests were rare. She was still rinsing the tea service from her visit with Yolanda Prince.

Her tentative "yes" was answered by the pleasant voice of the young policewoman who had been so kind to her on Monday. Could she and Detective Perrelli come up and talk to her again? Evelyn had a sick creeping sensation. Did they know about her slip to Yolanda Prince already? Were they angry with her?

Her immediate fears were put to rest when Detective Levinson greeted her warmly. "Mrs. Burhop, it's so good to see you again. Are you feeling any better?"

"Much, dear," she replied, much relieved. She looked up at Detective Perrelli, his handsome figure towering behind his partner, and gave him a weak smile. His fearsome expression only renewed her fear that she was in trouble.

Tony had put Karen in charge again, only because he knew she had established a rapport with the old woman, and it would work to their advantage. "Mrs. Burhop," she said, "we need to ask you a few more questions if you don't mind. About the missing cat."

"Chessie?" Evelyn asked. "What about her?"

"Do you think you could describe her for us?"

"Oh, yes. She's a beautiful cat. A mixed breed I suppose, you know, not one of those Orientals. But simply beautiful. And a loving cat . . . That cat was so loving."

"We need to be a little more specific, Mrs. Burhop. Like what color was she, how big was she, did she have any distinguishing markings?"

"Well, she was an unusual color, sort of the shade of coffee with cream, and she had a white marking on her chest if I remember correctly. And I guess she was about the normal size for a cat."

Tony interrupted. "Do you think Jennifer might have had a picture of the cat?"

"The way she loved that cat, I would think so."

"Do you still have a key to her apartment?"

"Why, yes," said Evelyn, shuddering to think of reentering that apartment. She went into her kitchen and removed the key from the drawer where she had always kept it, in among her measuring spoons and cookie cutters. She handed it to Tony, and the two detectives went back across the hall.

Karen felt an initial wave of nausea as she walked into the dark foyer. She couldn't help it; her memory triggered it. Thankfully, most of the sour smell of death had lifted, helped along by the cold wind that blew through the open windows.

"You look in the bedroom, I'll check the living room," Tony commanded.

Karen hesitated before entering the bedroom. She swung the door open slowly, reluctantly. She didn't know what she expected, but she was surprised to see that the bed had been stripped and she was staring at a bare mattress. Deep brown stains marred it, especially near the headboard. Then she remembered that the bedclothes had been sent downtown for further tests. The rest of the room was untouched, piles of books, women's things. Karen wondered if it would remain this way, and the rest of the apartment as well, until probate was completed and someone decided what to do with Jennifer O'Grady's worldly possessions.

Karen studied the shelves crammed with hardcover and paperback books. Among the titles was a biography of Picasso as well as books by Stephen King, Taylor Caldwell, Pat Conroy. There was a full set of the *Encyclopedia Brittanica* and a collection of great quotations. Other books were piled on the floor. No room for pictures of Chessie on these shelves.

Next she looked at the deceased model's dressing table. There she scored. Amid the clutter of expensive makeup and perfume stood a small silver frame holding the photograph of a beige cat wearing a jeweled collar. The cat stared out at its photographer with an impatient look as if to say, "All right, I'll be still for the moment, but let's get this over with."

"Bingo," called Karen, retreating from the bedroom and joining her partner in the living room where he was investigating the contents of a credenza. He took the picture from her and nodded, removing it from the frame and leaving the frame on the cocktail table.

They closed up the apartment and returned to Mrs. Burhop's.

"Is this Chessie, Mrs. Burhop?" asked Tony, showing her the photograph.

Evelyn nodded sadly, her proud old shoulders sagging as a sigh escaped her lips. "Oh, Jennifer loved that cat so. Just look at that collar she bought her."

Both Karen and Tony stared at the glittering collar, encrusted with large white stones.

"That isn't real, is it?" asked Karen.

"Yes, it is," replied Evelyn. "Jennifer had it made especially for Chessie. She said that Chessie had given her more pleasure and love than anyone else in her life, and so who would she rather spend her money on."

Tony let out a low whistle. Karen knew what it meant. A diamond collar was somewhere out there in the city. Now they really had something to look for.

"Let's go," said Tony, and he headed out into the hallway. Mrs. Burhop lingered in the doorway to say good-bye to Karen.

"Call me sometime, dear," she said. "Perhaps we could have tea."

"I'd like that," said Karen, feeling sorry for the old lady who seemed so alone in the world.

Mrs. Burhop smiled a weak smile and said, "Fine." She started to close her door, but before it was completely shut she thought of something else she wanted to say. "And we could invite Miss Prince to join us. Wouldn't that be lovely?"

"Miss Prince?" Karen's voice was guarded.

"Yes, Yolanda Prince. She was just here earlier. She is such a nice woman, young and professional just like you. I'm sure you would like each other."

The elevator doors slid open as the carriage arrived. Both Tony and Karen ignored it. Tony was groaning.

"Mrs. Burhop," he said, "you didn't by any chance mention what you found in Jennifer's apartment to Yolanda Prince, did you?"

Tony's driving was more than erratic, and actually quite frightening, as he swerved through the city traffic with little concern for anything or anybody who ventured into his way. "What the fuck," he said angrily as he sped up, projecting his wrath onto the accelerator. Karen held her breath as they squealed through the traffic with near misses occurring every few blocks. She found herself praying that they would survive the trip to Brooklyn and Sylvester Wolfe's decaying abode. "If that bitch, Yolanda Prince, takes this on the air then we're screwed. We'll have copycat nuts, and animal nuts, and people confessing to this crime all over the place. Not to mention the media on our backs. Before it was just your average New York murder . . . Now it will be all over the tabloids. God I hate the press!" he exclaimed fervently.

He swerved to avoid a car that had ventured out at a green light. "Son of a bitch," he shouted at the driver. Karen applied her imaginary brake and huddled low in her seat. "You stupid women have such goddamn big mouths," he continued on, his tirade nowhere close to spent.

"I'm sick to death of your opinion of women," Karen shouted back, enraged herself now. "I'll tell you what . . . Let me talk with Yolanda. Maybe I can reason with her and keep this off the air."

"Hah!" Tony hooted. "Reporter with a big story? Not a chance. You'll see snowballs in hell before you see that one."

"Well, it wouldn't hurt to try. You're the one who's always warning me about jumping to conclusions." She was still yelling.

"All right, you try. As soon as we finish with the nutcase here," he yelled back as they screeched to a halt in front of Sylvester's house. He slammed the car into park with such force that it rocked on its chassis. "But I can hardly wait to say 'I told you so.' "

Sylvester's home loomed dark and foreboding and even eerier than before as they stood pounding on the door. The only response this time was the maddened howling of the dogs from inside. No shade moved from behind the one unboarded window, no voice called from within to ask who they were.

"There aren't any lights on, Tony," said Karen finally. "He's probably out picketing."

Tony pressed his ear up against the door a last time, listening for any sounds of human life. "I can't hear squat over all that barking," he said with disgust, turning away from the door. "We'll just have to check for the cat later. If you're ready, I'll take you to see Yolanda Prince now, and we'll see if you can't just save the women of New York from the truth about the 'mad snatcher.'"

XXVI

As soon as Yolanda returned to the newsroom, she beeped Suzy Harking who wasn't in. Within a few minutes her phone rang and Suzy's tough Brooklyn accent came on the line.

"Suzy," said Yolanda, "I think I might have something important on the O'Grady murder. I'd like to discuss it with you."

Suzy sounded excited. "What is it?"

"I'd rather not say over the phone. When are you coming back to the studio?"

"I'm on my way now, I'll be there in half an hour. Talk to you then," she said, and she hung up as abruptly as she talked.

A half hour later Yolanda was still making notes from her conversation with Mrs. Burhop when a young woman about her own age walked up to her desk and identified herself as New York City police, detective Karen Levinson. She looked a little too chic to be a detective, with her straight, silky black hair, full lips coated with red lipstick and casual but obviously expensive clothes.

But she flashed a genuine badge. Yolanda glanced at it and looked back up at the woman. She didn't sound anything like most New York cops Yolanda had encountered, either. Most of them sounded like Suzy Harking, with the rough edges of native

New Yorkers. Karen Levinson's voice had the polish of education; it bore none of the marks of a city upbringing. It spoke to Yolanda of the rich suburbs outside the city, of Westport, Connecticut.

"I need to speak to you, about the O'Grady case," she said.

As a matter of reflex, Yolanda looked at her watch. She knew that Suzy Harking was due back at any moment, and that if they got it together she might be able to break her story on the late news. They could start writing the promos—"Startling development in the Jennifer O'Grady murder, news at eleven." An exclusive. A great big kudo for Yolanda.

"I know all about the O'Grady murder, Detective Levinson. Even the details you've hidden from the public."

"That's what I need to talk to you about, Ms. Prince."

"The pubic hair? The note? The literature from S.T.S.?"

"Yes," admitted Karen.

"So it's true then."

"Look, Ms. Prince. There's some kook out there who killed and mutilated a woman. He's sick and dangerous and we want to get him. But if you release these details, you'll make our job harder— and it could bring out a pack of sick copycats."

Karen was telling Yolanda exactly what she didn't want to hear. Here she had in her hands what could be one of the hottest stories of recent memory, and this cop wanted her to keep it under her hat.

"Sorry," said Yolanda, "but the public has a right to know."

"Jennifer O'Grady had rights too. If you could have seen what I saw in her apartment, if you could have seen what was left of her . . ." Karen stopped. She was having too difficult a time dealing with the image of Jennifer's body that kept popping back into her mind. "To see that happen to another woman. It would be too horrible. I'm begging you."

Yolanda was taken aback. In all her years in the Bronx, and in her professional years since, she had never heard a cop "beg" for anything.

"Give us a couple of days," Karen pleaded. "We think we're close to someone. Please don't put this on the air."

Yolanda gazed evenly into Karen's face, dark eyes meeting dark eyes. Between them at that moment something sparked, something that said from one woman to the other, I respect you for what you are trying to do, for what you have risen above. "All right, two days," surrendered Yolanda. "But so help me if I hear this story on another network . . ."

"You won't," Karen assured her. "Evelyn Burhop isn't going to say a thing to anyone else, that's for sure. Not since my partner put the fear of God into her. But I do think she would tell you or me just about anything in the world." Karen winked. "She wants us all to have tea someday."

It was just then that a red-faced, somewhat harried Suzy Harking burst into the room. "Here I am, Yolanda," she called out, eager with anticipation. "Now what is it that is so hot?" Karen held her breath, waiting to hear what Yolanda was going to say.

"Nothing, I'm afraid. Detective Levinson here has just explained to me how I had been misinformed. It's lucky she caught my mistake before it made it on the air."

Suzy shrugged and rushed back out of the room. Her schedule was too hectic to allow for idle chitchat when it wasn't connected to hot news.

"Thanks," said Karen earnestly. "I owe you big time, and believe me, if the opportunity ever presents itself, I'll pay you back tenfold."

Karen hummed as she left the newsroom, full of herself and her accomplishment. She was happy for what she had achieved from a professional standpoint; it would make the ongoing investigation easier. But if the truth were to be known, she was even happier for a second reason. She could hardly wait to throw it in her partner's smug, handsome face.

XXVII

Emily Wiggins was doing something that could be considered nasty, but she didn't really care. She was walking around her apartment naked underneath her new ranch mink coat. She rubbed her hands sensuously up and down the soft fur of the sleeves and moaned with the pleasure of it. She felt sexy and glamorous and she adored it.

She positioned herself in front of the full-length mirror in the hallway of her small Greenwich Village apartment. Slowly she dropped the left shoulder of the coat, exposing her bare breast. She poked a slim leg out the front opening of the coat and smiled, tossing her head back, posing for an imaginary camera. Not too bad for forty-five years old, she thought.

She had always planned to own a fur coat. It was to have been a gift from a devoted husband or, at the very least, a smitten lover. Unfortunately, neither husband nor lover had appeared in her life thus far, and this year she had decided that if she was ever to be draped in the richness of fur, she was going to have to buy it for herself.

After a summer of comparison shopping, she had finally settled on a Swank Fur. She bought it during their August sale and put it on layaway until the day she could actually afford to take it home. It hadn't been easy on her secretary's salary, but that day had finally come. Today she had brought her coat home.

I've waited a long time for this, she reflected, and nothing is going to ruin it for me. She thought about the creeps outside Swank yelling their ridiculous slogans at her, and the tall skinny one who had followed her for blocks sharing his philosophy with her. "It looked better on the animal's back," he kept saying.

She reexamined her image in the mirror, her blonde hair set off nicely by the ebony black fur. She couldn't have disagreed with the hippie more. The mink coat looked much better on her.

A bubble bath was running in the tub, and she went into the kitchen to get the bottle of California champagne she had picked up on the way home. She was going to celebrate by luxuriating in her bath, sipping champagne and staring at her coat. Afterward, she would model it for an imaginary lover. Who would it be today? Her boss perhaps? He did look at her from time to time with interest, but he was married with four kids. In real life, that is. It didn't have to stop his imaginary visits.

She had just popped the champagne and poured herself a glass when her buzzer rang. She wasn't expecting anyone. She put the bottle down on the kitchen table and went to the intercom.

"Who is it?" she asked.

"I have a delivery for you," said a man's voice.

"I'm not expecting any deliveries."

"This is from Swank Furs. It's a hat to go with your coat. Special promotion. They forgot to give it to you today, I guess."

Emily smiled. This *was* her lucky day. Not only did she have a new mink coat, she had a hat to go along with it. A free hat with the purchase of a coat. What a great promotion! Gleefully, she pushed the buzzer to admit her caller.

Still wearing nothing but the mink, she unlatched the deadbolt and, at the sound of a knock, she started to open the door. Suddenly it was thrust in upon her with such force it threw her to the floor, the heavy fur cushioning her fall. She looked up and felt a surge of terror as he stood over her, bringing his foot down on her chest, a heavy length of wood in his hand. And then it was all black, terror being the last sensation she would ever know.

XXVIII

THANKSGIVING DAY

Leslie had never seen such familial chaos as at the home of Neil's parents. There was so much family, brothers and sisters flanked by spouses and scores of noisy children running about, slamming doors in every corner of the modest suburban tract house. Everyone was good-natured and friendly, but she was overwhelmed by the sheer number of them; people were streaming everywhere like insects coming out of the woodwork.

She had been welcomed at the door by Neil's smiling mother, a harried-looking grey-haired lady who palmed back strands of damp hair, making her excuses about the heat in the kitchen as she greeted Leslie warmly. "Welcome to our house, it's not always like this, believe me," she said. But her lips betrayed a smile at the secret memory of a time gone by, and Leslie suspected that it had been like this a great deal of the time when Mrs. Harrigan's children were young.

Mrs. Harrigan pushed them off to the bar to get a drink and meet Neil's father as she swept a few children out from under her feet and made her way back toward her hectic kitchen. Leslie thought about how different Neil's mother was from her own.

Mrs. Harrigan was loud and boisterous, probably the kind of person who hugged you often and hard when you were good and gave you a smart hit when you did something wrong. Her own mother had been quiet and restrained. Leslie thought of holidays with her parents and the quiet, very proper meals they had shared together. She still missed them so.

Mr. Harrigan was a broad-chested man of medium height. He was tending bar in the den, and it was obvious that he had already had more than a few drinks himself. Blue eyes twinkling merrily, he poured Leslie a glass of white wine and handed his son a beer, cuffing him affectionately on the shoulder.

Leslie and Neil made small talk with Neil's brothers and had a few more drinks before dinner was served. When the call was sounded to "come and get it" they adjourned to the combination living and dining room where folding tables had been set up.

Dinner was more chaos as grown-ups and children alike feasted on turkey, two kinds of dressing, mashed potatoes, rutabaga, salad, rolls and two different Jello molds, recipes that had been handed down from the fifties. Leslie discreetly helped herself to vegetables and salad, hoping not to draw any attention to herself. Her hopes were dashed, however, when one of the children sitting at their table asked loudly why she wasn't eating any turkey. Conversation came to a sudden halt, and all eyes were on her.

"Leslie's a vegetarian," Neil explained to his curious nephew.

"What's a begetarian?" asked the undaunted young man.

"It's a person who only eats vegetables," said Neil, making a sour face at the child.

"Yuck," he responded, looking at Leslie as if she were diseased. "I'll never be one of those."

Everybody at the table laughed except Leslie, who turned beet-red and wanted to crawl into a hole.

After dinner, most of the family adjourned to the den where drinks were once again served. Everyone seemed to be partaking, the one exception being Neil's brother, Paul, who explained to Leslie that it was either drinking or his marriage, and he had opted for his marriage. She liked Paul. He was closest in age to Neil and seemed more subdued and serious than the rest of his siblings.

Neil's father now sat in a large, cushioned chair with a drink in his hand that miraculously stayed upright even though his head kept drooping forward as he struggled to stay awake. "Don't mind Dad," said Neil, gently removing the glass from his father's hand when his eyes finally shut. "He's been like this since he retired."

The energy level among the rest of the family remained high, and after hours of listening to them chide one another good-naturedly and laugh hysterically at family stories, Leslie was worn out. She was glad when Neil touched her hand with his own and said, "Let's head back." She looked into his glowing eyes and couldn't help but glow a little herself. He was so handsome, certainly the best-looking one in his family. And she saw how good his disposition was; he had taken merciless ribbing from everyone all evening, and it had just rolled off him like water off a duck.

As they stood at the door holding hands and saying their good-byes, Leslie felt as though she were a part of it all. She turned to Neil and found herself regarding him with a sense of possession, as if in some way he belonged to her. She was feeling so good that nothing could ruin it, not the jokes she had endured about being a vegetarian, not the comments about how refreshing it was that Neil had finally brought a nice girl home. "And one not named Heather," his sister Anne had added. Crazy as it was, she felt like she belonged.

There was a light sleet falling as they got into Neil's rented car and headed back toward Manhattan. Leslie was still warm from the wine she had consumed, talking about what a nice family he had and what a good time she had had. She was feeling a part of the world for once, part of a greater plan that included happiness.

They had just entered Manhattan and were still on the highway when the car in front of them slammed on its brakes, and suddenly the new world around her started to spin. It happened so quickly that she didn't have time to be afraid until she realized that their car was out of control, heading toward the shoulder of the ice-slicked road. Traffic was heavy but, miraculously, they hit nothing until the car careened off the pavement and slammed sideways into a guardrail. The world suddenly came to a jolting stop.

Leslie's first reaction was to look at Neil. He sat there, hands on the wheel, eyes forward, his face a picture of shock. He turned slowly toward Leslie. Her eyes were wide, brown pools of undisguised fear. Cars continued to speed past them as if nothing out of the ordinary had occurred. But it had. They had just traveled in

360s across four lanes of inbound traffic and they had emerged unscathed.

"Somebody was looking out for us," Neil said finally, his eyes raised upward. It was then that Leslie broke into tears. Neil tried to take her head and pull it to his shoulder. She pulled away. "Leslie, I'm sorry. The car spun out of control on the ice. I couldn't help it."

"You shouldn't be driving," she said between tears. "You've had too much to drink. We could have been killed." Her hysteria increased, and Neil, not knowing what to do, sat mutely behind the wheel.

The engine had died when they hit the guardrail, and he turned the ignition to see if the car would start. "No!" she screamed. "No." She tried to open the door on her side, but it was snug against the railing. She leaned across the driver's side, trying to climb across him and get out of the car. She was mad, frenzied, her hands clawing at the air. Neil had to grab her wrists to calm her down.

"Leslie, it's okay. We're all right. We'll get out of here and walk to the exit. Calm down." He seemed entirely sober to her now.

They got out of the car carefully, staying close to it to avoid the passing traffic. Once they were on the shoulder, walking toward the ramp, Neil put his arm around her protectively. She was still sobbing, making sounds so heartrending he didn't know what to do. Finally, when they were away from the traffic, she calmed down and started to talk.

"I'm sorry," she sighed. "I know I must seem weird, but you see, my parents were killed in a car accident and what happened just now made me think that I was going to end the same way."

Neil, not knowing what to do, remained silent.

"I've never really talked about this before with anyone, about their accident, it hurts too much. I can't help but imagine the way they died. It's with me practically every minute of every day." She took a deep breath, and pulled herself together before continuing.

"They were passing through an intersection when they were struck by another car going fifty miles an hour. It hit them broadside. The impact flipped the car over and it burst into flames immediately. The window on my mother's side was open, and people saw her arm waving for help. But no one could get near them, the flames were too intense. They were . . . burned . . .

alive." Leslie had to stop again to regain her composure, and Neil looked at her in horror.

"The woman who hit them was arrested for drunken driving. There were witnesses who saw her leave a bar after fighting with her husband, and I'm convinced she had put the pedal to the floor in a fit of anger.

"She said the pedal stuck, and she hired a flotilla of lawyers to keep her out of jail. I was angry about it at first, but I don't care anymore. It won't bring them back or change the way they died."

She looked up into Neil's eyes. "When we spun out just now on the highway, I saw my own life flashing before me, and for the first time in a long time I didn't want to lose it. Not now, I was thinking, not when I'm so happy."

Embarrassed by what she had just revealed, she bowed her curly head. Neil pulled her small frame closer to him, holding her fast against him. He felt helpless as he stood there with her, the noise of the traffic all around them, the sleet hitting them in the face.

Holding her ever tighter, he found himself wondering what he was getting himself into. A feeling of protectiveness had come over him and it scared him. This was not how it was supposed to happen, not for a slick guy like him. He wasn't the type to get emotionally involved with a woman like Leslie. Racier women with legs up to there and breasts that pushed against tight-fitting sweaters were more his style.

"C'mon, let's go," he said, suddenly hurrying her along to the busy street ahead where they would be able to catch a taxi. He thought about his rental car, abandoned at the side of the road, and then chuckled. Leslie looked up at him.

"Why are you laughing?" she asked.

"Oh, I was just thinking, it's a good thing I took out the collision coverage on the car."

They walked on, Leslie clinging to him.

XXIX

The interior of the Montclair mansion was quiet and staid as ever. Michael stood in front of the roaring fire, sipping a Scotch and thinking that he had little to be thankful for this Thanksgiving. Being in the presence of his father made him miserable, and his wife wasn't talking to him. Of course, she had good reason to be angry. He had defied her yesterday by leaving Swank right after their conversation about Jennifer and not coming home until late last night. And then he had been very, very drunk.

He had let himself into their elegant residence as quietly as his intoxicated state permitted, but when he tiptoed past his study, he saw her in there waiting for him. Sitting in the same chair where he had been sitting the fateful day that he and Jennifer first made love. He remembered how he had felt like such a man that day. Seeing Bunny in that chair only reminded him of what a pathetic man he truly was. She was the one with the strength.

"I'm glad you're home," she had said coolly. "I was worried." Then she had gone to bed without another word, the scent of her expensive perfume lingering in the room long after she left.

He had fallen into the chair and tried to quell the urge to cry once again. He cried more than any reasonable man should. How pitiable he was! He was nothing but an untethered sail left to luff in the wind, a rider who had lost his reins and was desperately trying to stay on his horse. He had poured himself another brandy, like throwing gasoline on a fire, before curling up and falling asleep in his chair. He awakened with the first light of morning, his face pressed into the fine Italian leather, still wearing his street clothes.

And now, Thanksgiving Day, his neck ached from the position he had slept in and his head pounded with a hangover. While Bunny chatted softly with his father in front of the fire, Michael stood before the imposing mirror that hung over the mantel and sipped at his drink, struggling to regain equilibrium. He stared at his reflection. It gave no indication of what he was feeling on the inside. He appeared to be the epitome of sartorial splendor with his immaculate clothes of perfect cut and proportion, his perfectly groomed hair, his strong distinguished features. What a sham, he thought. Inside this false front a man is crumbling to pieces.

He was gazing into the mirror still, offering no conversation, when he saw the reflection of two people entering the room. It was the General and his wife. He watched Bunny get up from the wing chair in which she had been stiffly sitting, and he saw his father raise his good arm in greeting. Michael felt obligated to turn and face them.

"Dan, it's good to see you," his father called to his longtime friend. "So glad you could make it."

"Could I ever break with our tradition, Lars?" bellowed Daniel Taylor, his voice filling the room. He was a man of great stature, and even at his advanced age, he stood militarily erect, with a slight favoring of his right hip and knee. He had long been retired, but Michael still found it startling to see the General in a business suit rather than a uniform.

Behind the General trailed Mary Taylor, his wife of fifty years, a petite woman of exquisite proportions whose quiet demeanor reminded Michael very much of his own mother. The two couples had shared Thanksgivings together for as long as Michael could remember. They had always been a perfect match, the two men domineering and aggressive, their wives always content to remain in the background.

"Bunny," the General said warmly as he took her hand. It disappeared between his two large ones. "It is always a pleasure to see you." He turned to Michael and gave him an imaginary cuff on the chin before shaking his hand with a firm strong grip.

Lars rang a bell, and Maria appeared to take a cocktail order. The General asked for a Manhattan, his wife a glass of white wine. Maria returned within moments with their drinks upon a silver tray.

"So how are things with you, Lars?" asked the white-haired man after taking a healthy swig of his drink, the crystal glass almost obscured by his massive hand.

"Aaach," Lars sputtered. "Terrible. I'm trapped here in a goddamn wheelchair while my business crumbles. My main model's been murdered and fanatics picket my stores while I sit here and can't do a goddamn thing."

Michael felt his cheeks burn. He looked at Bunny, who appeared to be uneasy herself. Lars was angry at her for not having the anti-hunger campaign in place yet. He felt they had lost the impact that making such an announcement on Fur Free Friday might have had.

"Things are never easy, are they Lars?" asked the General. Michael chuckled inwardly at his words. The General had never had it too hard. He enjoyed a comfortable living, courtesy of his wife's huge inheritance, and being married to a Bellingham certainly hadn't hurt his chances back when he was working his way up through the ranks.

"I don't know," Lars countered. "Ask the young people here. They seem to have it too good. Too easy. It's a damn shame, because it makes you soft. They spend too much time in an office crunching numbers. I used to be everywhere, in every store, at all the plants. I would check skins with my bare hands, and anything not good enough was sold to competitors. Not that there was much, because I was always out there checking the quality of my suppliers.

"I spent so much time in the Canadian bush in the early years of Swank that I should be dead three times over. Flying around from camp to camp in old puddle jumpers, checking the quality of the trappers' harvest. I would ride a dogsled with old Jean McInerney, and we would go out on his trap line for days where I would freeze my butt off. And after he died, I carried on with his son, young Jean.

"These young people won't put up with that," he said, indicating Michael and Bunny. "Now they want the trappers to come down to see them."

"Father, you know Jean only started to come down here after your first stroke," Michael protested. "It was your idea, so that you could still keep your hands on things. Besides, our problems aren't with quality. The problem is the times, and public sentiment. It's beyond our control."

"That's ridiculous," countered Lars fiercely, his voice as close to a roar as his condition would permit. "I've already told you one way you can combat this scourge. There must be countless others. Hold the animal rights idiots up for scrutiny. Show them to be the fools that they are. What kind of people would release hundreds of laboratory animals and ruin years of medical research? I must assume that none of them are diabetic, because without animal research there would be no insulin. They certainly can't be peace lovers since they feel free to firebomb fur shops in England. Doesn't that make them terrorists? They aren't ecologists. Fur wearing poses no threat to the environment. Man-made materials do. We know they aren't humanitarians. If they were they would have realized what they did to thousands of Eskimos when they got Europe to ban the import of baby seal pelts. Unable to pursue a living, they've been destroyed by drugs, alcohol and suicide. What about the Cree or Dene or the other tribes that depend on fur trapping? What's to save them from these misanthropes?

"We must stop these radicals. We can't allow them to ride roughshod over our rights." He glared at his son.

There was an uneasy silence as all in the room digested Lars' words. Then, tactfully, it was broken by the General. "Speaking of riding roughshod, do you think George Bush has the balls to deal with Saddam Hussein . . . ?"

The discussion turned to politics, a much more digestible subject as far as Michael was concerned.

They dined on perfectly roasted turkey served with giblets and a rich brown gravy so smooth it was practically silken. Glazed baby carrots and steamed brussels sprouts accompanied the chestnut dressing and roasted potatoes. Conversation was polite and subdued as they drank vintage Meursault, and in the European tradition the salad, dressed with a clinging vinagrette, was served afterward. They finished up with traditional pumpkin pie, smothered with whipped cream, and cups of steaming espresso. Cook had outdone herself, thought Michael, as he watched Maria clear the last of the plates from the table.

They returned to the living room where the General enjoyed a cigar with his cognac under the envious gaze of Lars Nilsson, who was no longer permitted to indulge in such pleasures. Michael sipped at a cognac too, and was listening to the bantering of the old men when he realized Mary, the General's wife, was talking to him, her polite voice so soft that it was barely a whisper.

"They are so alike, aren't they?" she said. "Even with their differences, even after all these years. Your mother and I got along just as well. How I do miss her," she added.

"We all do," said Michael wistfully. He wondered at Mary's

meekness, so like his own mother's. The two of them had simply been raised to let the man take charge, and sit in the background.

Not quite like my wife, he thought. She never minded taking charge.

Maybe Bunny had read his mind, because she spoke to him warmly for the first time all evening.

"Your mother certainly was a wonderful woman," she concurred.

As he eased the Jaguar onto the Jersey Turnpike, he apologized to her.

"Bunny, I know I shouldn't have disappeared like that yesterday. I owe you an explanation, but there really isn't one. I just needed to be alone."

"And drink." She spoke drily at first, but then warmed to him, her voice regaining its usual charm. "I forgive you, but I can't say I understand. You shouldn't have taken off like that. It's important for us to stay together now. The past is dead and buried."

He winced at her choice of words, thinking of Jennifer's remains still at the mortuary. She was dead, but not yet buried. Not until tomorrow.

Bunny realized her faux pas. "What I meant to say is that whatever's happened in the past is behind us, it was behind us a long time ago. The important thing for us now is that we work to save our business. That's our life."

It's sure your life, Bunny, he thought, but he said nothing, only took her hand in his and squeezed it.

When they arrived home he tried to make love to her, but was unable to perform. It didn't alarm him particularly, it had happened before, and Bunny didn't seem disappointed. He lay in the dark listening to the steady breathing that told him she had fallen asleep. Thoughts of his father's tirades over the business and thoughts of Jennifer swam about in his head. Unable to sleep, he finally slipped out of bed and went into his den, pouring himself a stiff brandy, and sipped it alone in the dark.

XXX

There was no turkey at Ellie's place in the Bronx, but there was a big old ham on the bone that Yolanda had sent up earlier in the week. Ellie had fixed it up just the way Yolanda had always liked it, with lots of gravy and swimming in grease. Fifteen people were crowded around the living room eating; those who didn't fit at the small dinette table were eating from plates in their laps, plates piled high with sweet potatoes and collard greens and black-eyed peas and, of course, thick slices of ham. Fresh corn bread and biscuits sopped up the gravy.

This is real down-home cooking, thought Yolanda, not like the stuff I eat most of the time. Eating with gusto, she felt a pang of guilt as she thought of the thick thighs and generous rear end she was constantly struggling to keep in line. The plate before her probably used up her fat and cholesterol allotment for the rest of the year. But it was so good, this comfort food.

It was a relief in a way to be free of the white world today. At times the world in which she aspired to succeed could be so tedious. Everything was go, go, go. Sometimes she looked back at the simplicity of poverty nostalgically.

What a laughable notion, she thought to herself. There was no going back. She was married to a new life, to a new world, and her forays into her old world would become fewer and farther in between.

Except for Ellie. Ellie she could never leave behind. Yolanda loved Ellie with all her heart. Ellie had been a mother to her, had raised her and nurtured her, had introduced her to the other world that existed out there. Her biological mother had never ventured past the ghetto, had fallen into the trap of drinking and drugs there, had birthed all her babies there, and would probably die a premature death there. She had been expected for dinner today, but had not shown. It came as no disappointment to Yolanda; her mother could never be counted on, and they had never been particularly close. How could they have been? They were both children growing up together. But Yolanda had grown out of a dead-end life while her mother had not.

Now that Yolanda was making some money, she was going to see to it that Ellie was always taken care of. Well taken care of. There would be no more creaky tenement where towels had to be put in the window cracks during the winter to keep out the wind. No more living in neighborhoods so dangerous that a woman always had to keep her money in her bra because a purse was so easily snatched. No more of the cheapest cuts of meats for Ellie. She would be dining on steak.

Yep, Yolanda was headed for the big time, and she would be taking Ellie with her. She thought about her future, and was troubled momentarily by the decision she had made yesterday about the Jennifer O'Grady story. She hoped she hadn't made a mistake by not going on the air with what she had learned. Well, what was done was done, and there was no sense in worrying about it now.

Not when she could be enjoying a second helping of Ellie's delicious cooking. She refilled her plate, taking ample servings of just about everything, and looked up to see her great-aunt's face beaming at her across the room.

"Girl," she said proudly, "ain't nobody with an appetite for good soul food like you. No matter where you be livin'."

XXXI

Karen's hopes for a quiet Thanksgiving Day on Long Island were dashed by the phone call she received in the middle of dinner.

"Karen," her mother called from the kitchen. "It's for you."

She pushed herself away from the linen-draped table, heavy with good china and sterling silver, and excused herself. The all too familiar voice on the phone was that of her unsupportive partner.

"Hope you haven't started eating yet," he said unceremoniously.

"What?"

"Because you may end up seeing it again. I just got the call. The mad snatcher's at it again. Down in the Village. I'm on my way there now, meet me." She rapidly scribbled down the address he gave her.

Her mother was fit to be tied when Karen announced she was leaving.

"What do you mean you're leaving? Howard, do something. Tell her she isn't allowed to leave."

Her father chewed his turkey. "She's a big girl, Jackie. It's her decision."

Karen said a quick good-bye to her younger brothers and her sister, the princess, all of whom barely looked up from their plates. Her mother followed her to the front door.

"Karen, I don't know why you are doing this to yourself. What are you trying to prove? A college graduate working for the police department? In New York City yet? Why don't you get a nice job where you'll meet a nice Jewish man and settle down. Life doesn't have to be so tough, you know."

"Mother, I have to go." She gave her mother a quick peck on the cheek and was out the door. The argument was an old one.

As she backed out the driveway away from the huge sprawling house, the one her mother had fallen in love with and had to have, she thought about why she was a cop. Because I don't want to be anything like you, Mother, she thought. God, the last thing she ever wanted in the world was her mother's life. Her mother's hobbies were buying furniture, having her hair done, eating out, and spending her husband's money. She never seemed to do anything that didn't involve spending money. Let her sister follow in her mother's footsteps. Karen wanted a life of her own.

She looked down at her hands on the wheel and her red lacquered fingernails. All right, so that was one trait she had inherited from her mother, weekly manicures. The rest, you could keep.

Traffic was light and she made good time getting into Manhattan. The midtown streets were deserted. Even the derelicts were having Thanksgiving dinner somewhere. It was cold and grey and sleeting lightly as she pulled up in front of the Village address that Tony had given her.

There were three squad cars parked in front of an old walkup subdivided into twice as many apartments as had originally been intended. Karen flashed her badge at the two uniformed cops who were stationed in front of the building and rushed past them. A few people milled about trying to learn what had happened, but for the most part it was quiet out front. A few police cars with their lights flashing didn't draw much of a crowd in the Village.

Karen walked up the three flights to Emily Wiggins's apartment. The scene inside was an eerie replay of the one at Jennifer O'Grady's earlier in the week. The forensic people were there, the coroner Nathaniel Bradlee was present, a mutilated female corpse lay on the floor. The only thing missing was the smell. Emily's body hadn't been lying there as long as Jennifer's had. Karen's eyes traveled to the red spot at the top of the legs where the hair had been cut away, and she shut her eyes tight.

When she opened them she tried to look at the scene more clinically. The dead woman's head had been battered almost beyond recognition, and she lay on the floor naked except for her mink coat.

"It doesn't appear that she struggled," she heard the voice of Nat Bradlee saying. "Probably hit her fast, before she knew what was happening . . . Mercifully," he added.

Karen nodded and hoped he was right. The coroner stared at her with serious brown eyes. "For the life of me, I don't understand why a girl like you would want to get involved in the likes of this."

Her partner emerged at that moment, coming from the short hallway that led to the bedroom and bathroom. He was talking loudly to a uniformed officer who followed him, and he stopped upon seeing Karen.

"Was I right that you would be better off doing this on an empty stomach, Levinson?" he asked brusquely.

She grimaced. "It's a little easier this time." Though the memory of Jennifer's body still stimulated her gag reflex, she had to admit it was growing less and less nauseating over time. How quickly we grow used to violence and death, she reflected. She thought of a paramedic she talked to once who had said death had become such a normal part of his life that it was hard to take it really seriously, even when it touched his personal life. A corpse just gets to be an everyday occurrence, he had said.

"Her family got nervous when she didn't show earlier today to help her mother with Thanksgiving dinner. They called the landlord, who let himself in. He found her just like this," said Tony, pointing toward the victim and looking at her for a minute before turning his eyes back toward Karen. "There are no signs of forced entry, so maybe she knew her attacker. The bathtub is full, and there is an open bottle of champagne on the kitchen table. She had no boyfriend that anyone knew of, and none of the neighbors who are home today saw or heard anything unusual yesterday."

"It was yesterday?"

Tony deferred to Nat. "Near as I can tell right now, I figure it was sometime yesterday afternoon or early evening. I'll know better when we get her downtown."

Karen looked clinically at the naked body sprawled in the fur coat. "Was there a note?"

"Same as last time, next to the pubic hair." Tony signaled one of the cops, who brought over a plastic bag that contained a single sheet of typing paper. On it was the same message that had been typed onto the same kind of paper at Jennifer O'Grady's.

HOW MANY OF THESE WOULD IT TAKE TO MAKE A FUR COAT?

"What about the coat pockets? Was there a flyer this time?"

"That's the only thing missing. No flyer this time."

Karen eyeballed the apartment. None of the trappings of wealth here. The small living room was tastefully furnished, but with inexpensive pieces that appeared to have been purchased over a long period of time. There was no central theme—the sofa was contemporary, a couple of chairs were older with material that showed signs of wear. Two end tables were probably thrift shop specials.

"Mind if I look around?" Karen asked her partner.

"Knock yourself out," was his reply.

She wandered into the bedroom. There was a traditional brass bed, a functional nightstand, a large, heavy chest of drawers and a small dressing table. Like Jennifer's dressing table, it was covered with perfumes and makeup. Karen found herself wanting to see a picture of Emily. She wondered what she had looked like before she was so brutally murdered.

Karen slid the closet doors open and looked inside. What she saw was a typical woman's closet. Suits, blouses and slacks pressed altogether too tightly against one another. The floor littered with shoes, and the shelf overhead overflowing with handbags.

The bathroom held nothing special. Prescription medicines in the cabinet, toilet paper and Kleenex under the sink. The bathtub was full of cool water and an opened bottle of bubble bath sat on its porcelain edge.

Karen returned to the living room, where the victim was about to be wheeled away on a gurney. As the body was removed, Karen noticed a tiny double door near the entry. She opened it. Another closet. Like the bedroom closet, it was packed to capacity. Spring and winter coats shared the same space along with boots and umbrellas and whatever other paraphernalia Emily Wiggins had managed to wedge in. Looking for anything that might be of interest, Karen noticed the garment bag with the Swank logo on the side, and read the receipt stapled to it.

"I think I know what she was celebrating," Karen said excitedly.

"Yeah, what?" said Tony, only half listening. He was busy with a forensics man.

"That mink coat she was wearing . . . She just bought it yesterday. I'll bet she was having her own little celebration." She waited for her partner to say something and when nothing was forthcoming, she added, "It's a Swank Fur by the way."

That got Tony's attention. "Those kooks still demonstrating out in front of Swank?"

"They were yesterday."

"I wonder if Mr. Keith Geiger was there yesterday," said Tony.

"Or Sylvester Wolfe," echoed Karen, thinking along the same lines.

They first tried Keith Geiger's residence, a seedy walkup on the lower East Side. After getting no answer there, they headed out to Brooklyn to pay another call on Sylvester K. Wolfe. Karen started getting a clammy shiver before they were even halfway there. She was not looking forward to this visit; she had a very unsettling feeling about Mr. Wolfe. She shuddered at the thought of him and the stench of his ramshackle house. Reluctantly she admitted to herself she would again be grateful for her partner's strong masculine presence.

"Feeling a little leery?" asked Tony, his voice for once not laced with cynicism.

"Just not looking forward to all those dogs and the smell of that house."

"Yeah, that place sure does stink. And to think, right now I could be at Ma's feasting away. Instead we're going to be standing around in a room full of dog shit. Why do these things always happen on holidays? I think the wackos do it on purpose, just to drive us cops nuts."

Karen noticed that he had said "us cops" and she quietly appreciated being included for once.

"Is your mom a good cook?" she asked, feeling they might be on the brink of some sort of camaraderie.

"My ma. The best. When I think of my brothers right now, stuffing their faces with turkey and calamari and mostaccioli with gravy, it makes me wild. Luckily, my ma will save some for me. Yeah, she'll put a big plate aside. She's a wonderful woman. All women should be like her."

He looked directly at Karen, and she realized she had led the conversation in the wrong direction. She should have stuck to business.

"Yep," he repeated. "All women should be like my ma. Taking care of their men and raising their kids instead of taking the jobs away from guys who need them. That's what's the matter with this world nowadays. Women leaving home and neglecting the kids."

"You think so, huh? Why don't you talk to some of the women who've been deserted by their men. You don't know what you're talking about."

"All I know is that it used to be a better world before you broads started thinking you were men. It used to be just kind of fucked up. Now it's totally fucked up."

He turned off the car, and Karen realized they had arrived. She looked nervously at Sylvester's building. It looked more forbidding than ever. She really had a bad feeling. She swallowed her anger with Tony, and hoped he would lead the way.

But Tony wasn't going to let her off that easy. If she wanted equality, she was going to get equality. As they stood at the curb in the pale yellow of the street lamps, Tony extended his arm with mock civility. "After you," he said, bending at the waist.

Cursing silently, Karen led the way.

Lights burned somewhere within; it was evident as a dull glow through the drawn shade of the one unboarded window. Neither she nor Tony noticed that the shade was drawn back slightly for just a moment. They walked onto the sagging front porch and

Karen rapped sharply at the door. The baying of dogs could be heard.

The door opened slightly, stopped by a chain on the inside. Karen peered into the dimness, expecting to see Sylvester's blood-shot eye staring back at her. Instead she saw something that looked familiar, but she wasn't quite placing it. As it suddenly dawned on her that she was looking at a cylinder of steel, she felt herself being hurled to the rotting wood floor of the porch as the deafening boom of a gun's report filled her ears. Terrified, she buried her face against the side of the building. She could feel the heavy weight of a body atop hers, and fearfully she turned to look. It was Tony. He was pressing his body along the length of hers.

Her eyes shifted rapidly to the front door. It was open all the way now, with dogs and cats streaming out helter-skelter in the aftermath of the gunshot. Calmly standing in the doorway was Sylvester K. Wolfe, oblivious to the menagerie around him, his stance unwavering as he leveled his shotgun at her and Tony. Tony rolled over quickly and grabbed a nearby cat, throwing it at Sylvester.

The animal hissed as it flew through the air, catching its owner with outstretched claws and clinging in panic to his tattered shirt. Wolfe screamed and wrenched the cat from his arm.

Karen heard the sound of more gunshots and screamed before realizing they were coming from her partner next to her. She watched in horror as Sylvester's grimy T-shirt darkened with first one, then two, then five big blots of red. The shotgun fell from his hands, discharging into the night, and then he fell too, narrowly missing a whimpering dog. The other animals had scattered in all directions. The entire exchange had taken maybe ten seconds.

Karen started trembling uncontrollably, her eyes welling with tears. She felt a gentle touch on her shoulder and rolled away from the building, forcing herself to sit up. She managed to staunch the tears before they could get started.

"Are you all right?" Tony asked.

"Yes," she replied, her entire body shaking.

"You're damn lucky that I saw the barrel of that gun. You would have been mincemeat."

"Thanks." Karen brushed dust from her sleeves in an effort to look casual and to calm her trembling body. She pushed herself shakily to her knees and then stood up on legs so wobbly she was sure she would fall. Tony stood beside her, leaning over the body of Sylvester. A couple of the dogs had returned and were nosing at the body as it lay there on its side, its eyes wide open, the T-shirt soaked with blood.

"The cats scattered all over creation, damn it," said Tony. "How the hell are we ever gonna know if Chessie was one of them."

Karen wasn't thinking of the cats. She was thinking of her own skin and how glad she was to still have it. And then she was thinking of the way she had responded in the crisis. She had frozen, paralyzed with fear. She never even drew her gun.

Tony was now bent over Sylvester, examining him closer, obviously not disturbed by the condition of the dead man. Karen felt she had to say something.

"Tony," she said. He looked up at her. "I'm sorry. I'm sorry I panicked. That's no way for a partner to behave."

In his eyes she saw the same resentment she had grown so used to. He stared at her directly for three long seconds and then in a voice that cut to the quick with its coldness, he said, "I wouldn't expect any more from a broad."

Within moments backup squad cars began arriving, and there was no more conversation between them.

XXXII

Larry paid more attention to his wine than he did to the food before him. He barely touched the elaborately prepared cornish hen with *haricots verts* and cranberry puree. When the waiter returned to inquire if everything was all right he asked that his plate be removed. Then he ordered a second bottle of Pommard.

"Larry!" his mother admonished him. "Are you sure you want more wine?" She picked over the remains of a quail, going back to the tiny bones to be sure she had secured every morsel of the tender sweet meat. Like her son, Sheila Warning tended to be soft and plump, and in recent years had reconciled herself to her single status, surrendering to her fondness for fine food and her disdain for any activity that might serve to burn off any of it. But her plump face still showed signs of her former beauty. Her intense grey eyes were her most remarkable feature. Dramatically framed by long dark lashes and ample dark brows, they served to draw attention away from a rather weak chin and undersized nose.

"Mother," said Larry, draining the last drop of wine from his glass, "it's Thanksgiving and what better way to give thanks than by appreciating what the French can do with the grape. It's absolutely the American way."

"Don't be ridiculous, Larry," she said. "You're getting drunk."

"Does it matter, Mother?" he asked, looking her straight in the eye. He was flushed from having finished most of the first bottle, and his fat cheeks were rosy.

"It's a shame Leslie didn't join us," said his mother, changing the subject.

He bristled at the mention of his half-sister's name. "Yes, I'm sure you miss her as much as I do, Mother. The little mouse. Did I tell you she was actually dining with the family of a boyfriend?"

"No, you didn't." She looked disturbed. "How nice for her."

"Yes, I'm sure you think it's as nice as I do. Sweet little Leslie, dowdy little thing. There may be some hope for her after all."

The waiter returned with another bottle of wine and opened it for Larry, pouring a taste into a fresh glass for his approval. Larry swirled the wine in his glass and took a mouthful of the rich, red fluid. "Ah, lovely. Blueberries and currants. Wonderful structure. Excellent tannins. You may pour."

After the waiter had poured the wine for Larry and his mother, he retreated and Larry sat back in his chair and mused.

"Yes, Leslie, wonderful Leslie. The wonder child. The child of true love." He saw his mother wince. "I'm sorry, I didn't mean to offend you. But it offends me that I was only half as important to my father as she was. Even with her strange ways, her total lack of social graces, her bizarre vegetarianism, he really loved her so much more than he ever loved me. He certainly showed that in his will. She controls everything. I can't even sell my stock without her approval."

His mother cut into a pumpkin tart the waiter had brought for her, and waved off any more wine. "It is a shame that the estate is tied up the way it is. Isn't there anything you can do to get your half free and clear?"

"Not unless Leslie agrees. It's ridiculous that I should be worth so much money on paper and unable to touch any of it. I barely exist on my trust fund."

His mother chose not to mention his uptown penthouse, his fancy cars and his flamboyant spending on a string of women. She was worried about herself and who was going to watch out for her as she got older. She did not want to do anything that might alienate her son.

It had been bad enough when she lost her husband. When he divorced her and married that shrew Amanda Smith, she had become permanently embittered. What did it matter that she and Edward hadn't been civil to each other for years—she had enjoyed her status as Mrs. Edward Warning. A selfish woman, she had been so venomous after the divorce that she transmitted her poison to her son, turning him into a mean, spiteful creature at a young age. Now that her beauty was gone, her biggest concern was to see that her son got his fortune so that she could get hers.

"Tell me about Leslie's new boyfriend," she said. "Does he have any influence over her?" Her greatest fear was that somehow an outsider might come in and take control of the Warning fortune.

Larry shrugged. "I haven't met him, but he's obviously a fortune hunter. She met him in Central Park when she was feeding the pigeons. Good God! Who feeds pigeons? Rats with wings is what they are." He paused to drink more wine. "I know the type. Came from nothing, made some Yuppie money, and has a taste for more. Probably wears wire-rimmed glasses and designer labels on everything. I see dozens of these guys every day." He thought about the scores of ambitious young dreamers who lined the bar at Mulligan's at the end of each work day, drinking beer with limes shoved into the bottle necks and talking about stocks and market swings as if they had fortunes affected by such things. Women swarmed around them, incredible bright, attractive women, cunning as they come, drawn to their bullshit like flies. Larry hung around these jerks too. He appreciated their drawing power, and picked up on their leftovers.

Of course, the girls were never too interested in Larry at first, that is until they found out who he was. When they did, their eyes lit up like little diamonds and their body language changed from the cold shoulder to a warm open front. Then he would take them home and screw them, they were that easy once they knew he had money. He shuddered to think how lonely his life would be if he didn't have any.

"You know," he continued, "if I ever get my hands on my fortune, I think I'll go and live on the Riviera or the Costa del Sol—leave New York and its slime big mouth know-it-alls. I'll live where the sun is hot and the girls bathe topless.

"Lawrence!"

"Sorry, Mother."

"And what about me, your mother? Would you think of me at all?"

She was the person in the world most like him, and he felt a strong obligation to her. "I will always be sure you are provided for."

His mother looked relieved. She drank coffee as Larry finished off the second bottle of wine. Larry knew what he had to do. He had to keep working on Leslie, wear his stubborn little half-sister down. And if that didn't work? He didn't know. He just knew he had to have what was his.

After the taxi dropped his mother off, he told the driver to take him to Mulligan's. He knew there wouldn't be many people there since it was Thanksgiving, but he wasn't ready to go home. Truth was, he felt like getting laid. To hell with his sister and his mother and everything else; tonight he just wanted to find the lonely bitch who was out there waiting for him.

XXXIII

The room was tight and claustrophobic—a prison. As he paced back and forth across the threadbare carpet, his ears were assaulted by the clatter of the city streets fifteen floors below. He had the room's one window wide open, and yet it still did not bring in enough air.

Finally, he could take it no more; he needed to breathe. He grabbed his key and left the room. The decrepit elevator took forever to get to his floor and the ride down in the confining quarters that smelled vaguely of urine made him even more anxious than he had been in his crackerbox room. He was relieved when he finally stepped out onto the pavement.

Walking along for miles, he was one of the obscure millions of the decaying city. He walked farther, faster, unable to escape the trapped feeling. He was surrounded by tall buildings that seemed to be closing in on him.

It was hours before he returned to his hotel, his feet sore from pounding the unforgiving pavement, his head aching from the unfamiliar pollutants in the city air. As he entered the seedy lobby, the claustrophobic feeling worsened and he decided to take the stairs instead of the elevator.

He climbed the fifteen flights to his floor only to find the door to the hallway locked. His first instinct was to kick it down, but then he thought better of it. It was best not to draw attention to himself. He walked back down the narrow stairs and reemerged in the lobby. He took the elevator back up.

As he lay on his bed, the sheets and blankets pushed aside, he stared out the window. All he could see was the backside of another building. He wondered if there was still a sky. As he drifted off into an uneasy sleep he asked himself the same question he had asked since he had arrived . . . How much longer must he stay?

XXXIV

FUR FREE FRIDAY

Karen awakened with a start. There had been a man standing over her with a gun, peering down at her through bloodshot eyes, making her squirm with fear under his scurrilous gaze. She was soaking with sweat, and it took her a moment to realize it had only been a nightmare and she was safe at home. But there was something unusual in the early morning darkness. There was the rhythmic sound of breathing right there in her ears, the comforting warmth of another body only inches from hers. Oh yes, she recalled, rolling onto her back. *I guess you just don't hate someone that much without there being another underlying emotion.*

She looked at his dark head laying on her printed pillowcase, his perfect features tranquil in sleep. She was sticky and sore between her legs, and seeing him there stirred the primal feelings she had experienced the night before.

She thought about how it had come to happen. He had been kinder to her after they finished up at Sylvester's house. He saw she was still shaken, and he asked her if she wanted to go for a drink. Over a Scotch she broke down, all of her pent-up emotions finally surfacing, the fear, the insecurity, her anger with him. He listened for a change and at one point put his hand out to touch hers reassuringly. At that moment something electric passed through them, and there was no question where it was going to go. They began to kiss in the car, deep, hard, desperate kisses. She was in a vacuum, being sucked into a soft, dark, bottomless place. He had barely been able to park, and they had begun to tear off each other's clothes as they rode up in the elevator. It had been sublime; he was the lover she craved, strong and confident and enduring. He had conquered her entirely, and she loved it.

But that was last night. Now as she lay beside him in the first inkling of day's light, she found herself hoping she hadn't made a mistake. She lay quietly for a while, watching him sleep, before creeping silently out of bed. She went into the kitchen and made herself some coffee.

She was on her second cup when she heard him come in behind her. She turned and smiled. He was wearing his pants and nothing else, his well-defined upper body covered with a blanket of thick dark hair.

"Is it all right if I use your shower?" was all he asked.

Her smile receded. "Of course."

He disappeared into the bathroom without another word, and she felt her stomach roil with the sick, sinking feeling that she had, indeed, made a mistake. She was still sitting at the small kitchen table when he came back fully dressed.

"What are you doing?" he asked. "You'd better get a move on, we've got a lot to do today, partner." His words were neither warm nor chiding. They were matter-of-fact, as if last night had never happened.

Karen wanted to say something, but the words would not come. Before her stood a man with whom she had shared the most passionate of human experiences only hours before, and he wasn't even acknowledging that it had happened. She felt her blood begin to boil much the way it did when he humiliated her at the stationhouse, and this time her anger overcame her humiliation.

"What the hell is it with you, Tony? Have you forgotten what went on here last night?"

"Nope, but that was last night," he said coldly. "This is today. I'm a cop, and I've got work to do."

"I'm a cop too."

"No, you're not," he said firmly. "You're a chick trying to play cop. Don't you know that, Karen? Look at what happened yesterday. If I hadn't been there to protect you it would have been your ass. You're a nice gal, a good-looking woman, an okay person, but you are not a cop."

"And what was I last night then? The nice gal? An okay person?"

"You know what you were last night."

The room echoed with the sound of her drawn-in breath. And then she said words that surprised even her. "You're telling me that I'm just a cunt, is that it?"

"You said it, not me." He shrugged his shoulders.

But Karen was not to be put off easily. "Then what does that make you, a dick?"

Tony laughed, the laugh coming easily, dispelling some of the animosity that hung in the air.

"You know, Levinson, you're something else. I got to admit, I'm attracted to you, otherwise, well, it couldn't have happened. But I'm attracted to the woman. We could spend time together, but not while you're a cop and certainly not while you're my partner."

He turned and went to the door. "See you at the station. One half-hour."

By the time she got to the precinct, some of her fury had died down, and Karen had decided that if she was going to survive this she was just going to have to act as if nothing had happened. She was conscious of eyes upon her as she crossed the squad room, and she wondered if anyone knew, and if so, how much? She avoided meeting anyone's eyes, bowing her head as she hurried to her desk. Tony's was empty. A few minutes later she saw him coming out of the Lieutenant's office. He walked directly over to her.

"I want you to know, I've given the Lieutenant a full accounting of what happened last night."

Karen turned crimson. "What?" she managed to sputter.

"At Sylvester Wolfe's house. Lighten up. But I told him about you freezing and I want you to know I have put in a second request for a new partner."

Her eyeballs burned hot as she felt the usual female response of immediate tears. Why did she have to react like this so automatically? she thought, cursing herself.

"Fine," she said. "And what did he say?"

"Lucky you, he didn't seem too concerned. Not when my ass is on the line. He said I'll just have to wait, so it looks like we're still together . . . for now."

"Great," she said sarcastically. "I can't tell you what that does for me. So, partner, what now?"

"I want to go talk to Keith Geiger. Find out where he was on Thanksgiving Eve. Then I want to talk to the Nilssons and see if they have any idea why someone would want to kill one of their customers."

"Then you aren't satisfied that it was Sylvester Wolfe who killed those women?"

"Don't you remember on our first day together I told you: Don't believe the obvious. If it turns out that it was Sylvester Wolfe, then fine. The world is rid of a menace and the public has been spared the expense of a trial. But there are a few things that bother me. One, no typewriter in his house."

"Maybe he used one at a copy center or the library."

"Possibly," Tony admitted. "Two, we need a weapon. A club, a bat, a two-by-four. We didn't find anything there."

"Maybe he threw it out."

"That's possible too. But what really bothers me is the flier."

"What flier?" Karen said. "There was no flier."

"That's what I mean," Tony smiled.

"Why didn't he leave one of those S.T.S. fliers like he did at Jennifer's?"

"Well, if it was Sylvester Wolfe, maybe because he knew we'd seen the flyers at his house," said Karen.

"Maybe, but there are still too many loose ends as far as I'm concerned. You know what I'd like to see? I'd like to see that cat of Jennifer's turn up. We've got patrol cars scouring Wolfe's neighborhood looking for it. Finding it would satisfy me."

He grabbed his jacket from the back of his chair. "Well, let's get going," he said sharply, and then, looking at Karen, he added, "Partner."

Karen ignored the jibe and drew her coat on. She couldn't figure him out. One minute he was hot, the next cold. She thought about the feel of him the night before and how confident and competent a lover he was and a shiver ran up her spine. This is just too weird, she thought, and with a sudden change of heart she found herself hoping that his request for a different partner would be granted.

XXXV

It was basic chaos at the S.T.S. headquarters Friday morning. The Soho office was packed with people stopping in to pick up placards and literature or just looking for camaraderie on the big march. The phones wouldn't stop ringing and Leslie heard herself repeating the same answers to the same questions over and over again. "The demonstration starts at twelve. No, you'll have to bring your own sign, we are down to very few. Yes, we do have literature available for handout." And then she would add, "Be sure to dress warmly."

And rightfully so. For the first time in days the sky was clear, the grey clouds that enshrouded the city had finally lifted. In their wake had come a bitter cold front, and temperatures hovered in the twenties. A cruel wind blowing from the north made things worse, barreling down the avenues and causing pedestrians everywhere to pull their jackets ever tighter about themselves.

This same wind was gusting in the door of the S.T.S. office with the arrival of each new marcher, and Leslie saw her breath escape in little white puffs as she answered the phone. She shivered with the chill. She was coming down with a cold. She had awakened with the beginnings of a cold this morning, but it hadn't bothered her much, her head was in the clouds. For the first time since losing her parents, she was happy, and all she could think of was the source of that happiness, Neil Harrigan.

Neil and his strong arm about her last night as they walked from the highway. Neil and the comforting warmth of his body as she huddled against him in the cab on the way home. Neil and the feel of his hand in hers. Her heart was filled with such a happiness that she felt it might fly from her chest.

Maybe dreams really do come true, she thought, as she recalled him kissing her good night softly, but with a telling firmness, at her door. He had told her he would call her tomorrow and they would have dinner. After he left she had leaned against the door, her breath coming rapidly, her heart beating like a small child's. She wondered if she should have invited him in. She was so immature in these matters.

Leslie realized she was smiling to herself. She was feeling such wonderful things inside, sensations she had never experienced. She had known girlish crushes before, but this was so different. She and Neil were actually sharing something.

She was embarrassed a little by the things she found herself dwelling on, like how would it feel the next time he kissed her? Would it be deeper, more passionate? And what would the caress of his hands on her body feel like? She wondered about his body, how it looked under the starched white shirts he always wore.

She was both tantalized and frightened by her feelings, and she wished her mother were there to give her advice. But no, this would not be something for her mother. This was Leslie's special moment. Her thoughts raced ahead to marriage and family and babies. She would never be alone again.

Mary Ellen's high-pitched voice brought her out of her reverie.

"Leslie, what is it with you today? Are you on another planet or what?" Leslie had been ignoring the ringing phones. More inquiries about the march. That's right, twelve noon. See you there.

Mary Ellen was leaping around the office like a gazelle, unable to contain her enthusiasm. She shouted orders gleefully, rallied everyone for the cause. "I'm willing to bet we double last year's turnout," she cried out to no one in particular.

It was nearing eleven o'clock and the push was on to get everyone out the door and on their way to Fifth Avenue where Mary Ellen was to kick off the march with a speech in front of the Swank store. Keith disappeared into the inner office and returned a couple of minutes later swathed in layers of polypropylene outerwear and synthetic scarves. In his hands he held Mary Ellen's traps. They would be using them as props.

They had just herded the last of the stragglers out of the office and were about to leave themselves when the office door opened and a fresh burst of cold air blew in, followed by Detectives Levinson and Perrelli.

"Hello," said Mary Ellen glibly. "I hope you're here to join our march, because we could use a ride uptown."

"I really wish we had time to save the animals," Tony responded, "but we're kind of busy trying to save some humans. We need to ask a few questions of Mr. Geiger here. Keith, you got a second?"

"Do I have a choice?" he asked.

"This is America." Tony didn't wait for Keith to exercise his right of choice, but instead pulled out a photo and passed it around. It was of an attractive woman in her forties. She didn't look familiar to Leslie, but when she passed it to Keith she noticed him exchange glances with Mary Ellen.

"Her name was Emily Wiggins," said Tony. "Maybe you saw the story on TV. She was found murdered in her apartment in the Village yesterday. Her family called the building super when she didn't show up for Thanksgiving dinner. The coroner thinks she was killed late Wednesday, some time after she picked up her new mink coat. Recognize her, anyone?"

"I recognize her," said Keith reluctantly. "I saw her come out of Swank on Wednesday."

"Oh, is that so?"

Keith looked nervous, his face had turned an ashen grey.

"Is that all? You just saw her?"

"Not exactly."

Karen was standing off to the side mesmerized as she watched Tony stalk his prey. He was after Keith Geiger, no doubt about it, and he was letting Keith know it. Trying to make him nervous.

Playing it as if he had plenty of time and nowhere to go. He had timed their arrival at S.T.S. today for exactly when the S.T.S.ers would be leaving. They would want to be there for the march. If Keith wanted to keep his appointment for the salvation of animalkind, he would have to speak up quickly. That was when people made mistakes, Tony knew.

"Look," said Keith, "I saw her coming out of Swank on Wednesday with a garment bag in her hand and I followed her for a few blocks, just to exchange rhetoric. Maybe I gave her a little bit of a hard time, but it certainly wasn't as hard as what the animals she was going to be wearing went through."

"A friend of Emily's said she told her she was harassed on her way home with her new fur coat. By someone who got awfully close to her."

"Look," said Keith. "Maybe I did get a little too close, but I certainly didn't kill her."

"But you say you did get pretty close?"

"Maybe," Keith said guardedly.

"Close enough to notice the address stapled to her garment bag?"

"What?" Keith was beginning to get defensive. "Hey, man, you aren't going to do this to me . . . don't try and railroad me. I know what you guys are like."

"Why? Have you been through this before? Maybe in the military? I was a Marine, maybe you can tell me about it. Was that why you were court-martialed?"

The air in the office hung thick with silence, but Tony's words were echoing in everyone's memory. Karen nodded to herself in sudden understanding. No wonder he was after Keith Geiger. He didn't like his military record.

Leslie was shocked and confused. Keith was white as a ghost. Only Mary Ellen seemed to have her wits about her, and she grabbed Keith by his free arm, the other still holding the traps.

"Excuse us, officers, but we have someplace very important to go."

"I just have one more question for Mr. Geiger, here," said Tony in a tone no one dared challenge. "Where were you the rest of Wednesday afternoon?"

"I was demonstrating in front of Swank until about three." He looked around, embarrassed. "Then I went to see my shrink at the V.A."

Tony was nonplussed. "And after that?"

"After that I went home," he said nervously.

"And you were there alone?"

Before Keith could reply, Mary Ellen chimed in. "We were there together. I met him right after his therapy and we spent the night together."

Everyone looked at Mary Ellen, who just stood there smiling. "I guess our secret is out now."

Tony wasn't put off. He had handled this type of situation before. Mary Ellen was obviously lying to help Keith. It wouldn't be hard to trip her up. Ask for details of the evening, and it wouldn't be long before one of them screwed up. What did you watch? What did you eat? What time did you go to sleep? Separate them and compare their answers. Just as a probe he asked Mary Ellen, "And what did you do that evening?"

Keith interupted before Mary Ellen could utter a word. He knew what the detective was trying to do. "We made love all night long, from the time she arrived until we fell asleep. Didn't even take time for dinner." He grinned victoriously and Mary Ellen laughed aloud. Tony looked deflated. What could he ask them about that? The positions?

Karen was trying not to laugh herself as she absentmindedly folded an S.T.S. pamphlet into tiny squares.

"Is there anything else, Detective Perrelli," asked Mary Ellen, still smiling, her long-toothed grin hyena-like, "because we really do have to get going."

"No," he said angrily, losing his cool. He didn't appreciate being made a fool of in front of his partner. He turned and stomped out the door. Karen followed like a Chinese wife, paces behind.

After they were gone, Keith and Mary Ellen broke out into laughter.

"What was that all about?" asked Leslie, confused.

"Those pigs," said Mary Ellen. "They'll stop at nothing. They're trying to connect Keith to that murder."

"By the way, thanks, Mary Ellen," said Keith, a hint of a smile on his lips now, his color beginning to return to normal. "That was pretty quick thinking."

"Me? How about you?" she laughed. "We must be exhausted after all that lovemaking." They laughed together again.

Leslie was still lost, and the talk of lovemaking embarrassed her. As she locked the office door behind them, she couldn't help but feel uneasy at what had transpired, or maybe it was the prospect of encountering Bunny Nilsson in front of Swank today that was making her feel strange. She sniffled, her cold beginning to worsen, and wondered where the good feeling she had been enjoying earlier had gone. But then she thought of Neil and of seeing him tonight and it began to return.

XXXVI

What better day to bury his former lover than Fur Free Friday, the day they would probably bury his business as well. Actually, Jennifer wasn't going to be buried. She had already been cremated, and her ashes stood before them in an exquisite antique urn that Bunny had selected. Michael wondered what they should do with Jennifer's ashes. Should they spread them around Times Square and the sordid streets from which she had come?

Very few people were gathered to acknowledge Jennifer's passing. Mrs. Burhop was there dressed in her widow's black. A couple of men Jennifer had dated briefly, a few fellow models, some of her photographers, and a number of people from Swank made up the bulk of the mourners. Michael wasn't surprised at the meager turnout. Jennifer never had many friends. She preferred it that way, opting to bury her head in her books and relate to people and things on the page instead of in real life.

As he listened to the minister speak, Michael was acutely aware of his father's presence. True to his promise, Lars Nilsson had shown up for the service, and he sat rigidly in his wheelchair at Michael's side. Even in his weakened state he still exuded power and strength, and just being around him made Michael uncomfortable.

After the last words were said, and people began to file out of the small memorial chapel, Lars turned his whitened head toward his son.

"Are you ready for today's hysteria, son?" he asked.

Michael shrugged. He wasn't surprised that his father's concern had already shifted from Jennifer and her service. He was more worried about the marchers.

"Rise above them, Michael. Let people see what they're really like." He turned his attention to Bunny. "What about the 'feed the hungry' bit?"

"That's my priority, Dad."

"Today," he stated unequivocally, locking his eyes with hers. Then he patted her on the hand with his good one before signaling to his nurse that it was time to go. He grunted a sour good-bye, and Maureen wheeled him off to his limousine to be whisked back to his estate and away from the hell Michael was going to face later.

Michael felt his wife's hand upon his sleeve, that soft and possessive touch he had grown to know so well. He looked into her green eyes. They were mossy and cloudy today, and appropriately red-rimmed with grief.

"Are you all right, Michael?" she asked him.

"Fine," he responded, marveling that despite all that he had put her through, her principal concern was still his welfare.

"Let's go then," she beckoned.

As the driver drew nearer to the store, the traffic on Fifth Avenue grew more congested. Michael steeled himself for what he knew was coming. Already he could see that there was a great crowd in front of his store. They were chanting something. He instructed the driver to turn up a side street, so that they could enter the store through the receiving dock. Bunny stopped him.

"No, Michael. We will go in through the front door. We are proud of our business, proud of what we do. We have nothing to be ashamed of. If we allow these people to force us into hiding, what can we expect from our customers?"

He knew she was right, so they proceeded down Fifth Avenue and into the heart of the demonstration, stopping directly in front of the store entrance and the intimidating crowd. Michael found himself wishing that Bunny hadn't chosen to wear her sheared beaver coat to the service today.

Bunny seemed unconcerned, however. She emerged from the limousine as if she owned the world, and she strolled leisurely through the crowd of taunting demonstators. Someone slapped a sticker on her back that read THE REAL OWNER OF THIS COAT DIED IN IT. Undaunted by cries of "shame" and "murderer," Bunny walked straight ahead with her head high. Michael followed close behind, trying his best to look like her protector when in actuality he was riding in the wake of her fearlessness and confidence.

Once inside the store, Bunny's cool facade melted quickly. "Those bastards," she cried out in red-faced fury as she tore the sticker off her coat. "Something has to be done about them."

"But what?" Michael heard himself whine. "How can you fight a mob like that?"

"As your father said, 'fight fire with fire.' "

She looked around the deserted main floor, empty save for the salespeople who stood at their posts, anxious to get to work. It made her physically sick that the store should be without any customers on what should be the busiest day of the year. She prayed that the branch stores were doing better.

"Well, I'd better go find some hungry to feed," she said, not permitting any tone of defeat to enter her voice. "I'm going up to my office."

She climbed the spiral staircase that led to the second floor showroom, and sighed as she passed through the deserted salon. Her mind racing with things she had to do, she reached the hallway outside the offices and discovered the two homicide detectives waiting for her. She glanced at Sarah, who only shrugged.

"Good morning, Mrs. Nilsson," said Tony. "I hope you don't mind our waiting for you, but your secretary had said you would be in soon."

"We were at Jennifer's memorial service. What is it? Have you learned something new?" she demanded.

"Well, a lot has happened. We'd like to speak with you and your husband. Is he here?"

"Sarah, will you call for Mr. Nilsson?" Bunny commanded. Without waiting for an answer, she led them into Michael's office and shut the door behind them, much to Sarah's obvious dismay. Michael joined them within the minute.

"Michael, you remember Detectives Perrelli and Levinson," said Bunny.

"Of course," said Michael, his face open and interested. "What is it?"

Tony cleared his throat. "Well, I've got some bad news actually. There has been a second murder and we're pretty sure that it was done by the same person or persons who killed Jennifer O'Grady."

Both Michael and Bunny turned pale. "Is it anyone we know?" asked Bunny, her voice filled with trepidation.

"Her name was Emily Wiggins. Do you recognize it?"

"No," said Bunny. Michael shook his head no.

"The corpse was discovered yesterday afternoon, she was murdered sometime Wednesday night. There are some striking . . . similarities . . . between the two murders, things we can't tell you.

"But we can tell you that Emily Wiggins purchased a coat here the day she was killed, and we think her murder was connected to it. Do either of you know someone with a vendetta against you or Swank?"

Michael laughed aloud. "Are you kidding? Have you looked outside?" He walked to the window and pointed at the marchers below. Their numbers had swollen to fill the street. "You might find more than a few down there."

Tony nodded sympathetically. "There sure are a lot of loose nuts and bolts running around this city, aren't there? Well, this may make things a little brighter. One of our suspects was killed yesterday. An animal rights fanatic. Now we've got a second suspect. Another one of them," he said, jerking a thumb toward the window. "Anyway, I'd like you to look at their pictures and tell me if either one looks familiar."

He gestured to Karen, who had been silently watching the proceedings. She produced two mug shots they had procured earlier that morning, one of Sylvester K. Wolfe, the other of Keith Geiger.

She handed them first to Bunny, who looked them both over carefully and tapped her finger on the picture of Keith Geiger. "This hippie looking one—I've seen him outside the store." She reexamined the shot of Sylvester. "I've never seen him, and I can't say I'd want to. What a horrible looking creature!" She shuddered and handed the pictures to her husband.

Michael pointed at the photo of Keith. Yes, he'd seen him outside the store. Many times, as a matter of fact. He looked at the second mug shot. The bloated face of Sylvester K. Wolfe with its stubbly beard and bloodshot eyes stared directly at him. He drew back in shock as he realized that it looked hauntingly familiar. But why? He strained to remember. It wasn't from outside the store, it was somewhere else. And then, unhappily, it came to him.

"I've seen this man too." He looked at Bunny apologetically. "I saw him a week ago, standing on the street in front of Jennifer O'Grady's building."

Both Tony and Karen straightened up in their chairs as if they had just been slapped between the shoulder blades with a ruler.

"You mean last Friday?"

"Yes," said Michael.

"The day Jennifer was murdered?"

"Yes."

"You mean to say that you were at Jennifer O'Grady's apartment last Friday?" asked Tony incredulously. "You never told us that."

"I wasn't at her apartment. I only rang the buzzer. There was no answer so I left."

"Why were you there?"

"Jennifer wanted to speak to me about something important."

Tony leveled his dark eyes at him. The eyes were cold and piercing, and Michael squirmed under their accusatory gaze. "Why didn't you tell us about this before?"

Before Michael could answer, Bunny Nilsson got up from her seat and walked behind her husband, draping an arm loosely around his shoulder in a show of support. "I think it's for the best that you know this. Michael had an affair with Jennifer years ago. I believe he went there on Friday to try to rekindle it. He never told you about it because he didn't want me to know." Michael's body tensed under his wife's arm as she spoke. Otherwise he showed nothing.

"I wasn't hiding anything from you, from the police," he insisted, "and since I never did see Jennifer I didn't think it would matter. Until now . . . until you showed me that picture. I did see that man outside her building. I remember him very well because he was so odd looking. And he seemed to be watching me very closely.

"I'll bet he was the one who'd been harassing her," Bunny volunteered. "Do you think he killed her? And the other woman too?"

"We don't know, he's dead now," said Tony, taking the pictures back and getting up from his chair frustrated. "Before we go, is there any other little detail you may have neglected to tell us?"

"No," said Michael, ashamed.

"Absolutely not," his wife said confidently.

Michael shook himself out from under Bunny's arm and stared out the window, at the demonstration. Like a great snake, it slithered along Fifth Avenue, and like a mouse in a snake's belly, a large bulge of humanity remained in front of his store. He sighed aloud.

"Why did you have to tell them, Bunny? Why did you have to share our personal problems with the whole world?"

"It wasn't that, Michael. I just didn't want them to think that we had anything to hide. That's all."

He looked into his wife's emerald green eyes and he saw in them a strength and a single-mindedness he would never possess. It was at that moment that he realized that he didn't love her and never really had. But she remained his friend, his partner, his strength. He couldn't be angry with her now—he had put her through enough already.

As if she was reading his mind, the hint of a tear formed in her eyes, and he reached out to her, giving her a kiss. For all her toughness, she too had a breaking point.

"It's all right, Bunny girl," he said, using an endearment he hadn't uttered for a long time. "Everything is all right." She lay her head against his shoulder.

"I love you, Michael," she said.

Tony was smacking his head with his fist as he marched ahead of Karen, his herringbone coat flying open in the wind, flapping wildly about him. Taking two steps for every one of his, she struggled to keep up with him, feeling sheepish about the night before and resenting that he had once again excluded her from his thoughts. Finally, she shouted at his back, "What, Tony? What is it?"

Amazingly, he stopped dead in his tracks and turned to her. She almost piled into him. As she stood beneath the glowering face that towered over her, she couldn't help but realize how attractive he was. This is asinine, she thought, as she waited transfixed to hear what he had to say.

"You have to ask me 'what?'" he shouted at her. "The affair, that's 'what.' All this crap about her being like a daughter. That's a pretty strange family, where the father's banging the daughter."

"So they had an affair. Does that mean he killed her?"

"I don't know what it means, but it could be significant."

"But how? How does it fit with Emily Wiggins? And what about Sylvester Wolfe? If he was following Jennifer O'Grady he probably followed Emily Wiggins too!"

"Karen, you don't get it, do you? You just don't get it. It's too obvious. Haven't you listened to anything I've said?"

He turned on his heels and continued his forced march to their illegally parked Dodge. As she scrambled to keep up again, her mind was a kaleidoscope of facts and images. Sylvester Wolfe, Keith Geiger, Michael Nilsson, Jennifer O'Grady, Emily Wiggins. Did they all fit together somehow? Well, if they did, it certainly wasn't "obvious" to her.

What was obvious, though, was that she was on an emotional roller coaster as far as her partner was concerned, and if she was going to survive at this job, she had just better get off it.

XXXVII

Leslie, Mary Ellen and Keith finally caught a cab a block from the Soho office. More than a few taxis had passed them by after noting the ominous hardware they were carrying. The Middle Eastern driver who finally stopped eyed them skeptically as the trio piled in and dropped the steel traps to the floor with a clang. Mary Ellen plunked her huge nylon shoulder bag on top of them and attempted to settle back in the seat. It was difficult for her to relax. She was tense and edgy, like an athlete before a key game. She chattered on nervously about the march and the tremendous impact it was going to have.

Keith, on the other hand, had been subdued ever since his encounter with Detective Perrelli, and he sat gazing out the window, lost in his own thoughts. When Mary Ellen realized that he wasn't listening to her, she became concerned and asked him if he was all right. He turned toward Mary Ellen and Leslie, and in his eyes they saw a familiar look, one they saw often on the faces of the trapped animals on their posters—a look of fear and confusion. Keith said nothing.

"Keith!" Mary Ellen repeated. "Are you okay?"

"Yeah," was his distant reply. "Do they really think I could hurt somebody?"

"Oh, that," said Mary Ellen. "Who cares? They're pigs and that's their problem. We told them we were together and no one can dispute it—right? So relax and don't worry so much. We've got more important things going on here today."

If he was relieved by her words, it didn't show in his face. Still, he made an honest effort to placate her. "You're right," he said halfheartedly. "We have work to do, and they aren't going to take away from it." But it was a somber face that he turned back toward the window as he added, "I can't be put away again. I don't think I'd make it."

Leslie was more confused than ever, and she looked to Mary Ellen for some kind of explanation, but things were just fine now as far as Mary Ellen was concerned. Her concentration was on the scores of people carrying placards outside their cab.

The taxi was standing still, brought to a stop by the hundreds of people spilling off the sidewalks and the drivers who slowed to watch them. "Let's get out of here," Mary Ellen cried, the captain rallying her troops. She grabbed her bag and jumped from the cab, waiting impatiently as Keith gathered up the traps and Leslie paid the driver. As they surged through the crowd, Leslie was relieved that they hadn't been let off in front of the Swank store. She was terrified of running into Bunny Nilsson, and when she thought about their brief luncheon encounter her skin crawled. She had seen Bunny's ire only once, and that had been enough for her.

When they reached the front of the Swank store, it appeared the festivities had begun. A famous game show host was speaking from a makeshift platform, pontificating about the evils of wearing the skins of dead animals and swearing that no such product would ever be given away on his show. He was applauded loudly by the crowd.

Camaraderie ran thick amongst the demonstrators. Leslie could pick out Donna Segura from the Humane Society, Della Richards from P.E.T.A. and John Cline from the Animal Liberation Front. She recognized people from the Friends of Animals, the Animal Rights Alliance, and the Radicals to Remove Animals from the Public Domain.

All around her people brandished signs proclaiming that FUR KILLS and YOU SHOULD BE ASHAMED TO WEAR FUR. The S.T.S. slogan IT LOOKED BETTER ON THE ANIMAL'S BACK was seen on many a sign, but most had tastefully removed any pictures of the late Jennifer O'Grady. She saw a couple of placards bearing the likeness of Nancy Reagan with the slogan FAKE PEOPLE WEAR REAL FUR and more that said simply FUR IS DEAD. Three particularly dedicated young women shivered against the cold in fleshtone body suits under a banner that read, WE'D RATHER GO NAKED THAN WEAR FUR.

Leslie watched as Mary Ellen took her turn at the podium. Shrieking above the crowd and waving her trademark animal traps, she was able to mesmerize her audience with tales of injustice in the wild. They stared at her transfixed as she told gruesome stories of severed paws and shattered bones. She finished to applause, holding her bear trap high above her head.

Mary Ellen returned to where Keith and Leslie stood waiting for her. The march was about to begin. She looked disappointed and said, "I figure there are about a thousand of us here. I had hoped there would be more." They joined the parade, which wended its way for a mile down Fifth Avenue, and then turned to head back up Madison Avenue. Along its route, anyone they passed who was insensitive enough to wear fur on such a frigidly cold day bore the full brunt of their fury. Showered with taunts, the fur-wearers scurried out of sight.

The march had made a complete circle and was passing in front of the Swank store again when an attractive young blonde woman in a full length mink coat happened past. Her hands were filled with brightly colored shopping bags, her bounty from hours of

Christmas shopping. Undaunted by the insults from the marchers, she slowed her pace and strolled in step with them. She appeared to take pleasure in teasing them until one of the demonstrators slapped a sticker on the back of her coat. She swung her
leather shoulder bag at him. "You keep away from me," she cried,
shaking her frizzy blonde head into the wind.

"Murderer!" he cried out at her, and the crowd echoed, "Murderer!"

The blonde turned to her accusers and gave a shrill laugh.
"Sticks and stones may break my bones, but names will never hurt
me!"

It was then that Mary Ellen, the huge bear trap slung across
one shoulder, her own ungainly shoulder bag draped across the
other, broke ranks with the marchers. She ran up to the mink-clad
shopper, screaming like a banshee. "It's people like you who give
people a bad reputation." She unzipped her bag and pulled out a
small aerosol can. As Leslie and Keith watched in horror, she
aimed the nozzle at the woman. Bright red streaks of paint appeared all over the dark mink as Mary Ellen kept spraying everywhere, coloring the woman's hair as well as her coat.

"Mary Ellen!" shouted Keith, charging up and wresting the
spray can from her. Many of the marchers stood there aghast,
stunned and silent. A few enthusiasts in the crowd called out,
"Way to go!"

Keith just looked at Mary Ellen with disbelief. "Are you crazy?"
he shouted.

The blonde was in shock by now, and her treasured coat was a
sticky mess of red. Strands of her golden hair blew in the wind
while entire clumps of it stuck to the tacky mess on her coat.
"What have you done?" she wailed. "My coat, it's ruined. My hair.
I'll have to cut my hair."

Two policemen, alerted by a passerby, joined the scene. Seeing
Keith holding the paint can, they immediately grabbed him. "No,
it was her," the blonde cried and pointed a gloved hand at Mary
Ellen. "It was her."

One of the policemen grabbed hold of Mary Ellen, who showered him with curses as she struggled to break away. Leslie stood
off to the side as he tried to subdue her. Mary Ellen, spotting
Leslie, tossed her purse and the bear trap at her. "Take these for

me," she shouted as more police arrived. Leslie watched as Mary Ellen, squirming against the policeman's grip, was loaded into a squad car. In spite of her situation, she appeared to be smiling. Keith followed behind her, but his face showed none of her enthusiasm. A few other demonstrators were arrested, and within minutes the crowd had dispersed and police had the entire situation under control. A young, eager-looking cop escorted the blonde victim, now sobbing loudly, to his waiting squad car. Solicitously, he opened the door and helped her in.

Keith had dropped the traps he was carrying, and Leslie went over and picked them up. The weight of Mary Ellen's bag was heavy on her shoulder, and she felt ridiculous standing there with all the extra hardware. She had had enough for one day. She was chilled to the bone, and she could tell that her cold had gotten worse. Her whole body ached, and her throat was sore. She walked away from the remaining handful of marchers and hailed a cab.

As she settled into the glorious warmth of the taxi, she thought about Neil. He was supposed to call her for dinner tonight. She wanted to hurry home to wait for his call. She was tired of demonstrations, and she didn't want to think about Bunny Nilsson and the Hunger Exchange and Keith and Mary Ellen sitting in jail. All she cared to think about now was Neil.

XXXVIII

"Hey, Tony, they want you downstairs. Something about a wino with a diamond cat collar."

Tony nearly knocked his desk over pushing his chair away from it. "Where is he?"

"They're holding him for you in detention."

"Thanks, Bob." Tony practically ran the uniformed cop over as he bolted from the room. Karen was up and fast on his tail.

"Hey, wait," she called out to his back. "Remember me? I'm on this case too."

His reply was a barely audible grunt accompanied by no discernible slowing of his pace. She scrambled to catch up with him at the elevator. As she waited beside him, in uncomfortable silence, Karen absentmindedly slipped one of her nails into her mouth and began to click it back and forth across her front teeth. How she hated him, she thought. This silent treatment was the worst yet. Their communication had peaked today with the unpleasantness this morning in her apartment and it had gone steadily downhill ever since. Now he was acting as though making love last night had totally absolved him of having to treat her as a peer. Silence was his way of telling her that everything he had ever said about women cops was true.

The elevator was slow in coming. That was nothing unusual. It serviced far too many floors with too many people. Karen continued to click away at her teeth as they impatiently waited. Tony shifted his weight from leg to leg.

"Will you quit that?" he snapped.

It took Karen a moment to realize that he was referring to her nervous habit. Quickly, she withdrew her finger from her mouth.

"Sorry," she said icily.

A minute later the elevator still hadn't arrived. He was still ignoring her, his only word an occasional "damn" uttered under his breath. His abrasiveness was finally driving her to the breaking point. She decided to review her situation.

Is it my fault, Tony, that I was teamed up with you? Is it my fault that I'm a woman? So I slept with you last night. Big deal. Big fucking deal. What difference does it make? You were against me before and you're still against me now.

Karen thought about how she had put his life in danger at Sylvester Wolfe's house. Was it all her fault? He knew she was green; he should have gone first. How could she learn anything if he wouldn't help her?

He had put in for a new partner. Fine, but she suspected that because of department politics, his request would be turned down again. Not unless she requested one too. There were just too many cops on the job who resented working with women. Well, too bad for them, women were there to stay. They would have to learn to live with it. She felt a certain surge of power as she realized that is was she who held the cards if he wanted to be free of her.

She deeply regretted that they had been teamed together in the first place. She had been warned that this "seasoned veteran" was a macho creep, but she had viewed it as simply another challenge. Now it had grown to be tiresome. What did she have to prove to him anyhow? If anything, he was holding her back, not teaching her anything except for his cliché "look past the obvious."

More than ever, she regretted sleeping with him, even if he did have a fabulous body. Had she been in a normal state of mind last night it never would have happened, but the tangle with Wolfe had left her shaken. Compound that with the fact that she and Tony shared the necessary ingredients for passion: attraction and revulsion, affection and animosity, a desire to control and be controlled.

She thought of the exact minute when he had slammed her to the ground, protecting her from the deadly barrel of Sylvester's gun. In that one crushing moment when he pressed the entire length of his body along her, she experienced an electricity unlike anything she had ever known before. All that was quickly forgotten in the ensuing hail of bullets, but it had sparked right up again when he touched her hand in the bar. There had been an ember smoldering there all along, and last night it flared and burned hard and fast. Too hard and too fast. She was standing in the ashes of it now.

As he stood there beside her, his body language showing her nothing but disdain, she viewed him in a different light. Why should she be intimidated by his male role playing? Sure, they had slept together, but she had slept with him the same as he had slept with her. She had used him last night to play out the biggest myth of all, that men, with their strength and power, were women's protectors.

What a fairy tale that was! Like her parents . . . Her father had never really run the household. He may have been the bread-winner, but it was her mother who was the strong one. It was she who called all the shots, made the final decisions. Her father was only a figurehead.

And she had seen the same things with her friend's families too. It always seemed to be the women who held things together even with husbands who drank or left them or showed them no kind of respect at all. Karen had been an observant little girl and she had seen all this from an early age and wanted always to remember it. The women were the ones who really cared—they were the protectors.

That was the real reason she had become a cop—she wanted to take care of things, not wait for some man to do it. Not when she could do it herself. And no one, especially not Tony with his Neanderthal world view, was going to keep her from it. Sure he was walking cocksure today, but the truth of the matter was that she had fucked him as much as he had fucked her. Well, she wasn't going to put up with his posturing anymore. She had tried to play the nice way, now it was going to be hardball.

The elevator doors were opening, and she and her partner squeezed into the crowded car. Karen's dander was up, and she realized if she was going to make the most of her anger, she had better do it now.

"Goddamn it, Tony," she said, ignoring the sidelong glances of the other passengers, mostly cops and mostly men. "I don't care anymore what you think of me, or last night, or working with a female, or anything else. I care about one thing, my job. And you are not going to ruin my chances for a promotion by pigeonholing me or ignoring me or making me look bad to the Lieutenant. We're partners? I don't like it anymore than you, buster, so I'll make you a deal. I'll go along with your request for a new partner if you promise me one thing. I want to stay on until we resolve this case. After that, you'll be free of me."

There were a few muffled snickers in the rear of the elevator, and Tony's face reddened visibly. Karen couldn't tell whether that was from anger or embarrassment and frankly, she didn't care. Not anymore. Not one iota. He had pushed her too far. He shot her what was meant to be a withering glance and said gruffly under his breath, "Let it wait a minute, okay?"

Karen turned eyes forward in the elevator and didn't say another word until they reached the ground floor.

"What did you go and do that for?" Tony blasted as they stepped off and the other passengers quickly dispersed. "I knew some of those guys; they're laughing their dicks off at me."

"Too bad," Karen retorted. "That's how I feel, like everybody's been laughing at me ever since I've been teamed with you, walking like a Chinese bride twenty paces behind. I've had it with you.

What do you say about my offer? You include me in this case, and when it's through, I'll put in for the change."

"As soon as we finish this case?"

"The very moment."

"Well, then let's get to work, partner." He extended his hand and they shook on the deal, Karen matching his firm grip. He held her hand a minute too long. Disgusted, she yanked her hand from his, and in her action, she felt she had scored a victory.

The wino was a white-haired, red-nosed man named Tim who looked about sixty and was actually about forty. He sat in an interrogation room, looking about nervously. He wasn't fearful of the police; he had dealt with them many times and the prospect of being roughed up a little held no particular threat for him. The cops were nothing compared to the overzealous neo-Nazis running around the city these days who might kick a sleeping drunk in the stomach or set him on fire.

No, Tim was more worried about how much longer he would be detained, and that was causing him discomfort. He had to get out of there and find himself some hooch before he started getting sick. Very sick. Already, his hands were shaking.

Tim was relieved when the door finally opened and a man and a woman walked in. They introduced themselves as detectives, and Tim was surprised, he had never seen a female detective before. Oh, well, nothing shocked him anymore. Maybe she was a soft touch, and he could hit her up for a few bucks after they were finished here. Go out and buy that bottle of Thunderbird he was dreaming about.

"Would you like to take charge of this, Detective Levinson?" the big guy asked of his partner. Tim thought he detected the trace of a smile across her lips.

Karen sat down and sized up Tim. It didn't take more than a moment for her to recognize that there was no way he was their murderer. He was a rumpled bum, his rheumy eyes staring at her from the face of someone who wasn't all there. She deferred to Tony.

"No, Detective Perrelli. If you don't mind I would be happy to observe your expertise."

"As you wish, Detective Levinson." Tim was confused, he had

never seen cops act like this before. Usually they squared off, with that ridiculous good cop, bad cop routine that everyone had seen a million times. He just wished that they would get on with it. Time was of the essence. His stomach was beginning to churn and he feared it wouldn't be long now before the shakes came.

"Tim, we want to ask you a few questions about that collar you tried to hock this afternoon."

"What about it, officer?" said Tim politely, trying his best to be agreeable.

"Do you remember where you got it?"

"Yeah, sure. I pulled it out of a dumpster in the east eighties."

Karen and Tony exchanged knowing looks. Jennifer's apartment was in the east eighties.

"When?" asked Tony.

"It was a while ago. I've been saving it for an emergency."

"You wouldn't happen to know when a while ago was, would you?" Tony asked patiently. He realized this was going to take a bit of deductive work.

"Oh, a while ago," Tim repeated. He was shifting uncomfortably in his chair now, his grizzled face reddening. He clutched his stomach and began to moan. "Oh, I'm not feeling so well," he said. Oh great, thought Tony. Just what they needed.

Karen looked at him with concern. "I think he's sick. Maybe we should call a doctor."

"Maybe you should grab the garbage pail and put it in front of his face," said Tony. "I'll be right back." He rushed out the door and Karen found herself face to face with Tim, who was looking worse with each passing second.

"Don't worry," she assured him. "Detective Perrelli has gone to get a doctor." She opened the door and stuck her head out. Tony was nowhere in sight. Tim stared at her with disbelief and doubled up over his chair. "I don't feel good at all," he said and as Karen looked on horrified he began to spew vomit on the floor, a dark coffee-colored stream that splattered on the grey tiles. She turned her head away, and noticed the trash can in the corner. That was what Tony had meant, damn him. Where had he gone anyway?

He was gone for ten minutes, during which time the bum retched again, but this time it was into the wastepaper basket that Karen had finally placed before him. When Tony reappeared his face was flushed as if from running and the smell of fresh cold air radiated off him. He was carrying a brown paper bag, and he immediately assessed the situation, taking in the moaning bum and the reeking puddle on the floor. "Too late, I guess," he quipped.

Tim raised his ashen face and was looking with a great deal of interest at Tony as he withdrew a bottle of Old Irish Rose from the bag and twisted the cap off. He placed it on the table. "Here's the doctor."

Tim grabbed the bottle and drank from it greedily, a man who had spent days in the desert with a powerful thirst. Karen watched with amazement as the color returned to his face almost immediately. He sat up straight and belched.

"Now, Tim," Tony continued as if there had never been any interruption. "Tell us about finding this collar."

"Like I said, I was rummaging through a dumpster looking for cans or whatever when I felt something furry. I jumped near a mile. I was sure it was a rat. But when I calmed down, I looked closer and I saw it was a kitty, a dead kitty wearing this fancy collar. I figured the cat didn't have no use for it, so I took it. I didn't know I was breaking any law."

"The cat was dead?" asked Tony, keenly interested.

"Yes sir. Poor little thing. It's head was bashed in."

As if on a single wavelength, Karen and Tony stared at each other. Tony turned back to the wino.

"When was this?"

"Sometime late last week. Could've been Friday. That's the day I usually work uptown."

"All right, Tim. You can go after you clean up that mess. I'll get you some paper towels."

"Thanks, Captain," said the wino good-naturedly, his equilibrium restored for the time being.

XXXIX

Bunny peered down from the safe haven of her second story office. She couldn't believe what she was seeing. That maniacal harpy who had been leading the marches in front of her store all week was spray painting the mink coat of a passerby. Would this ever stop? She applauded loudly as the police arrived and watched as they made several arrests, loading the demonstrators into waiting squad cars.

I must get the name of that poor woman, thought Bunny. Offer to replace her coat or something. See if we can't get a little positive publicity out of this, turn a bad situation into an opportunity.

As the police closed the doors and drove off with their prisoners, Bunny's eyes fell upon a familiar figure poised on the pavement. She could tell by the timid, unassuming posture that it was Leslie Warning. Bunny watched with interest as she juggled an ungainly shoulder bag and a pair of animal traps while trying to hail a cab. It's too bad she wasn't arrested too, thought Bunny. Let that little bitch who has never had to worry about a cent in her life spend some time in prison. That might give her a taste of what the world's all about.

The excitement over, the march continued peacefully in front of her window, but it appeared to have lost much of its momentum. Disappointed that the police hadn't used the spray paint incident to break the whole thing up, Bunny finally vacated her perch and returned to her desk. She flipped open her ostrich skin briefcase and took out a thick organizer. She had promised her father-in-law that she would come up with something today—the charity program they were going to use to offset the ill-will created by the animal rights people. She thumbed through the organizer, looking for the name of someone who would be a good liaison. Finally, she came upon the name of Kimberly Johnson, who was involved in a number of shelters for battered wives and their children. That was a timely cause, and one sure to appeal to women, thought Bunny. Perfect for their purposes.

She arranged to meet with Kimberly Johnson that afternoon. Bunny had explained most of the program on the phone. She wasn't going to make the same mistake twice—assuming that people would be grateful for her help. But Kimberly had been so enthusiastic that, when Bunny hung up, she called Swank's P.R. firm to start the ball rolling. She wanted to get as much mileage out of this as she could. Then she called Sarah in and instructed her to contact the police for the name of the woman who had been assaulted with spray paint in front of the store.

Feeling good, because she had killed off two major birds so far this day, she took a break and headed down the hall to the lounge.

Swank's powder room had been designed with the furrier's upscale image in mind. Mirrored vanities with silk upholstered stools lined one wall of the waiting room, and upon their glass tops were packaged brushes and combs, atomizers of popular colognes, and samples of lipstick and other cosmetics, for the use of their patrons. The thinking at Swank was that if a woman felt good about herself, she would be more apt to want to indulge that self with a fur coat.

There were a couple of private rooms off the lounge. One was Bunny's personal dressing room where she kept changes of clothes for all occasions and duplicates of all her toiletries. The other room had belonged to Jennifer, the place where she could keep her makeup and extra clothes as well as her personal belongings. Bunny unlocked the door to Jennifer's room and peered in.

She hadn't entered it since that Monday, the day she had spoken her last words with Jennifer. As she looked around the little room with its tidy stacks of books and magazines, she mused about how Jennifer would lock herself in here to kill time between shoots or in store modeling sessions. She used to hide up here like a hermit, closing off the rest of the world. Jennifer had been a real loner in the end. Almost as if she had lost interest in people.

A canvas tote bag filled with books was slung over the back of Jennifer's low dressing table chair. Curious, Bunny pulled the topmost book out. *The Animal's Treatise* glared at her from the cover, the words striking deep into her heart. How dare Jennifer bring this sort of tripe in here, she thought angrily. She flipped through it chapter by chapter. The author decried everything from animal testing of cosmetics to using animals for food. A large section was dedicated to the use of animal skins for fur coats. There were pictures of birds and domestic pets that had stumbled into traps meant for fur-bearing animals. Bunny slammed the book shut. She dug through the rest of the bag. The other books were innocuous, some contemporary, some classic. At the very bottom of the bag, Bunny discovered a leather-bound diary. It was locked. She began to rummage through the drawers of the dressing table, and far to the back of one she found a tiny gold key. It fit the gold lock, and Bunny opened the book. She turned to the back of it. The last entry was dated Monday, November 12—the same day they had talked. As Bunny read it, her face turned scarlet. She slammed her fist down on the dressing table in an act of fury, and then calmed herself. She closed the book, and slipped it under the jacket of her suit.

She walked stiffly back into her office, holding her arm so that the bulge of the book would not be visible to her secretary. As she walked past, Sarah called out to her, "Mrs. Nilsson, I got that woman's name. It's right here," she said, holding a slip of paper out toward her boss.

"Fine, Sarah, fine. Thank you. I'll come back for it in a moment," Bunny responded distantly, walking past the befuddled secretary and into her office. Once inside, she locked the door behind her and withdrew the diary, hurriedly secreting it inside her briefcase. She locked it carefully, and removed the key from her key ring, putting it in her pocket and returning the rest of her keys to her purse. She slid the briefcase under her desk, and returned to her earlier perch in the window. She was glad to see the marchers had dissipated by then, the cold having driven the last of them off.

She would have to destroy the diary as soon as possible. This weekend she would burn it page by page in the fireplace. Thank God she had found it before anyone else. She couldn't believe she hadn't thought to check Jennifer's things before.

That little bitch, thought Bunny, staring at nothing out the window, her eyes glazed over. In fact there was a far better word Bunny could apply to her. Suddenly she felt old and tired. She thought again about what she had read, and she knew there was someone else she had to share it with. And he would not be happy. She did not want to anticipate what his anger would be.

XL

Leslie climbed the steps wearily and went into her quarters where the two cats meowed happily at the sight of her. She was exhausted. She threw Mary Ellen's heavy bag and the assortment of traps into the corner and flopped down upon a chaise lounge. Her body ached and she felt as though she had been hit by a truck. She knew if she weren't still so frozen it would be worse.

She cuddled the two cats close to her, appreciating their softness and warmth. "What a day I had today," she said to them. She pulled a handknit throw blanket over herself where she lay and closed her eyes. Within moments, she was asleep.

When she awakened to the sound of the phone ringing, it was dark outside. She regretted having rushed to pick it up when her eager hello was answered by the dour voice of her brother. She gazed out of the blackness of the darkened room, thinking about how much she hated this time of year, the time when the days grew ever shorter.

"So how was it?" asked Larry, his whiny voice chiding as always. "Should we watch for you on the news?"

"No, but you can watch for Mary Ellen as usual," she conceded. "She and Keith were arrested after Mary Ellen spray painted a woman's mink coat."

"That's vintage Mary Ellen for you. I've never known anyone who enjoyed making an ass out of herself more."

"Leave her alone, Larry. It's just her way. She is so dedicated to her causes."

"Was Keith spray painting innocent people, too?" he asked.

"You know Keith. He's too much of a pacifist for that."

"Still waters run deep," he countered. "I'm surprised you're not down there bailing them out."

"Some of the others are taking care of it," said Leslie. With her money, she thought, but she didn't bother to pass that information on to Larry. He would be wild if he ever knew how much money she poured into causes like S.T.S. and the Hunger Exchange. "I'm sure you didn't call to talk to me about Mary Ellen, Larry. What is it?"

"I wondered if you had given any more thought to signing the papers we discussed."

"My God, Larry. Do you ever give up? I gave you my answer. I really don't want to discuss it anymore."

"But think of what you could do with all that cash. You could single-handedly support five or six major charities."

"Leave me alone, Larry." Leslie was growing impatient, and was irritated with him in the first place for not being Neil. "I said I don't want to discuss it and I meant it. Now good-bye," she said, slamming the receiver down. She knew she ought to be ashamed of her outburst, but in fact she felt excited and relieved. She was finally able to stand up to her brother. Maybe being with Neil was giving her more confidence.

She turned on some lights in the sitting room and noticed it was almost six o'clock. Yolanda Prince's "In Depth" interview with Mary Ellen should be coming on. She flipped on the television just in time to catch the beginning. She wondered if Mary Ellen had made it out of jail in time to watch herself.

The show opened with Yolanda giving a short introduction about the fur industry. "No small business by any means, it is a 1.8 billion dollar industry that employs 250,000 people in the United States and another 80,000 in Canada at its various levels, not to mention the thousands of ranchers and trappers who supply the raw skins.

"But in recent years, the sale of fur has dropped off as much as twenty percent in this country as more and more people take exception to the wearing of animal skins. The fur industry argues that they are working ever harder to insure that treatment of all animals used in the making of fur coats is humane.

"Tonight on 'In Depth' we hope to explore both sides of that issue."

Next, Michael Nilsson spoke proudly of the history of the business, how it was fur traders who actually explored and settled this country, and that his industry, one so very intrinsic to America, was operating under higher standards than ever before.

Leslie stroked Edward and Amanda protectively.

Mary Ellen was shown next, explaining with a great deal of emotion what a "wring off" was. "The frantic animal leaves his paw behind in the trap, chewing it off in his quest for freedom. Is this humane?"

Yolanda addressed the issue of "wring-offs" with Michael. "The actual number of 'wring-offs' is far fewer than the animal rights enthusiasts would have you believe. And now we are working with more humane traps like the conibear trap, which kills the animal instantly. Also, new legislation requires trappers to check their traps frequently."

Mary Ellen came on and compared the fur trade to the slave trade. Leslie winced. Michael Nilsson spoke of the 100,000 Canadian trappers, half of whom were aboriginals and depended upon their income from trapping to support their families. Mary Ellen pointed out that it could take twenty minutes for a beaver or muskrat to succumb inside a drowning set, a weighted trap set in deep water.

A segment of the show consisted solely of people on the street giving their opinions. "I used to wear fur until the animal rights people scared me away from it. You can't be sure what these people will do." "I have a fur coat, but I won't wear it anymore. Think of all the suffering that went into making it." "I think it's a shame that people are putting animal rights before human rights these days."

As the show wound up, Leslie had to admire Yolanda for showing both sides of the issue fairly. She presented information and let her viewers draw their own conclusions. Leslie only hoped they could see it her way, that to cause pain to God's creatures was wrong.

There was a commercial, and then Yolanda came on to announce the topic of her next special.

"In recent years there have been attacks on some of New York's most celebrated fashion models. In my next show we will explore some of these attacks and the lives of the victims—Charlene Wright, a poor little rich girl whose face was slashed by hooligans, and Sophie Tochowitz, who reigned as the glamorous Jennifer O'Grady until she was found murdered earlier this week. Until next week then, I am Yolanda Prince."

Leslie straightened in her chair. That name. Sophie Tochowitz. Where did she know that name from?

Before she could solve that particular puzzle, her thoughts were interrupted by the sound of a door slamming downstairs in the kitchen. She sat frozen in her chair, the cats asleep atop the blanket on her lap, listening to the unmistakable thud of footsteps crossing the ceramic tile floor. Next, the unseen visitor mounted the back stairs, and Leslie listened with her heart in her throat, as the rhythmic footsteps came closer and closer. The steps were not tentative; the intruder walked at a steady and sure gait. Paralyzed with fear, she gasped as she saw the silhouette of a man move into the doorway. She grabbed Amanda and held her tight. Edward had jumped to the floor.

The figure in her doorway rapped two times against the door frame.

"Anyone home?"

"Larry!" she cried at the sound of his voice. "You just scared me half to death. Why didn't you tell me you were coming?"

"After you hung up on me, I didn't know if you would let me in. But I couldn't have my favorite sister mad at me, so I came over to iron things out."

"Still, you could have announced yourself. Look at my hand," she said, holding it out. "It's shaking."

"I'm sorry," said Larry, his soft, weak face falling into a fleshy pout, making him appear all the more comical. "Did I scare oow? I'm sowwy," he teased in a baby voice. Then, switching back to his usual high-pitched whine, he added, "Next time I'll announce myself from downstairs."

"I'd appreciate it, Larry," she said, ignoring his sarcasm. At times she regretted that he still had a key to the house, but she had never had the nerve to ask him to relinquish it, even after her parents' death. In many ways he had as much right to be there as she did.

Larry settled himself down in an armchair opposite her and petted Edward, who was sniffing at him curiously. The cat jumped back from his reach and hissed at him. "Stupid animals, I don't know how you can stand them," he huffed.

"That's odd," said Leslie. "I've never seen him do that."

The phone rang, and she grabbed it eagerly. Her heart fluttered as she heard the sweet sound of Neil's voice.

"How are you today?" he asked.

"Fine," she said, then after a loud, involuntary sneeze, she added, "Except I'm coming down with a terrible cold. I think it's from spending too much time outside this week."

"Poor baby," he said. "Then I guess you won't want to go out for a bite to eat. How about if I bring over a veggie and goat cheese pizza?"

The thought of being in the house alone with Neil made her nervous, but it was a good nervousness.

"That sounds great," she said as she sneezed again into the phone. "Aren't you afraid of catching my cold?"

"I'd catch anything you want to throw me. I'll see you in about thirty minutes."

She was grinning as she hung up. Larry was staring at her. "You do look a little green around the gills," he said.

Her face fell. "It's this nasty cold." She put the back of her hand to her forehead. "I think I'm starting to get a fever. Oh, maybe I should call Neil back and tell him not to come."

"So Neil's coming over here? Don't cheat me of the opportunity to meet your mysterious lover."

Leslie flushed red. She knew Larry was teasing her, but he was always teasing her. "He's not my lover," she snapped, "but I'll let you meet him anyway. In fact, I'm glad you'll be meeting him. I want to know what you think of him." Larry was, after all, her only living relative.

They watched television then without conversation, this un-usual brother and sister, who had nothing in common but their late father and some complicated financial interests. Leslie stud-ied Larry as he sat there beside her. Despite the way he worked so hard to irritate her, she really did love him. He had his own sad-nesses and disappointments, she thought. Maybe if they spent more time together they would talk more and get along better.

Oddly enough, Larry was having thoughts along the same lines, but for entirely different reasons. He should spend more time with the painfully boring mouse, he was thinking, because per-haps if he befriended her instead of fighting with her all the time, he could get his way. What was it that his mother had tried so hard to teach him? Oh yes, you catch more flies with honey than with vinegar.

When the doorbell rang a half hour later, Larry jumped to an-swer it. Laying idly on the chaise beneath the throw blanket, Les-lie really was beginning to feel feverish, and she wondered if hav-ing Neil come over had been a big mistake. Her doubts were dispelled when he entered the room, his face red with the cold, his auburn hair tousled by the wind. He wore a heavy wool jacket, still buttoned all the way up, and in his right hand was a large pizza box. She thought her heart would break with love, and she was suddenly conscious of her own red nose and watery eyes.

"Reinforcements," he called out casually, but the words seemed forced, unusual for him. He appeared nervous as he bent over to give Leslie a peck on the cheek, a simple gesture that filled her with warmth. She was aware of a smirking Larry hovering near the door.

"Did my brother introduce himself?" she asked, sorry now that he had stayed.

"I didn't need to, Leslie," said Larry smugly. "We already know each other, Neil's a regular at Mulligan's and we've raised more than a few glasses together there. Isn't that so, Neil?"

"Right, Larry," Neil conceded cheerlessly. He looked uncomfortable.

Larry was thinking of some of the girls he'd seen leaving the bar with Neil at various times. They were the type he never got to first base with. Good-looking guys like Neil had all the luck. He bet Neil got laid plenty. What then was he doing with Leslie? Larry knew there wasn't any action there.

"In fact," said Larry, "we've even talked about you, Leslie. I told Neil all about my vegetarian sister who loved to spend Saturday afternoons in Central Park." This was true; however, at the time, Larry was lamenting being hooked to "a wacko rich sister who wasted her Saturdays feeding the pigeons."

"And you two end up dating! Is it a small world or what?"

Neil cleared his throat and the sound echoed in a room suddenly quiet. Leslie stared at him in disbelief. From her semi-reclining position on the chaise lounge, she began to feel her entire newfound world of happiness and love slipping out from under her. It was sliding away in one brief eye-opening moment.

The look on Neil's face was apologetic. He reached out to touch Leslie's arm, but she sat straight up, withdrawing from his reach. Even Larry could feel the changed climate in the room.

Her eyes welling with tears, Leslie felt as though she couldn't breathe, could barely see. She looked at Neil through the blur. "I think you better leave," she said, without anger but with plenty of grief. "Just go away."

"Leslie . . ." Neil pleaded. "It looks bad, I know it does, but it's not the way you think. Not entirely. Give me a chance to explain."

"Go away," she repeated, and without another word she rolled off the chaise and ran into the bedroom, slamming the door shut.

"Leslie!" Neil called.

"Leave me alone. Get out of my house, right now!"

Neil turned to Larry. "Help me out here, Larry."

Larry was amused and puzzled. "I don't even know what happened," he said. "One minute she's fine, the next gaga. But I do know she's obstinate as hell, so whatever she's mad about, I don't think you're going to get her to change her mind about it tonight."

"What set her off like that?"

"Damn you, Larry," said Neil. "You are a social Neanderthal. You did, by what you just told her about me. It just so happens that we met in Central Park, while she was feeding the birds!"

After she was sure they had both gone, Leslie ventured out from her bedroom and went into the bathroom to rinse her face. She had never been a beauty to begin with, and she certainly looked the worse for wear now. She hadn't felt like this, hadn't cried like this, since the death of her parents, and she was feeling the same way she had felt then. Like she was trying to climb glass. She was helpless, betrayed, alone. How could he? she thought. He had been using her all along. He only wanted her for her money.

She blew her nose hard and felt some temporary relief of the pressure in her head. The combination of her cold and crying had given her a throbbing headache, and she felt so miserable of body and heart that she wanted to die. Everybody wanted something from her, everybody. Larry, Mary Ellen, Bunny Nilsson, and now Neil. Doesn't anyone just want me for me, myself? she wondered.

Neil's pizza was still unopened in the sitting room, and she decided that despite her misery, she was hungry. She opened the cardboard box and looked at the cold pie, its top a congealed mess of broccoli, onions, mushrooms and little white pieces of goat cheese. She picked up a piece and took a bite, chewing slowly, and as she chewed she thought about how considerate Neil had been, never trying to force meat on her, going out of his way to accommodate her diet.

Tears began to flow again, and unable to swallow, she spit the partially chewed piece of pizza into her palm. She stood there holding the messy glop of vegetables and tomato sauce in her hand, her small body wracked with sighs. Throwing herself down onto the chaise, she cried her eyes out once again with no one to hear her and no one to care except for two worried cats who climbed beside her and rubbed their bodies against her with concern.

XLI

It was well after two A.M. by the time Keith and Mary Ellen made bail and were released. The judge had stated in no uncertain terms that he was disgusted with Mary Ellen and the overzealous tactics she employed in her quest for animal rights, and he set an unusually high bond for both of them. It was obvious that Keith wasn't happy with the situation as he and Mary Ellen stood outside the courthouse, the chill wind railing at them, blowing their hair across their faces.

Mary Ellen, unfazed as always, pulled wayward strands from her mouth as she shivered against the cold. "Well, that was an adventure, wouldn't you say?"

Keith remained quiet. He was disgusted with her for getting them arrested and detained in cold holding cells crowded with undesirables who made sport of tormenting him. Getting arrested in New York City was no pleasant experience and the detention cell brought back many unpleasant memories. Keith stuffed his hands into the pockets of his army coat, and started to walk away from Mary Ellen.

"Wait," she called to him. "Where are you going?"

"Home. To get some sleep. Why don't you do the same?" he said, impatiently.

"I'd like to, but Leslie has my keys. She has my purse." She waited for an invitation to stay at Keith's, but none came. After pondering for a moment, she said, "Lend me your office key. I'll stay there."

Keith hesitated a minute as if he had undergone a change of mind, but he then went ahead and pulled a keyring from his pocket. He removed a key and tossed it to Mary Ellen, who caught it with some difficulty in her mittened hand. Keith turned his back on her and walked away.

"Thanks, Keith. Night, Keith. Don't worry about me, I'll be fine," she called to his disappearing figure. He never even turned around. He must be real mad, she thought.

She didn't have much money on her, but she did have enough for a cab to Soho, so she flagged one down and gave the driver the S.T.S. address. She only had a quarter left after paying the fare, and this she tipped to the driver, earning herself a searing look that she shrugged off with her usual aplomb.

The office was toasty warm, a delightful contrast to the bone-chilling cold outside and the dank chill of the holding cell where she had just spent so many hours. She had been crammed in with dozens of other female offenders, most of them reeking of booze, and having the musky scent of bodies that hadn't seen a bar of soap in months. She wouldn't miss the cold cement floor where she had sat in close quarters with her fellow detainees for so many hours, her nose never quite adjusting to the more odoriferous of them.

There were extra coats in the office and a few blankets in the back room, and she piled these up on the floor near the hissing radiator. An exhausted Mary Ellen turned out the light and flopped down onto her makeshift bed. It was quite comfortable actually—a hell of a lot better than some of the places she had slept in her life. Within minutes she was asleep.

She was awakened an hour later by a sound at the office door. Her senses heightened by the quiet and the dark, she lay still and listened. It was quiet for a minute and she thought that her mind had been playing tricks on her. Then she heard the noise again. Someone was fiddling with the office door. Of that she was now sure. She could hear scratching. She got to her feet and was trying to think of what she could use to protect herself when she heard the undeniable sound of wood giving way as the doorjamb separated from the door frame. Her heart pounding, she dropped to her hands and knees and crawled into the inner office. She huddled in a corner, thinking that the intruder was probably just a burglar and if he didn't see her, he would just go away. For a crazed moment she regretted her stand for gun control.

The light came on in the outer room, and she could hear the sound of drawers being ransacked. Take the typewriter, she thought. Take the computer. Take it all. She drew further back into her corner, suddenly quite aware of her mortality. The intruder continued to open and shut drawers. After a few minutes that sound stopped, and she could see a large figure framed in the doorway as it hesitated before coming in. Fingernails bared, she leaped on it in the darkness.

XLII

SATURDAY MORNING

Karen and Tony stood in the Soho office of S.T.S., or rather what was left of it. It had been thoroughly trashed, stacks of papers strewn about, file cabinets overturned, typewriter, telephones and computer smashed and destroyed.

"Whoever did this did it with a vengeance," said Tony, shaking his head. The office was crowded with the usual complement of investigators, the forensics people, police photographers and once again, Nat Bradlee. He stood before Tony, an ashen cast over the dark chocolate tones of his face. His deep brown eyes had seen too much.

"It's a mess in there," he said, indicating the inner office behind him. "The girl must have fought like a banshee, but she was no match for this guy. He beat her to death with something. We haven't found the weapon yet. She probably died very quickly after the initial contact, after he was finally able to get to her."

"How do you know she fought?" asked Karen.

"There was a substantial amount of blood and skin under her fingernails. I'm willing to bet he's pretty scratched up."

Karen shuddered at the image of Mary Ellen clawing viciously at the air, at the face of an assailant. She closed her eyes against the thought, but was brought back to the very unpleasant reality by her partner's voice saying, "Well, we might as well go and take a look."

"Have you gotten tough enough yet, young lady?" Nat Bradlee asked her.

"I honestly don't know," she replied.

The inner office was a sea of red, blood everywhere it seemed, a testimony to the brute force with which Mary Ellen had been hit. Her life's essence had been sprayed about the room. In the far corner lay the crumpled body, the arms still raised above the head in a protective gesture. Karen stood mutely by as her partner examined the body close up. She averted her eyes and looked about the room. It too was a mess, papers all about, drawers pulled from the desk, equipment destroyed. Was this destruction an extension of the violence that had taken place? Or was the murderer looking for something?

"God, I'm tired of looking at the bashed-in heads of women," said Tony.

"Do you think this one is connected to the other two?" Karen asked.

"I know I think that it's more than a coincidence that the last three female homicides I've seen have all been killed by the same method."

"Yes, but the first two appear to have been done by some animal rights fanatic. Why would the same person then go after Mary Ellen?"

"I don't know, but one thing's for sure," he said.

"What's that?" she queried.

"We can't blame this one on Sylvester K. Wolfe."

Keith Geiger lived in a seedy section of the lower East Side. As they walked down the street, passing degenerates who shuddered in the gutters and others who leeringly checked her out from top to bottom, Karen felt the ambivalent relief of having the tall detective close by her side. She fingered her badge in her pocket, and wondered how much difference it would make to any of these people if she flashed it. Somehow, she thought, it wouldn't make much of an impression.

There was no buzzer on the door of the small walkup, so they went straight in the front of the building and up two flights of creaky stairs to the door marked 3R. "Somehow I don't picture this as a love nest," said Tony, checking out the peeling paint and the shabby condition of the building. He knocked sharply at the door, standing to one side of it. Karen followed his lead and stood to the other side.

There was a muffled voice from inside. "Who is it?" they heard.

"It's Detectives Perrelli and Levinson. We'd like to speak with you."

There was a reluctant pause and then the door slid slowly open. Karen looked toward it anxiously, ready this time for any departure from the expected. There was none.

Keith opened the door a quarter of the way. He was naked from the waist up and was wearing blue jeans. He was barefoot. She had the impression that they had awakened him.

Tony must have felt the same way. "Tired this morning, Keith?" he asked, his voice filled with skepticism.

"I didn't sleep too well last night."

"Something on your mind?"

Karen could practically see Keith's heart beating through his skinny chest as he fought to maintain his composure. He made little attempt to hide his disdain for the detective.

"Listen, Perrelli. I know you're after me for something, but whatever it is you're dead wrong. You've got the wrong guy, okay? Now is there something legitimate you want from me or are you just going to harass me?"

"What do you know about the death of Mary Ellen Fitzsimmons?" Tony asked coldly.

Karen could see the look of total shock appear on Keith's face. He started to speak, stopped for a second, then tried again. "What are you talking about, Mary Ellen's *death?*"

As far as Karen could tell he was genuinely surprised . . . either that or he was one of the finest actors ever born. She could even read the look of hope on his face—hope that he had heard Tony wrong. She could tell that he was praying that what Tony had just told him wasn't so.

Unlike Karen, Tony wasn't seeing it that way. He didn't believe the tears that were beginning to well in Keith's mysterious eyes. "Mary Ellen was murdered sometime early this morning in the S.T.S. offices," he said, without a shred of sympathy.

The look on Keith's face was that of a wounded creature. His cheeks fell even more hollow and his deep-set eyes became shrouds of pain. His face turned a ghostly white, its very paleness setting off the blue-green veins at his temples like rivers on a relief map. Karen thought he was going to faint.

"Come in," he said weakly, throwing the door open wide for them.

The apartment struck Karen as odd. It was clean and unsluttered, but decorated in such a somber fashion that she immediately had a sense of gloom upon entering. An old mustard corduroy sofa dominated the longest wall, a card table with a lamp sat beside it. Heavy old draperies were pulled open to let in whatever rays of light could find their way in through the two small windows. A narrow kitchen, its miniature stove and refrigerator ancient and yellowing, was visible to the right. Karen guessed that the bedroom and bathroom were down the narrow hallway to the left.

The only other furniture in the room were two folding chairs that Keith offered to them numbly. He seated himself in the center of the couch and placed his head in his hands, propping his arms up on his long legs.

"Tell me what happened," was all he said.

"Someone broke into the S.T.S. office with a crowbar last night. Made a mess of it. Finished up by making a mess of Mary Ellen."

"But how? How was she killed?"

"Bludgeoned to death."

"Uhmph!" The choked sound of pain emanated from Keith Geiger's throat.

"Keith," she said softly, "can you tell us what happened yesterday? When was the last time you saw Mary Ellen?"

"We were bailed out about two o'clock in the morning," he said, forming the words with difficulty. "We didn't really speak after that. I was angry with her for getting me arrested. I have this thing about jail . . . I can't stand being locked up . . . contained. She asked me for my key to the office, and I gave it to her.

"I think she wanted to come with me, but I didn't want to be around her, I was so angry. So I left her there on the street, just like that. Caught a bus and came home. Left her standing there . . ."

He looked as though he wanted to say more, but instead he

buried his face in his upturned palms and gave a high-pitched whine that tore at Karen with its primal rawness. Then he started to sob, his narrow shoulders wracked with spasms.

Tony was unmoved. He glanced at Karen with eyes that were trying to communicate something she was unable to read, and then he turned them on Keith. "Can I use the can?" he asked.

Keith nodded weakly, his head still buried in his hands, the gesture barely discernible. The folding chair squeaked as Tony rose; the only other noise in the room was the heartrending sound of a man crying. Karen felt the urge to go to Keith and put her arms about him. But instead she sat silently waiting for Tony to come back.

He was gone for an unusually long time, and when he did return, he had a hard look on his face, his jaw was set in a determined manner, and his gun was drawn. Without hesitation, he walked directly to Keith and ordered him to get up from the couch slowly.

"You are under arrest," he stated.

"Tony!" cried Karen, mystified. "What are you doing?" She whispered in his ear. "This man didn't kill anyone, I just know it. He doesn't have any scratches, the coroner said there'd be scratches."

"Nat's been wrong before," said Tony, his eyes never leaving Keith for a moment. "Why don't you take a look in the bedroom."

Karen walked tentatively down the short dark hallway. The bedroom door was ajar and she stuck her head inside. The room was dim and gloomy like the rest of the apartment. Along one wall was a twin bed, unmade.

The entire wall opposite was a collage of war. It was covered with photographs of war and newspaper headlines and articles. As Karen examined it further, her eyes were met by many gruesome scenes, snapshots of corpses of soldiers and civilians, women, children, old men. Newspaper articles dated March 1971 announced the conviction of Lieutenant William Calley for the murder of twenty-two Vietnamese civilians at My Lai. Other articles decried his conviction as a miscarriage of justice. And then she noticed an old photograph with two young soldiers standing side by side in fatigues and flak jackets. One she recognized from the newspaper pictures as Lieutenant Calley. The other was Keith Geiger.

There was a small table in front of the wall and on it was a pair of well-worn army boots, a set of dog tags and a small wooden box. Leaning against the table was a darkened piece of wood about two feet long. It appeared to be a piece of a tree branch, but thick and knotted at one end. She picked it up. It was heavy and dense, but not too large. Something that could easily be concealed under a long coat. An army coat? She looked at it more closely. The end was stained a deep rusty brown. The color of dried blood?

Her curiosity piqued, she reached out and opened the small wooden box. She had to stop herself from screaming when she saw that inside was an old dried piece of cartilage she recognized to be a human ear.

She closed the box quickly and hurried back into the living room where Tony had Keith laying face down on the floor, his hands cuffed behind his back. Still thinking of what she had just seen, she felt distanced from what she was watching in front of her. She only barely heard her partner as he instructed her to call in for assistance.

"But, Tony, what about his rights, a search warrant?"

"We don't need it. He let us in voluntarily. Can I help it if I had to go to the john and he left his bedroom door open with a murder weapon right in sight."

Keith was getting nervous. His crying had stopped and he looked anxiously from detective to detective. "Please," he begged. "You can't arrest me. I can't go into prison. You don't understand." He strained and pulled at his cuffed wrists, squirming about the floor. That was enough for Tony, who placed a foot on his back, keeping the whimpering man at bay.

He stood there like that until backup arrived. Then they escorted a struggling and cursing Keith from the apartment as a scattered assortment of curious neighbors watched from their windows.

XLIII

Yolanda was sitting in Mrs. Burhop's cozy living room, sipping tea and listening politely as the old woman recounted many of the same stories Yolanda had heard on her first visit and a few new ones as well.

"It was a kinder and graceful time," said Mrs. Burhop, referring to the days of her youth. "Things are so different now. Everyone is in such a hurry; there is no common courtesy any longer. It seems that so much of the charm has gone out of life." She sighed as she replaced her fragile teacup in its saucer and raised the porcelain pot to pour, first into Yolanda's cup and then into her own.

Yes, but in that gentler time, Yolanda was thinking, would a young black woman be sitting with you drinking tea? More likely, she would be serving it.

While Mrs. Burhop poured, Yolanda took advantage of the break in the conversation to turn it back around to the subject she had come to discuss. "I was just wondering, Mrs. Burhop, if there is anything else at all that you can think of about Jennifer? Something that would make people sit up and take notice, something that would serve her memory well."

"No, dear," the aged widow replied. "Jennifer was special, but she kept so very much to herself. I really believe the only thing she truly loved was that cat."

"Did she ever speak about her friends, her employers, the Nilssons? Wasn't there some fondness there?"

"Honestly, I don't think so. Nothing particularly outstanding anyhow. I think what Jennifer felt for the Nilssons was more of an obligation. After all, they had taken care of her, given her a start in the world, and she wasn't the type to forget that. But I don't think there was much warmth there."

Yolanda's disappointment was written all over her face. She had come back to visit with Jennifer's former neighbor in the hopes of learning something more interesting, more telling, about the deceased fashion model. Something that would illuminate her transition from simple little Sophie Tochowitz to fashion icon Jennifer O'Grady. And how it had led to her demise.

Yolanda's disappointment wasn't lost on Evelyn, and she regretted that she didn't have anything more to share with the friendly reporter. It was so nice that one of her kind was doing so well, and was so polished and spoke so properly. Evelyn wanted so to be of more help to her. And then she thought of something that might just be of interest to Yolanda.

"You know, Yolanda, would it help if you had the chance to look at Jennifer's apartment? I still have the key and they haven't moved any of her things out yet. Perhaps that will give you some of the answers that you are looking for."

Yolanda leapt at the opportunity. To be able to look around the dead woman's home, to rummage through her things, to feel the very essence of her by spending time in her personal space. Why of course it would help. It would help a lot.

"That would be nice, Mrs. Burhop," said Yolanda demurely, trying not to appear overeager even though she was chomping at the bit. Mrs. Burhop went into her kitchen and after rummaging around for a minute, she emerged with a key that she handed over to Yolanda with a trembling hand. "If you don't mind, dear, you'll have to go alone," she said. "Just remember to return the key."

Yolanda let herself into the apartment, the evening dusk just starting to set in, casting eerie light through the miniblinds. She threw on the entry light, and it shone off the polished marble at her feet. She walked into the living room and flicked on the switch in there. Soft lights illuminated the room. She sank into one of the silk upholstered sofas and took in her surroundings. The room was beautiful, expensively decorated, but it told her nothing about the model. She walked down the hall into the bedroom.

The first thing to meet her eye was a bare mattress stained with brown patches Yolanda assumed to be blood. It spoke of the violence that had occurred here. Yolanda studied the bed. Is that where he cut it off? The hair?

The rest of the room spoke of Jennifer's personality. Detailed feminine furniture and floral chintz were juxtaposed against crowded floor to ceiling bookshelves. There was none of the immaculate orderliness of the living room here; piles of books lay on the floor before the shelves, toiletries were crowded on a vanity. One full wall of closet opened up to reveal a cache of cocktail dresses and cashmere sweaters as well as shelves of blue jeans and T-shirts. She picked up the T-shirt on the top of the pile. Save the Whales, it read. For some reason she found that odd, but she wasn't quite sure why. She replaced the shirt where she had found it and looked around on the vanity, the makeup and perfumes still in place. There were no photos anywhere, and there seemed to be nothing of warmth to personalize the room.

She walked over to the bookshelves and began examining the titles, a little of everything from the classics to modern self-help. Yolanda was somewhat embarrassed as she looked at the titles and realized how little reading she had done since her graduation from college. It seemed the journalism game left little time for such self-improvement.

She scanned the books and noted there were many biographies, more than a few books on art, some on history and politics. A particular title caught her eye and she took it from the shelf to examine it further. *Slaughter of the Innocent*, the spine read. Must be a murder mystery, thought Yolanda, the title reminding her of Jennifer herself. As soon as she opened it, however, she realized it wasn't fiction at all, but a detailed accounting of animal abuse in medical research. Somehow, like the Save the Whales T-shirt, it didn't seem to fit.

Yolanda turned her attention to the stacks of books on the floor. These were probably the last Jennifer read, since the shelves were filled to capacity. The top two books were novels she recognized from the latest best seller lists, but the titles of the third book down and the fourth and the fifth surprised her. *Animal Liberation, The Case for Animal Rights, 67 Ways to Save the Animals.* Strange reading for a fur model thought Yolanda. She picked up one of the books, a glossy green paperback with the pictures of a raccoon, monkey and dolphin on its cover. The book fell open to a chapter entitled Victim of Vanity: Death by Fur Coat. Yolanda read the opening paragraph:

Nowhere is this indifference to animal cruelty and exploitation in the name of fashion more evident than in the case of fur products. Fur-bearing animals trapped in the wild inevitably suffer slow agonizing deaths. Fur farms severely limit natural movement, grooming and social behavior patterns. When we purchase the products of commercial furriers we support massive animal pain and death.

The next sentence had been highlighted in yellow:

Each year in the United States alone, at least 70 million animals suffer and die to produce fur garments.

Yolanda shut the book and went through the rest of the pile. There were several more books about animal abuse and a couple on vegetarianism. As she stacked them neatly back into a pile, she was obsessed with the thought that something was very odd here. Why would a fur model be so interested in animal rights?

She returned the key to Mrs. Burhop. "Did you find anything useful?" the old lady asked.

"I don't know," replied Yolanda, the question still nagging at her. "Tell me, Mrs. Burhop, did Jennifer ever say anything to you about her job, about maybe not feeling right about it?"

"Now that you mention it, yes. Why, in the last month, she spoke about it a couple of times. She said she was having a moral dilemma, that she felt responsible for creating a great deal of suffering for the animals that went into fur coats. I told her nonsense, that's what they're for. One of my prize possessions is the mink coat Mr. Burhop bought for me on my fiftieth birthday. I still wear it to this day . . ."

"Mrs. Burhop, may I use your phone?"

"Tell us, Keith," Tony was saying to a practically catatonic Keith Geiger, "tell us what you did to those bodies. Why did you do it?"

"I have no idea what you're talking about," he answered, his tired and empty face propped up on one of his hands.

Karen was feeling terrible for Keith, and feeling guilty about the grilling Tony was giving him. She wondered if he did have anything to say. The lab had the horrible things they had found at his apartment, but it would be a while before they would know if that was human blood on the club in his bedroom and if any of it matched that of the female victims. The ear was obviously old.

They were interrupted by a uniformed officer who told Karen she had a call. "It's from a reporter, that Yolanda Prince, and she insists on talking to you."

Karen shot Tony a glance. "I'd better take this one," she said. She went out into the hall and picked up the nearest phone.

"Karen Levinson."

"I'll trade you," said the excited voice of Yolanda Prince. "You promise me an exclusive on anything that develops in the Jennifer O'Grady case, and I'm going to give you a very interesting piece of information. Deal?"

Karen had no reason to doubt Yolanda's sincerity. True to her word, she had not revealed any of the gruesome details of Jennifer's murder. She wondered what Yolanda would do if she knew that the same details applied to the murder of Emily Wiggins. Would she remain as cooperative?

"Sure, if I get anything for you. What is it?"

"Did you know that Jennifer O'Grady was on the verge of becoming an animal rights activist herself? Her apartment was filled with books on the subject."

Karen didn't bother to ask Yolanda how she had gained access to Jennifer's apartment. She had a pretty good idea who had let her in. But she was trying to digest what Yolanda had said. Jennifer O'Grady, top fur model, a supporter of animal rights. It just didn't make sense.

She hung up the phone and stood in the hallway, angry with herself and Tony. How had they both overlooked the books?

Instead of returning to the interrogation room, she took the elevator up to the fourth floor and went to her desk. She opened a drawer and took out all the animal rights literature she had collected since the beginning of this investigation. She began to leaf through it until she found something that was of particular interest in one of the pamphlets.

She folded the pamphlet, put it in her pocket and went back down to the first floor and the room where Tony was still grilling an uninformative Keith Geiger.

"Tony," she said, calling him over, out of Keith's earshot. "I just learned that Jennifer O'Grady was more than casually interested in animal rights, and I also learned something else. Guess how most trapped animals are killed."

Tony glared at her. "I suppose they shoot them in the head."

"No," she said excitedly, trying to keep her voice down. "They are usually clubbed to death."

XLIV

It was six o'clock in the evening and pitch black outside. Leslie lay on the chaise, still wearing her flannel nightgown. She hadn't bothered to dress. She was totally cried out and felt as though there was no reason to go on living. Every breath she took was a chore, and hardly worth sustaining something as worthless as her life. Occasionally she would forget for a millisecond why she was feeling so bad, but then her thoughts would go straight back to Neil and the hurt would come back too, as sharp and as agonizing as ever.

Whatever could she have been thinking, believing that a man as special as Neil was in love with her? How could she have been so vain? What was she, after all, but a boring little mouse who unfortunately happened to have a lot of money that everyone wanted a piece of. Including Neil. Now it all made sense. That day he had approached her in the park. His offhand comment about her feeding the birds. She pictured that crisp October day and handsome Neil standing there in the weak autumn sun. She had fallen in love with him that very second.

The phone was ringing again and she put a pillow over her head to block out the sound. It had been ringing all day, but she had turned off the answering machine. There was no one alive she wanted to talk to. Oh, Mama, Papa, how I miss you, she thought. Isn't there anyone to love me? Her bones felt heavier than lead and her whole body ached, the misery of her cold expressing the misery of her heart.

The ringing stopped and she was glad. She halfheartedly wondered who it might have been. Larry? He was partly to blame for this whole thing. She never wanted to talk to him again. Could it have been Neil? That didn't matter either. What could he possibly have to say to her that would ease her pain?

As she lay there, her mind in a fog, her face swollen and red, she couldn't suppress the feeling that she had some unfinished business. It was a nagging notion that she had forgotten something very important, but she couldn't remember what it was. Then her eyes drifted to the corner where Mary Ellen's oversize shoulder bag and the animals traps lay in a heap. Oh my God, Mary Ellen! she thought. She must be the one who's been calling all day. Mary Ellen carried her whole world around in that purse. Without it she must be lost.

Listlessly, Leslie dragged herself off the chaise and went to the telephone. She dialed Mary Ellen's apartment. There was no answer, so she tried the S.T.S. office. She was surprised when an unfamiliar male voice answered the telephone.

"Is Mary Ellen in?" Leslie asked.

"Who's calling?" the voice demanded.

"Leslie Warning."

There was a pregnant pause. "Uh, Miss Warning, I'm afraid there's been an accident. People from the police department have been trying to get in touch with you all day. I'm afraid that Miss Fitzsimmons is dead."

No, thought Leslie, her head reeling at the sound of the words. It couldn't be. This was another terrible nightmare. In a minute her mother would wake her and she would be a little girl once again, safe and secure in her mother's arms. None of this would be happening.

"Detectives Perrelli and Levinson want to talk to you. Let me give you their pager numbers," the voice said. He read off a couple of numbers, and the next thing Leslie knew, she was alone again, cut off from the outside world.

Mary Ellen dead.

She paged the detectives, punching in her phone number at the sound of a beep. She hung up the phone and waited for them to return her call. Her eyes misted over as she looked at Mary Ellen's huge and battered nylon tote laying in the corner. She could picture Mary Ellen rummaging through its depths, pulling out S.T.S. literature, an extra pair of mittens or a scarf, or her disorganized appointment book to scrawl illegible notes or confirm an engagement.

Sadly, Leslie picked up the bag and peered inside. The appointment book lay on top. She opened it and began to thumb through it nostalgically, reviewing Mary Ellen's active days. Her fingers stopped at November's calendar. One date was circled over and over in red. FUR FREE FRIDAY. Yesterday. The Thursday before had been marked as Turkey Free Thanksgiving. Wednesday held a single illegible name. The appointment that had never shown. The one Leslie had waited for, the one who had made her late for her non-lunch with Bunny Nilsson.

Leslie stared at Mary Ellen's cryptic scrawl. On Wednesday she had been unable to read the name, but now she could make out that the first initial, at least, was S. And the last name, she could see now, began with T and o.

Suddenly something clicked and the rest was clear: The name was S. Tochowitz. Mary Ellen's Wednesday appointment had been with someone named S. Tochowitz. Where had she heard or seen that name before?

Then Leslie remembered. Last night's "In Depth." During Yolanda Prince's story about murdered models. She had mentioned that Jennifer O'Grady's real name was Sophie Tochowitz.

Could Jennifer O'Grady have been coming to see Mary Ellen? No wonder she hadn't shown—she was dead. And then an even more disturbing thought crept into Leslie's head. Could Jennifer's murder be related to Mary Ellen's death?

The sound of the front door opening downstairs distracted her. Not now, Larry, she thought. He was the last person she wanted to see. Why hadn't she made him give his key back yesterday? She didn't want him to see her red and swollen eyes, she didn't want to hear his comments about Neil, she didn't want to hear what she supposed would be his tasteless response to the news of Mary Ellen's death. She waited unhappily to hear the sound of his heavy footsteps on the stairs.

But there was only silence. Maybe it hadn't been the door after all. Her ears were stopped up from her cold. Then she thought she heard something again.

"Larry?" she called out. There was no response. She called out again. "Larry!"

Her voice echoed in the silence of the empty house. She walked to the head of the stairs and peered down. The kitchen was dark. Surely if Larry was down there he would have turned on the lights. She flicked on the switch in the stairwell and light flooded out into the kitchen. There was no sign of life in the empty room and yet she was sure that there had been someone there a second ago.

She flicked the light off as though the darkness could erase the existence of whomever was there in her kitchen. Her heart started pounding wildly as a rush of fear-driven adrenaline coursed through her body. Her nerves were sharpened and she could hear the flow of her blood as it pulsated in her ears.

Larry had always liked to torment her. Maybe it was only him playing a cruel practical joke. If this is Larry, she thought, I'll kill him.

But something inside her told her this was more than a joke. Somewhere in this house a predator was stalking her.

She retreated to her quarters and locked the door. The simple lock on the knob looked awfully flimsy. She stood in silence, straining her ears to hear any sound. A step creaked. Her heart raced even faster. A second creak convinced her that the intruder was moving closer.

She looked around the room for escape, feeling like a cornered animal. The phone! She raced to pick it up. It was dead. She clicked the receiver a couple of times and still she got no dial tone. Now she knew for sure that she was not alone.

She had to protect herself. Frantically she looked about the room for some kind of a weapon. How ironic that she had spent the whole day laying there wishing to die, and now she was desperate to save her life. Right now even losing Neil seemed unimportant. What was important was that she survive.

I have to take him by surprise, she thought. Perhaps if I were to hit him on the head with a vase or . . . Her eyes fell upon the animal traps piled in the corner.

Quickly she grabbed one of the smaller ones, opened it and placed it near the door. She looked in horror as Edward and Amanda went over to investigate. "Stop!" she cried, grabbing the cats. She hurled them into the bathroom and closed the door behind them.

She opened the two other traps, and placed one to each side of the door. The bear trap remained. It was much bigger than the others and its jaws were far tighter. She pushed against the sides with all her body weight until she heard them click into place. The jagged teeth of the metal monster certainly looked dangerous. Would they be enough to hold off whoever lurked unseen behind her door? She shuddered and turned out the lights, huddling in a corner. She faced the door and waited breathlessly.

She heard the sound of the doorknob being tested. At first it was a gentle rattle, but gradually it grew in intensity until she thought the door would give way. Then, abruptly, it stopped.

There were seconds of silence as, fear-stricken, her mouth dry as cotton, her throat practically closed, she waited in terrified anticipation of whatever was to come next.

She did not have long to wait. Within seconds the door burst open. Her eyes, having adjusted to the dark, could make out the outline of a man standing in the open doorway. She could see that he wore a long coat and held in his hand what appeared to be a club. She pulled herself closer to the wall and curled herself into a ball, willing herself to become invisible.

He took a step into the room and groped along the wall for the light switch. Thankfully, it was on the other side of the room. Leslie held her breath and prayed that he would take another step before he noticed the traps yawning wide before him.

A floorboard creaked as he turned in the dark. She heard a heavy boot take a cautious step in her direction and then a second, more deliberate one. Had he spotted her?

Then she heard the snap of the smaller trap. "Damn!" the man cried out, but from his tone Leslie could tell he was unharmed. She could barely make out his figure as he bent over casually to free his right foot, then fling the spent trap across the room. But the motion of throwing the trap had unsteadied him and his left foot moved forward, landing squarely on the trigger pan of the big bear trap. The groan of old metal was followed by another sharp snap as the bone-crushing steel jaws slammed shut.

"Eyaahh," screamed the intruder, his agonized howl penetrating Leslie's very core. His club dropped to the floor as he reached down with both hands to free his leg.

Leslie took the opportunity to bolt from her place in the corner. The intruder was on the floor in front of the door, blocking her escape, his hands working furiously to pull open the trap. She hesitated before bracing to jump over his hulking frame. His hand shot out at her and caught her leg as she went over him, and she landed with a crash on the other side of him. Quickly, she got onto her hands and knees and tried to crawl away, but he was holding the back of her nightgown. She clawed at the rug as she struggled to get away, but his strong grasp kept pulling her back. Desperately she lunged time and time again to pull the nightgown free, but her strength was no match for his. Frantically, she undid the top buttons of the nightgown and wriggled her shoulders out until she could reach the top of the stairs. With all her adrenaline-fueled strength, she escaped from the gown and, clad only in white panties, catapulted down the stairs and into the kitchen.

Trembling so badly her legs could barely support her, she struggled to her feet. It was dark in the kitchen and she knocked over a stool as she ran for the door. Her hands shook as she fumbled at the kitchen door, trying to get it open. She could hear him coming down the stairs, and her hands shook all the worse.

Suddenly the kitchen was flooded with light. He had thrown the switch. Reflexively, she turned and found herself looking into the cold and black eyes of her pursuer as he came across the room for her. The eyes were devoid of emotion. The rest of his face was obscured by a heavy black beard, except for a nose that appeared to be deformed, with part of it missing. She looked at his leg; his pants were shredded and soaked with blood.

She flung the door open and charged out. She hadn't gone more than a few steps when she stumbled over something and went down. Whatever it was she had tripped over was wet, and in the dim light cast by the streetlamps she could tell that it was a man. She cried out in anguish as she recognized the shaggy head of her brother. "Oh, Larry!" she cried, realizing that the dampness she felt was his blood.

For one split second she forgot the danger she was in, until she heard the sound of approaching footsteps. When she looked up he was there, looming gigantic over her. His club was poised over her head, and she closed her eyes, waiting for it to fall.

XLV

"Freeze! Right where you are!"

The sound of the sharp female voice rang out, and Leslie opened her eyes to see the figure of Karen Levinson standing twenty feet in front of her, her legs spread apart, gripping her gun with both hands. A momentary rush of relief spread through her as she looked up to see the man above her hesitate. But her relief was short-lived, for even as the detective stood before them with her gun drawn, he swooped down and scooped Leslie easily from the ground. He held her in front of him, her nude back pressed to his chest, his muscled forearm crushing her small breasts.

Karen watched with dismay as he backed into the house shielded by his immobilized victim, her feet dangling inches above the ground. Karen could read the fear in her eyes before she disappeared into the open door of the house. It had all happened too quickly for Karen to respond.

Tony, who was split seconds behind her, looked questioningly at Karen and the lifeless body of Larry Warning.

"What's happened?" he asked breathlessly.

"Some big Neanderthal has got her in there. He's carrying a club." Karen started into the house.

"Wait," said Tony. "We need to call for backup." The memory of Karen's performance at Sylvester Wolfe's was still on his mind.

"You call. I've got to get him before he kills her," said Karen, disappearing inside without waiting for his answer.

She paused in the empty kitchen, straining her ears for any telltale sound. A dull thump was coming from the darkened stairwell off the kitchen. She went toward the noise, working her way slowly up the stairs, keeping her body close to the wall as she followed the sound of the heavy, uneven gait.

It was dark at the top of the stairs. She stopped and listened again. She could hear the man breathing heavily as he carried Leslie down the wide hall. Karen heard the sound of a door open and close, followed by the click of a lock.

She hurried down the hall to the closed door and looked at it helplessly. A stream of light peeked out from underneath it. Karen didn't know what to do. She wished Tony would hurry up. She couldn't break the door down herself, and even if she could, who knew what awaited her on the other side. Was one policewoman any match for this kind of adversary? She pressed an ear to the door and strained to listen.

*   *   *

Inside the room, Leslie found herself once again on the floor, staring up at her captor. Despite her fear, she was embarrassed by her nakedness, and she used her arms to cover her breasts.

"I should have known, never assume your prey is docile." He spoke with an odd inflection she could not identify.

Grimacing, he tore open the leg of his blood-soaked pants, revealing the limb the bear trap had mangled. Pieces of his gouged flesh hung free, exposing raw muscle and bone. Ignoring her, he stooped to examine the leg, and then tore a piece of material from his pants and wrapped it tightly around the wounds. Leslie stared at his maimed nose. Noticing this, he wiggled it back and forth with a huge forefinger. "A coyote took it off for me years ago. Snapped it off with his teeth. Lucky for me I pulled back in time or it could have been worse." His black eyes gazed into hers, haunting in their coldness.

Abruptly, he broke eye contact. He went to the bedroom window and opened it, looking down into the courtyard below. There was a substantial drop, but there were hedges against the house— something to break his fall.

Leslie lay there unmoving, regretting that of all rooms he had chosen her former bedroom. Here, in the shadow of her childhood memories and in the presence of her beloved dolls, she was going to die.

The dark stranger pulled his head in from the window, and raised his club. "I have to do this," he said matter-of-factly. "It won't hurt. It will put you out of your misery."

Something stirred in Leslie and she shouted at him, "What am I? Some kind of an animal that you are putting to sleep? I'm a human being. Have some mercy . . ."

"Stop!" he cried out. "You people have no mercy. You should never have started this. It's your fault."

He was poised to let the club fall when suddenly the air split with the deafening sound of gunshots, and the bedroom door flew open. Her attacker's eyes darted to the door, and Leslie took advantage of his distraction, rolling frantically across the floor. A moment later the sound of splintering wood could be heard as he crashed the club down onto the hardwood floor.

Karen stood in the open doorway, poised in the same crouch position she had taken outside, her gun held steady in her hands. The stranger looked at her for a split second, and then, moving with the same lightning rapidity as before, he heaved his club at her with all his might. She dropped to the floor, barely evading it as it flew over her and across the wide hall, bouncing off the railing and landing noisily on the marble floor a level below. When Karen raised her head, he was gone.

"He went out the window." The timid voice was coming from under the bed. Quickly, Karen bolted to the window and looked out in time to see him get back on his feet and take a few steps. She could tell he was in a great deal of pain from the way he favored his bleeding leg. The fall must have injured it even more.

She hurled herself out of the room, back down the stairs. She could hear a commotion outside, and ran through the open door of the library, arriving just in time to see Tony and the intruder locked in hand-to-hand combat. Tony's gun lay on the ground feet away from him; the monster was brandishing a knife.

The two men fell to the ground and rolled about on the hard, cold concrete of the paved courtyard as they fought. First one would be on top, then the other, as they grappled for control both of the knife and of each other. Despite his condition, the big man was more than a match for Tony, and he made unintelligible grunts as he gained the advantage and pushed the hard steel of the knife ever and ever closer to Tony's face.

Karen watched helplessly, her gun frozen in her hand. There was nothing she could do; they were too close to each other for her to shoot. Her adrenaline was flowing ten-forty as she watched them struggle, and her hands were so clammy she feared she might lose her grip on the gun. She watched Tony gurgle as the knife slipped too close, his strength ebbing quickly. Karen's eyes never left them, and she prayed that the right moment would present itself.

And then it did. The assailant, sensing that Tony was depleted, lifted his body away and raised his knife as if about to plunge it into Tony's chest. Taking advantage of the momentary separation of their bodies, Karen aimed and fired.

The man's head snapped up as he looked in disbelief at the woman who had just opened a two-inch hole in his chest. The knife was still gripped tightly in his hand, and he attempted once again to stab Tony. Karen fired another shot into him.

He gurgled and fell over on Tony, who weakly deflected the hulking body to his side. As Tony lay there on his back gasping for breath, he turned his head in Karen's direction. "We're even," he gasped.

Minutes later, they were surrounded by uniformed police, and Tony tried to figure out where the dead man had come from and why. He had carried no identification. The only clue found on his body was a key for a seedy midtown hotel.

"He must have followed her brother in through the gate, and then killed him. He let himself in with Larry's key, and then took the phone off the hook in the kitchen so she couldn't call out," Tony said to Karen.

They went into the living room where Leslie sat wrapped in a warm bathrobe, drinking a cup of hot tea that Karen had made for her. She was surprisingly composed, considering all she had just been through.

"It's a good thing you beeped us when you did," Tony told her. "We recognized your number right away because we had been trying to get in touch with you all day. When all we could get was a busy signal, we checked with the operator. She said the phone was off the hook. That's when we decided to come over."

"Thank God you did," Leslie said weakly, taking a sip from her steaming cup. "Why was this man after me? Why did he kill Larry? Is he the same man who killed Mary Ellen?"

"We don't know," said Karen, "not yet, anyhow." Karen also wondered if the big man was connected to the deaths of Jennifer O'Grady and Emily Wiggins. But that didn't make sense. Two women with furs—two women without.

"There's something I have to tell you, something I just learned this evening. Before she was murdered, Jennifer O'Grady had set up an appointment to meet with Mary Ellen. She made it in the name of Sophie Tochowitz, so I never made the connection until Yolanda Prince mentioned Jennifer's real name on her 'In Depth' show."

A light clicked on in Karen's head and the same one must have clicked on in Tony's, because they exchanged knowing glances.

"Why would a fur model be making an appointment with an animal rights activist?" he asked.

"Maybe because she didn't want to be a fur model anymore,"

Karen responded. "Just maybe she was going to join the other side."

"And who would be unhappy about that?"

"Maybe the people she was representing," was Karen's reply.

XLVI

Michael Nilsson was seated in his living room on the sofa with Bunny at his side. Karen and Tony sat opposite them in a pair of antique chairs. In his hands, Michael held a Canadian passport, a passport that Karen and Tony had found a few hours earlier in a midtown hotel room. There had been nothing else of interest in the room. The man had a change of clothes in there and nothing else. There wasn't even a scrap of paper with a scribbled note or phone number to connect him to anything or anybody in New York.

"Yes, I know him," Michael said, referring to the man whose photo was embossed on the passport. The man was dark and bearded and missing part of his nose. "This is Jean McInerney. He runs our trapping operations in the Northwest Territories, or rather he coordinates all the trappers up there for us. He's been working for my father for thirty-five years. His family's been trapping for generations. They're the best. He has an unshakable loyalty to Swank. Makes sure that we get the quality and quantity of skins we need from up there. He's still one of the best trappers himself."

"Any idea what he might be doing in New York?" asked Tony.

"Jean in New York? I didn't even know he was here. In fact I find it hard to believe; it's their season up north. Bunny, did you know Jean was in New York?"

She shook her head.

"So you know this man too?" Tony asked her.

"Why, yes! He's been coming down to New York once a year ever since Michael's father got too ill to make the trip up north. Reports to him and lets him know what's going on in the Northwest Territories as far as trapping and prices are concerned."

"He only stays a couple of days," she continued. "New York makes him claustrophobic. But he always comes into the store—he is so proud of all the coats. And he used to be mad about Jennifer—"

"Is Jean in New York?" asked Michael. "Is he in some kind of trouble?"

Karen watched the faces of both Nilssons intently. His was placid, inquisitive. She seemed to have developed a nervous tic.

"He murdered a man today, tried to kill a woman, and is a strong suspect in the murder of another woman in the early hours of the morning."

"Jean!" Michael cried. "I can't believe it."

"Both the women were animal rights activists, by the way."

Michael's face turned ghostly white while Bunny's remained impassive. "This is nonsense," Michael said. "Utter nonsense. Where is he? I want to talk to him. I want to get him a lawyer and see if we can sort this whole thing out."

"I'm afraid he won't be needing a lawyer," Tony said coldly. "He's dead."

Ah, Tony, what a bedside manner, thought Karen.

Michael really looked floored now, and as he opened his mouth to say something, his wife cut him short.

"I don't know what you-all are looking for here," she said, slipping into her South Carolina drawl as she was prone to do when she was upset or angry, "but I, for one, resent your comin' in here and making inferences about our employees."

Tony looked at her coldly. "Oh, it's no inference. But speaking of employees, did you know, Mrs. Nilsson, that Jennifer O'Grady had expressed an interest in the animal rights movement?"

"What?" said Michael, aghast. "I don't believe it."

"She had a meeting scheduled with S.T.S. for last Wednesday. But of course, she never showed up."

Michael looked numb. He looked to his wife and then at the two detectives. "I didn't know about that," he said.

Bunny shook her head in silent agreement. Then she said sadly, "I can't believe it. I can't believe that our Jennifer could turn on us like that. It's too much."

Karen was still watching Bunny Nilsson. There was something odd about Bunny, something in her guarded Southern manner. She didn't see it in Michael Nilsson. Michael had been stunned and then outraged and finally defeated as the facts about his former mistress sunk in. Mrs. Nilsson hardly reacted at all.

The two Nilssons sat there in silence as if each were wrestling with their own personal demons.

Once they were outside the Nilsson penthouse, Tony took Karen by the arm in a personal way he never had before. "It's them, I know it's them. It's just figuring how we are going to make the connection."

"It's not him," said Karen.

"Why do you say that?"

"I can just tell, trust me. Call it woman's intuition. Give it a little credit."

"How about if I give credit to something else," he said, playfully lowering his hand to her derriere and giving it a squeeze. "You know our days as partners are numbered now."

She pushed his hand aside with feigned indifference. "There's another thing I don't understand here. Where does Emily Wiggins come in?"

"That's a good question," he agreed, and grabbed hold of her arm again. "You saved my life today," he said seriously. "Remember what happened the last time one of us almost died?"

Karen started to fend him off again, but she made the mistake of looking in his eyes. They were undeniably sexy eyes, dark and mischievous. She was both excited and perturbed by this presumptuous man who felt free to fondle her, a man who had recently slept with her, rebuffed her, derided her, and fought to get rid of her. She could feel his warm hand back on her butt. They weren't going to be partners for much longer . . . What the hell.

XLVII

There was an awkward silence between them after the detectives left. It was broken by Bunny. "That Jennifer," she railed. "That ingrate. After everything we did for her, to turn on us! It's a good thing someone killed her. Why, I could have killed her myself."

"Bunny . . ."

"And those detectives, acting as if one of us had something to do with it. That's the most ridiculous thing I have ever heard. I'd like to call the mayor and complain. I mean really."

She was on her Southern high horse, so Michael let her ramble on as she fluttered about the room, turning out lights, smoothing her hair back off her face with the palm of her hand, purposely avoiding any eye contact with her husband. When she had run out of chatter she finished up her monologue with a simple, "Well, I'm going to bed now, darlin'. Are you coming with me?"

"Bunny." Michael's voice held a tone that was new to her. It had an air of authority to it she had never heard before and it stopped her in her tracks. She turned toward him, and this time it was impossible to avoid his gaze. "What do you know about Jean McInerney being in New York?"

She met his eyes boldly and straight on, unflinching. "Why, nothing more than you do. What is that supposed to mean?"

He tried to read her eyes. They could be so cold, so inpregnable. "I guess nothing," he conceded. "You go on to bed, I'm going to have a drink."

He went into the study, poured himself a stiff brandy and then sat back in his leather chair, swirling the liquid about and inhaling the intoxicating aroma of fruit and cedar. As he sniffed deeply, the alcohol released by his swirling burned his nose in a pleasant, numbing sort of way. A taste of the brandy further numbed his senses.

He knew, but he didn't know. And he didn't want to. His life with her was too organized; she took care of him, she took charge. She alone was able to handle his father, to keep the mean old man he so loved and so hated at bay. She always watched out for him, since the day they were married. She had given him a lot.

Except his manhood. Jennifer had given him that and then she had taken it away. Who ever said life was fair?

He poured a second brandy and felt the fire of the alcohol course through his veins. He wasn't such a bad guy though; he had some fine qualities beneath his good looks. He was a man of vision, he could make his own decisions. It had just worked out so much easier over the years letting Bunny take the reins. She always took care of the difficult things for him—like his father.

His head was spinning as he filled the glass a third time. Alcohol seemed to affect him more lately, his tolerance for it was becoming lower and lower. But it still made him feel assured, strong and tough, as a man. He felt brave, he felt whole, he felt complete.

A sound at the door of the study disturbed him. It was his wife, wearing a long white whisper of silk, her ripe curves bathed in the flattering soft light. He thought she was coming to him, and he waited in his chair for her to come to his lap, lower herself down upon him.

Instead she headed directly toward the large leather-topped desk where her briefcase lay. "I forgot something," she said, picking up the briefcase and retreating from the room.

You forget me, he thought. He drained the last sip of brandy and padded down the hall behind her. She had already gone into their bedroom, and he was surprised upon opening the door to see that she had a fire going in the fireplace. That was odd, she never lit a fire in the bedroom. Her briefcase was open, and she held a leather-bound book in her hand. Upon seeing him, she slipped it back into the briefcase quickly and snapped it shut.

"Darlin'," she said, all honey and magnolias. "Are you coming to bed? Why don't you go and get undressed? I lit a fire."

"I want it."

"Want what?" she replied, looking amazed.

"Give me your briefcase."

"Why, honey, whatever are you talking about?" she said, still holding it tightly on her lap.

He walked over to her and pulled the briefcase from her hands. Her grip on it broke; tough as she was, her strength was no match for his.

"Give it back," she screamed, clawing at him.

He had never seen her this way, but it neither frightened nor surprised him. He held the case out of her reach and, pushing her back, went into the bathroom and locked the door. She pounded at it as he pried open the briefcase with one of her nail files. Inside were piles of her usually organized notes and the leather book he had seen in her hand. He opened it and recognized the writing inside as Jennifer's. He turned to the last entry. It was dated Monday, November 12. The Monday before she was murdered.

I told Bunny about my decision today. She reacted exactly as I expected. She wasn't exactly happy. She lectured me on what a mistake I was making, how I was throwing away my career. I told her that I didn't want to make my living at the expense of poor defenseless creatures and that I was sure I could find something else.

She begged me not to tell Michael right away. These are tough weeks for us with the holidays and all. Let me prepare him for this. She told me that I owed her at least that much. Something in the way she said it told me that she knew all about Michael and me. So I said O.K. I'd wait before making it public that I was leaving.

But the truth is, I can hardly wait to get away. The sooner I stop being a symbol for cruelty the happier I will be. I was handed a flyer not too long ago by the creepy guy who had been following me, and imagine how mortified I was to see my picture on it for the whole world to judge as an abuser of animals. I don't want this anymore. So I made an appointment at S.T.S. for next Wednesday, two days before Fur Free Friday. I want that to be my coming out—I want to be an active part of that demonstration. I made the appointment in my real name for a very important reason. From that day forward that is who I am going to be. No more of this whitewashed, Waspy good girl image. I believe in something more now. I believe in me.

I have just decided that if Bunny doesn't tell Michael by Friday, I am going to tell him myself. I don't think I can wait any longer. I feel kind of bad for him. I know he still loves me, I can see it in his eyes, and this is going to hurt him. But you know what, it is what I have to do. I am on the road to making myself happy. The dependent street urchin is breaking free.

Jennifer O'Grady is dead. Fur is dead.

Michael shut the diary without reading any other entries. He didn't need to, didn't want to. He walked out of the bedroom and stared coldly at his wife where she sat waiting for him on the bed.

"You knew. You knew about Jennifer's change of heart."

"Change of heart? That ungrateful little bitch was going to destroy our business. Don't you see that? Wasn't it enough that I turned my head while she was screwing my husband? Do you know why I never confronted you? To avoid scandal. To save the business. You should be grateful to me. You owe me for that." She had lost her cool and was crying, but her tears were tears of anger. She was finally releasing a rage that had been building up for years.

"What would you be without me, Michael? You haven't the guts to go for anything yourself. If you had been running the company alone you would have run it into the ground."

Michael stared at his wife. He had never seen Bunny so out of control.

"So you killed her?"

"No, I didn't kill her," she shouted. "But I didn't know what to do, and I knew you wouldn't be any help, so I called the strongest person I know."

"My father."

She nodded.

"And he told you what to do?"

"He told me to contact Jean. He knew Jean would do it, because Jean hates what the animal rights people have done to the fur trade."

"Who was Sylvester Wolfe then?"

"Just a demented creep who had a crush on Jennifer. A lucky coincidence."

Michael's face was ashen as he asked his next question. "What about the Wiggins woman? Did Jean kill her too?"

Bunny nodded. "That was all your fault. When you told the police that you had gone to see Jennifer the Friday she was murdered, I was afraid that they'd start looking at you more closely. I called your father again. He was incensed. He said we had to pick a second victim just to divert suspicion from you. A customer from the store being murdered would make it look like someone was after us. Fortunately, Jean was still here."

Michael sat on the bed, his head numb with disbelief.

"Bunny, this is unreal. How could you do this?"

"Do this? Michael, she started it, that bitch cunt whore, turning on the only people who were ever good to her."

"What about those murders the police asked about tonight? Are we involved in those too?"

Bunny rolled her eyes. "Michael, it had to be done. Sooner or later that Fitzsimmons woman would have figured it out. If only Jean had finished it with Leslie Warning, then he could have been gone, and there would never be any connection to us. Still, as it is now, all they know is that Jennifer had an appointment with Mary Ellen.

"There is no hard evidence to tie us to any of this. Any calls I made to Jean I made from a pay phone, and I only met with him twice, on the street briefly to give him money and the notes."

"What notes?" asked Michael.

For the first time, Bunny looked slightly ashamed. "Your father wanted to make the activists look as sick as possible, so he had me instruct Jean to . . . scalp . . . the women after they were dead and leave a note asking how many . . . of them . . . would it take to make a fur coat."

"Scalps? But the women were bludgeoned to death. How could he get their scalps?" He couldn't believe he was even asking these questions.

"They weren't those kind of scalps, Michael."

Michael was sick to his stomach now. He looked at his wife and couldn't believe he had shared a bed with this stranger for so long. Had she always been this evil? Or had his father corrupted her? Did it even matter?

"There is nothing to connect you or my father to any of this?" he asked again.

"That's right. Who could ever prove that we knew Jennifer was going to the other side? There's nothing that would tell about it except that," she said, pointing at the leather book in Michael's hand.

And then, quicker than a flash, Bunny grabbed the book from him and tossed it into the fire. His reflexes dulled from the brandy, he was too slow to stop her. He stood helplessly in front of the fire, watching the flames lick at the pages. Within seconds the book was consumed. In a fleeting moment of courage he tried to put his arm into the flames and take hold of his dead lover's memories, but he was still too weak and the fire was too hot and it was too late. Too late for so many things. Except one.

His strongest thought was that he was glad he and Bunny had never had any children. He would never want to put them through what would have to come next. No, he was glad he didn't have any children whose lives he could ruin the way his father had ruined his.

XLVIII

Karen's and Tony's beepers went off simultaneously. The sound was most unwelcome in light of their position in her bed at the time.

"Oh, Christ no," said Tony, frustrated, his body glowing with sweat, all of his muscles tensed and actively working. "Oh no," Karen echoed, her arms clinging dearly to his damp shoulders, her fingernails pressing into his flesh. "It can wait a minute, can't it?" she asked with urgency.

Tony stepped up the pace and finished in a minute something he had planned to be a long encounter. They lay on their backs panting, Tony's gentle mat of chest hair glistening with sweat, Karen's slim, toned body damp and dewy.

"Let's draw straws," she said breathlessly, referring to who would retrieve their beepers from her bureau. Tony dragged himself from the bed, giving her a playful slap on the stomach. He picked up both of the pagers. "Same number," he said.

The voice of Michael Nilsson answered the call. He was on his car phone. "I want you to meet me at my father's house in Upper Montclair. It's important." He gave Tony the address. "I paged your partner too," he added.

"That's all right, we're together," replied Tony. "We'll be right there."

"I'll wait for you out front," he said. They dressed quickly, and Karen was brushing her hair as they waited for the elevator. She hoped she didn't look like she had been doing what she had just been doing.

The ride to Jersey went quickly, the atmosphere in the car both upbeat and personal. They were both afire with anticipation. What did Michael Nilsson have to say to them? They pulled up in front of the large estate and parked behind the darkened Jaguar in which he was sitting. Upon seeing them, he got out.

"Follow me," he said simply, adding nothing more.

Though it was late the entry light was on, and Michael was surprised at how quickly Maria answered the door.

"Wake my father," he said curtly as he pushed past her into the foyer.

"There's no need, he's awake," she said. She escorted them into the living room where he saw his father looking small and vulnerable in his wheelchair in front of the fire. His nurse Maureen sat off to his side. She glared at Michael as if to say, how dare you disturb your father at this hour?

Lars did not seem surprised to see him. Of course, Bunny would have called. He did appear taken aback by the presence of the two police officers, however, and his cold blue eyes flared with anger.

"What is it, Michael? Why are you here so late? Your wife called me hysterical."

"Father, I want you to meet Detective Perrelli from the homicide squad and his partner Detective Levinson. Bunny told me everything, Dad, and now I am going to tell them."

Lars made a motion toward Maureen, dismissing her, and the nurse left the room without hesitation. He stared at his son as Michael began to speak.

"The murders of Jennifer O'Grady and Emily Wiggins, and the murders of other innocent people that occurred today, were all orchestrated by my father and my wife. Together, they schemed to kill Jennifer when they learned she was going to leave Swank because she felt she could no longer represent the fur industry. They brought Jean McInerney down from Canada to do the dirty work, and had him kill Emily Wiggins to throw any suspicion off me."

"Ridiculous," the old man boomed. "If your wife said this, then she's touched in the head. But I think maybe it's you, Michael. Maybe you're the one who's lost his mind. Do you realize what you just said. Why, if I could get out of this chair, what I wouldn't do to you . . ."

"Dad, don't deny it. Do you think I feel good about doing this? I have to do what is right. For once in my life I have to stand up to you. Don't you understand that?"

"All I understand is that you are an ungrateful son who is a disgrace to this name. Thank God your mother is dead, or this would have killed her."

Michael also thanked God his mother was dead; he would hate to have to put her through this. The air in the room was thick with tension. Michael began to feel uneasy as Lars turned his attention to the detectives.

"Officers," the old man said with measured calm, "I'm sorry to say this, but my son has always been a selfish and vindictive young man.

"I don't know why he's accusing me of these things. Perhaps it's a guilty conscience. God knows he's been unfaithful to his wife. Maybe he wants us both out of the picture. I honestly don't know."

As he spoke he looked directly at Michael, his voice growing more intense until it began to crackle with contempt.

"And now, if we are finished with the fairy tales, it's past this old man's bedtime." He rang his bell furiously and both Maureen and Maria appeared in the room.

"You may show these people out, Maria," he said with finality. "Maureen, I am ready for bed."

Karen stood there in awe. The arrogant old man was holding all the cards and he knew it. There were no witnesses. Bunny Nilsson was never going to repeat the story she told Michael, and the Canadian trapper was dead. They needed something solid here, some fact that might let them know who was telling the truth.

"Wait," she called to the nurse, who was beginning to push Lars from the room. "Mr. Nilsson, can I just ask you a question?"

He signaled to Maureen that it was okay.

"Mr. Nilsson, who do you think might have murdered Jennifer O'Grady?"

He was more than ready to answer that question. "Young lady, that's been very clear to me from the start. I have no doubt it was those animal rights people, only which ones I couldn't begin to guess. They're all unbalanced fanatics."

"I have to agree with you," said Karen. "There has to be something wrong with anyone who could mutilate a body in such a nasty way and then leave such a cruel note about it."

"That's what I'm saying, but of course they would leave a note. How else can they draw attention to themselves? And equating a woman's pubic hair with the making of a fur coat—it just goes to show how twisted they are."

There was a sudden silence as Lars realized he had just made a critical mistake. Michael looked confused as Karen smiled in triumph. It was Tony who said, "Mr. Nilsson, the police have never released any details about how those bodies were mutilated or the notes beside them. How did you know about them?"

"Well, Michael must've . . . or no, it was Bunny . . . Well, certainly somebody told me something about it," he said, frantically backpedaling. "I can't recall now. In fact, I can't even recall what I just said. I'm a confused old man and I'm going to sleep."

"I hope you do sleep well, Mr. Nilsson," said Karen, "because tomorrow may be a long day for you. There are five of us here who heard what you said, and the D.A. will want to know about it."

Tony let Karen do the driving back into the city, playfully chucking at her arm and side along the way.

"Stop it," she said. Her mind was nowhere near thinking about him. She was too excited about what had just taken place at the Nilsson estate.

"You know that was brilliant, what you did," said Tony, giving her the credit she was due. "You really got him good."

"Thanks," she said, grinning. She was proud and for the first time since she had come to homicide, she knew she belonged there. Her insecurities had faded, replaced by new confidence, new faith in herself.

Tony reached out to her once again, this time caressing her breasts. "Let's go back to your place and finish what we started."

She slapped his hand away. "If you don't mind, Tony, I'm really tired. I want to get a good night's sleep and be fresh for tomorrow when we present this to the D.A."

Tony tried not to show his amazement at her rebuff.

"Okay. Tomorrow then," he said, as she pulled up in front of her building. He got out of the car and came over to her on the driver's side. She slid past him and gave him a quick wave.

"See you in the morning," she said.

XLIX

Yolanda couldn't believe her good fortune. She was learning the system, that favors do pay off. Not only was she the first one to break with the story that Lars Nilsson and his daughter-in-law had been arrested in connection with four murders, she also had exclusive inside details . . . all courtesy of Karen Levinson. This was exactly the feather in her cap that would make the network boys sit up and take notice. Maybe she would get a regular spot on the nightly network news or, better yet, maybe they would want to take "In Depth" national.

Already she had been told that her boss wanted to speak with her, and she had a sneaking suspicion that it was going to involve money. Well, she was ready to accept a big, fat raise. She thought of the things she could do with the money, starting with Ellie.

She was waiting for her date to pick her up, a young black prince who was making a name for himself on Wall Street. Maybe there was a house in Connecticut in their future too.

She pulled on her big fox coat, the lustrous red fur gleaming in the lamplight. Then she sat the matching hat that Bunny Nilsson had given her atop her gleaming black hair, its unruly thickness pulled back in a neat chignon. She checked herself out in the mirror. Bunny was right. The red fox really did flatter her.

Yolanda wondered if she should feel guilty about wearing all this fur. Well, why the hell not, she thought. White people are so screwed up. They've been wearing fur for centuries and all of a sudden it's a violation of someone's rights. The animal's right. Maybe they should take a little look around their cities if they want to see some rights violated. Kids starving to death, old people freezing in their homes when their gas is turned off because they can't pay their bills. They choose to throw all their energy into saving the animals because they feel sorry for them. What about human rights? Didn't they count for anything?

She thought about it and decided that she would do a series of "In Depth" programs about the city's poor.

That still didn't stop her from wanting to be one of the rich and famous, however. Today she could laugh at the human condition. She wasn't doing too badly for a black, formerly fat girl from the Bronx.

L

Leslie was surprised at how many people cared. Dozens of people from the Hunger Exchange and S.T.S. had called to see how she was, and to express their condolences about her brother's death. Some of her mother's friends had visited, and even some of their daughters had sent cards and flowers.

Leslie was sitting in the living room of the greystone townhouse; the room a showpiece with a carved ceiling and wainscotting, period furniture and heavy velvet drapes. Mother and Father had sat there every evening and had a cocktail, always only one, and listened to classical music. Leslie had loved to sit with them, it was always so peaceful and serene.

Now she sat in the room with a couple of the volunteers from S.T.S. and Keith. Leslie found solace in the Brahms concerto coming from the CD player, each note acting upon her as a tranquilizer, something she much needed. She had refused to take any from the doctor.

She felt sorry for Keith, she could see he was in much pain. He had truly loved Mary Ellen. Despair showed in his hunched shoulders and rigid back. Still, he held her hand as he sat there beside her, trying to console her. Little did he realize that the loss in the forefront of her mind right now was the loss of Neil, and that window of happiness he had so briefly opened in her life.

"Was it terrible being locked up, Keith?" she asked, trying to bring him out of his silence.

"It always makes me feel like I'm going crazy. I've been that way ever since Vietnam. I was court-martialed for refusing to obey orders, and I spent a lot of time in the brig. Now I have a phobia about being in small places. That's why I got so angry with Mary Ellen for getting us locked up on Friday. If I hadn't been angry, I would have stayed with her and she'd still be alive."

"You can't blame yourself, Keith. Maybe you'd be dead too."

"When the police came and accused me of killing Mary Ellen and the other women, I couldn't believe it. I saw enough killing at My Lai. I swore I could never raise a hand against another living thing. That's why I became vegetarian. That's why I joined S.T.S.

"You know I keep a memorial in my apartment to the atrocities I witnessed. It's horrible, I know, but I want to make sure that I wake up every day and go to sleep every night with a reminder of how wicked man can be to man."

"I suppose we can," said Leslie, thinking of all the lives that had been so brutally snuffed out in recent days.

The bell rang and Keith went to answer it. Leslie closed her eyes and leaned her head against the back of the sofa. She felt so tired, her mind and body both drained. There was so much to do. She had told Larry's mother that she would help her make the arrangements. Life would be quite different without Larry around, the brother who irritated her so, but whom she had loved nonetheless.

She heard Keith talking and then another male voice. Her heart jumped as she recognized it. She was aware of Keith calling the other two women out of the room, and then suddenly Neil was standing before her. As always, her first thought was her appearance. She must look terrible, her face swollen, her eyes red.

"Hello," he said tentatively. For once, he wasn't smiling.

"Hello," she said, but unable to meet his eyes, she concentrated on the Oriental rug.

"I'm sorry to hear about Larry," he said guardedly.

"Yes."

"Are you all right?"

"I'll live."

"Leslie, would you look at me please?"

She kept her head down stubbornly for a minute and then slowly lifted it to meet his eyes.

"Leslie, I know I've hurt you deeply. Believe me, that's the last thing I wanted to do. I tried to call you all day yesterday, but you never answered the phone. Can I explain to you now?"

"It's a free country," she said, embarrassed at the childish words that slipped from her mouth.

"Leslie, it's true that I went to the park to meet you because Larry told me about you. I admit I want to have it all and have it fast, so I thought it might not hurt to score with a rich girl. But I'm also selfish in a lot of other ways. I always pictured myself with some good-looking babe who turned all the heads when she walked into a room. So after our first dates, I decided it was all wrong, you weren't the type for me no matter how much money you had. Shy, quiet, no flash, *vegetarian*. Definitely not my style. That's when I stopped calling.

"So I started going back to Mulligan's where the girls all wear the right clothes and do all the hip things, but somehow the long legs and big boobs didn't interest me any more. I missed you. Through my selfish, stuck-up Yuppie ways I realized why. Because you are real, you have heart. You shine through the fakeness and the flash and trash that is everywhere around us. Those other women started to seem like vultures."

He looked at her beseechingly, his blue eyes peering deeply into her brown ones. "I want you to believe me. You are the first thing in my shallow materialistic life that I really believe in. I can't make any guarantees, but I want to give this a chance. Give us a chance. Let's see where we can go."

Leslie didn't know what to do. Her first impulse was to shout out, "yes, yes, yes," but something inside her told her to slow down. Her mother had always told her to play hard to get. If she really wanted to keep Neil, she decided she had better not seem desperate.

"All right," she said simply.

The hangdog look on Neil's face lifted, and he beamed the easy smile that she so adored. Then, remembering the somberness of the occasion, and what had taken place in this house, he adjusted his expression to one more appropriate, and dropped down alongside her on the couch. He put his arms about her protectively and pulled her head to his chest, and kissed the top of her curls tenderly.

Leslie shivered at how he made her feel. Maybe some fairy tales did come true, she thought. Maybe the good little girl was going to get her reward.

LI

Monday morning the Lieutenant called them in.

"After the way you wrapped up this case, are you two still sure you want to change partners?" he asked.

Tony was the first to speak. "I don't know that a change is really necessary anymore, Detective Levinson and I . . ."

Karen interrupted him. "With your permission, sir," she said, addressing the Lieutenant, "I am still requesting the change."

The Lieutenant was kind of irked, but he kept it to himself. First, Perrelli initiates the change, but now he doesn't want it, and now the broad whose fault it was in the first place wants the change. Well, the department was learning to live with women and their ways, why should homicide be an exception.

He gave them their new assignments.

Karen recognized the name of her new partner, Ernie Flores, a seasoned cop reputed to be middle-of-the-road, not too easygoing, not too hard. She was happy. She sensed they would get along well.

Tony groaned when he saw that his new partner was Bob Cuneo, a virtual Tony clone. Those two egos clashing ought to be interesting, thought Karen.

As they stepped out of the office, Tony grabbed her arm and drew her aside. "Hey," he whispered. "What's wrong with you? Ever since Saturday, you've been like ice."

"Sorry, Tony," she said, repossessing her arm.

"I mean, I'm surprised you don't want to be partners. I thought we had reached a point where we were getting along."

"We were getting along fine, Tony. But the problem here is that I'm ambitious, and you'll hold me back. I know you, Tony, and no matter what I do that's right, every time I make a mistake you'll say it's because I'm a woman."

"Whoa!" he said, throwing up his arms in a gesture of surrender. "I give up. It's probably better this way anyhow. It'll be easier for us to go out."

"Sorry, Tony, but no to that too." She turned to walk away.

"What?" he called to her back. "What's the story here? It's obvious that you're attracted to me." She stopped in her tracks and turned on her heel.

"Tony, remember what you taught me? Don't go for the obvious." She left him standing there flabbergasted as she went off to introduce herself to her new partner.

LII

WOMEN'S WEAR DAILY—
February 1, 1992

SWANK FURS CLOSES DOORS

After more than 50 years in business, Swank Furs has gone out of business. The financially troubled retail chain had been plagued by scandal in recent months. A spokesperson for the firm cited the recession and the current animal rights sentiments as contributing factors in Swank's financial difficulties.

Former vice-president Bunny Nilsson, wife of the firm's president, Michael Nilsson, is scheduled to go on trial in connection with a number of sensational murders in New York, including the killing of one-time Swank model Jennifer O'Grady. Lars Nilsson, founder of the Swank chain, was also charged with the murders but he died last Wednesday after suffering a stroke.

According to the spokesperson, all the firm's assets, including the Fifth Avenue real estate, are to be sold off to meet financial obligations. All leftover funds will be donated to the Hunger Exchange, a non-profit organization that provides meals for the homeless.